Pieces of Home

A Hometown Harbor Novel

Tammy L. Grace

Pieces of Home is a work of fiction. Names, characters, places and incidents either are products of the author's imagination or are used fictitiously. Any resemblance to actual events, locales, entities, or persons, living or dead, is entirely coincidental.

PIECES OF HOME Copyright © 2016 by Tammy L. Grace

All rights reserved. No part of this book may be reproduced or transmitted in any form or by any means, electronic or mechanical including photocopying, recording, or by any information storage and retrieval system without the written permission of the author, except for the use of brief quotations in a book review. For permissions contact the author directly via electronic mail: tammy@tammylgrace.com

www.tammylgrace.com
Facebook: https://www.facebook.com/tammylgrace.books
Twitter: @TammyLGrace

Published in the United States by Lone Mountain Press, Nevada

ISBN 978-0-9912434-8-8 (paperback)
ISBN 978-0-9912434-9-5 (eBook)

FIRST EDITION

Cover design by Kari Ayasha, Cover to Cover Designs
Interior Formatting by Polgarus Studio

Printed in the United States of America

ALSO BY TAMMY L. GRACE

Below you will find links to the electronic version of all of Tammy's books available at Amazon

Cooper Harrington Detective Novels

Killer Music

Hometown Harbor Series

Hometown Harbor: The Beginning (FREE Prequel Novella)

Finding Home

Home Blooms

A Promise of Home

Pieces of Home

Tammy would love to connect with readers on social media. Remember to subscribe to her mailing list for another freebie, only available to readers on the mailing list. Follow this link to her webpage and provide your email address and she'll send you the exclusive interview she did with all the canine characters in her books. **Follow Tammy on Facebook at this link**, by liking her page. You may also follow Tammy on Amazon at this link, by using the follow button under her photo.

Dear Readers,

I enjoy writing the Hometown Harbor Series. It's always relaxing to return to Friday Harbor and surround myself with some of my favorite characters in the picturesque setting in the San Juan Islands. *Pieces of Home* (Book 4) picks up where the third book ended. Its emphasis is on Ellie Carlson, the gifted baker at Sweet Treats.

I recommend you read the series in order for the most enjoyable experience. In case it's been too long since you've made the trip with me to Friday Harbor, I wanted to refresh your memory with a quick summary of each book. **Be advised there are spoilers so don't read any further if you haven't yet read Books 1-3.**

*Spoiler alert: The first book features Sam and her move to Friday Harbor after finding herself divorced at fifty years old. She opens a coffee shop and bakes delicious pies. She discovers comfort surrounded with new friends and falls in love with Jeff, the owner of Cooper Hardware.

The second book focuses on Linda, the local florist. *Spoiler alert: She and Sam's best friend, Max work together on Sam and Jeff's wedding. She suffers a broken ankle and Max tends to her injuries. Jeff is the victim of a shocking accident resulting in a traumatic brain injury shortly after returning from his honeymoon with Sam. While Sam keeps a vigil at Jeff's bedside, Linda and Max fall in love.

I'll summarize, in more detail, the third book, *A Promise of Home,* which focuses on Regi. *Spoiler alert: She moves to the island shortly before her 40th birthday in an attempt to fulfill a youthful promise she and her high school sweetheart, Cam, made with each other. While she's occupied thinking about a reunion with Cam, she barely notices the local delivery man, Nate. He's attracted to her, but has a hard time competing with the man from Regi's past, who occupies all her waking moments.

Regi's journey is littered with disappointment and a tragedy involving her daughter, Molly. As it turns out Cam is a no show, but a chance encounter in Seattle brings them face to face. Cam has a very good reason for not showing up on the island to celebrate Regi's birthday. His daughter was killed in a horrific car crash, at the hands of his wife. After struggling to come to terms with the loss, his wife commits suicide. Regi's heart goes out to Cam, but she soon realizes he's not the same young man she fell in love with decades ago.

Two new characters, Kate and her best friend, Spence, are introduced in *A Promise of Home*. Kate is in her early sixties and opens an art and antiques shop. Regi's tumultuous relationship with her own mother causes her to seek the guidance of Kate, who she looks upon as a mother figure.

Regi's brother, Leon, fresh from prison, comes to live on the island. She blames Leon for the death of her oldest brother and struggles to forgive him for his life of crime. She finally convinces herself he's changed, only to find he takes advantage of her kindness by stealing from her friends and fleeing the island. Regi's strained relationship with her mother intensifies after Leon's latest betrayal.

She resolves her feelings about Cam and eventually commits to Nate. The book ends with Regi and Nate's wedding near Christmas. Although her mother refuses to attend the wedding, Regi's father makes the trip and gives indications he may be ready to leave his wife.

Fix your favorite reading drink and settle in for another escape to Friday Harbor where you'll catch up with all your old friends in *Pieces of Home*.

Happy Reading,
Tammy

P.S. I'm working on my second book in my new private detective series. If you enjoy reading whodunit mysteries on the cozy side, check out *Killer

Music: A Cooper Harrington Detective Novel. It's available now in both print and e-book formats.

These books are set in Nashville, Tennessee, and feature Cooper "Coop" Harrington, an irresistible bachelor detective, who lives with his wealthy aunt. Coop's faithful friend and assistant, Annabelle and his loyal golden retriever, Gus, both lend a hand during his investigations. The second book in the series will be released in the summer of 2016.

For my mom, my biggest fan

One

Alerted by the chime, Ellie looked up from the bakery case and saw a young woman gazing around the empty shop. With sunrise an hour away, the residents of Friday Harbor were still cocooned in their beds the morning after Christmas. The girl hesitated and then made a timid approach. Ellie greeted her with, "Good morning, you're out and about early."

The welcome earned her a shy smile as the girl focused on Ellie's bright green apron, adorned with blotches of flour. "Are you visiting your family for Christmas?" asked Ellie, as she finished loading the case and deposited her pan on the counter.

The girl nodded her blonde head and directed her eyes to Ellie's name, embroidered on the apron. "You're Ellie? Ellie Carlson?"

"That's me, I own this joint." She paused and then asked, "What can I get you this morning?"

"Um, I don't know yet." The girl glanced down at the case and gazed at the pastries and confections. The dark circles supporting her eyes punctuated her pallid complexion.

"Take your time and give me a shout when you've decided." Ellie gathered the pan and took it in the back. She watched the girl take another look around the shop and wander to the bulletin board. She scanned the photos of Ellie's cakes and various celebrations and meandered to the collection of pictures showing the Carlson family working at Sweet Treats through the years.

Ellie checked the clock and gathered donuts to box for a few standing orders. Charlie would be coming by to pick up his dozen for the hardware store and one of the deputies would be in soon to retrieve the daily box for the San Juan Sheriff's Office. She had the order for Sam's shop ready and waiting, expecting one of her helpers to arrive before seven. She plucked a warm strawberry cream cheese croissant from the pan and put it on a plate.

The girl was still studying the photos when Ellie said, "I need a second opinion on this new flavor I'm trying. Would you be interested in sampling it?"

Ellie set the plate on a table, along with a fork, a bottle of juice, and a napkin. The girl gave her a weak smile and nodded. She sat and said, "It looks good, thank you."

Charlie came through the door, followed by a deputy. "Good morning, Ellie," said the officer. "How was your Christmas?"

She pushed his box across the counter and shrugged. "It was quiet." She collected his signature and he hollered out a promise to see her Monday.

Charlie grasped his box and signed for his order. "Are you ready for your trip?" she asked.

His smiled widened. "Yeah, we leave tomorrow. I can't wait to hit the slopes."

"Have a great time and be careful. I want to see pictures when you get back."

"Will do," he said grinning. "Dad's covering for me, so you'll have to deal with him for the next week." Charlie slid his box off the counter. "Have a Happy New Year, Ellie."

While she was waiting on Charlie three more customers came through the door. She bustled behind the counter and after she rang up the last order, scanned the table where the girl had been and saw only an empty chair.

She frowned as she put the money in the register, but didn't have time to dwell on the mysterious visitor. The shop was soon packed with all her regulars, plus their relatives visiting for the holidays. She didn't get a break until early afternoon.

She took advantage of the lull and called in her lunch order while she scanned her recipes. She wanted to make something special for Regi's open house party on Sunday.

While she was thinking about a few ideas she had culled from the group, she whipped up a batch of dog cookies and put them in to bake. Her lunch arrived from Soup D'Jour and she made herself a glass of iced tea before slumping into one of the booths to enjoy her meal. Her new helper, Nicole, was out of town until January and Ellie was looking forward to shorter days once she trained her.

As she ate, she mulled over the girl from the morning. Over half of the croissant had been left on the plate. The girl's sunken cheeks and wrists no bigger around than her smallest biscuit cutter led Ellie to believe the girl was hungry. Although clean and well dressed, the girl struck her as troubled and wary. Ellie knew everyone on the island and didn't recognize her. Usually relatives came in with their family. Plus she knew Ellie's last name. *Weird.*

As she finished her lunch, Spence walked through the door. "I'm craving one of your cupcakes. I'll take a few to the shop and share with Kate and Mitch."

Ellie gathered her dishes, tightened her ponytail, and washed her hands. "I enjoyed visiting with Mitch at Regi's wedding. I bet Kate's going to miss him when he goes back."

"The holidays are tough for her and having her son around makes her smile. I don't think a parent ever gets over losing a child. Even though Karen's death was so long ago, the sadness lingers. He leaves tomorrow, so it'll be a tough day."

Ellie felt tears form in her eyes and blinked several times to keep them at bay. She turned and collected a small box. "What can I get you today?"

He scanned the case and chose half a dozen cupcakes. "We'll see you at Regi's on Sunday, if not before," he said, waving goodbye.

Between spurts of customers, Ellie spent the rest of the day baking and making sure pans and bowls were cleaned and lined up for tomorrow morning. She decided on four different cupcakes to make for Regi's new house celebration and scanned the storage room to make sure she had everything she needed. She used her laptop to start her weekly order before it was time to close.

On the drive home her thoughts drifted back to the girl. Her serious eyes haunted Ellie as she pulled into her garage. The guys from Linda's nursery had installed Christmas lights and she was glad to see them. They were a welcome sight after the long days of going to work in darkness and getting home after the sun had set.

Oreo, her faithful border collie, bolted through the dog door to greet her, as she did each night. "How's my sweet girl?" Oreo answered with a quick spin in a circle.

The aroma of her dinner welcomed Ellie as she hung her coat in the closet. She caught her foot in the strap of a scarred leather bag on the floor under the rack of coats. She flicked the errant strap with her foot and gave it a kick, thrusting it deeper into the corner of the closet. She shut the door and wandered to the kitchen. She was too tired to cook when she got off work and did her best to put something in the slow cooker on winter mornings. She flicked the remote for the television and listened to the news anchor jabber in the background as she stirred the rich stew. After pouring Oreo's dinner, she changed into her warm pajamas.

She ladled the stew into a bowl, added slices of homemade bread and an apple to the plate, and trudged to the living room. As was her habit, she put her meal on a tray by her chair and lounged in the recliner while she ate dinner. She poked the remote, in search of something to watch.

Oreo plopped onto her bed next to the recliner and rested her head on her paws. Ellie finished her dinner and with nothing worth viewing, instead considered the tree. The colorful twinkle of lights lifted her spirits each night, but she was glad Christmas was over. This was the first year she had been alone, without a visit from her family. She glanced at a photo of her on the wall, sandwiched between her aunt and uncle on the day she took over Sweet Treats, five years ago. Their arms were wrapped around Ellie and she was holding her new black and white puppy. What a happy day it had been.

She scanned the spacious living room, with its tall rock wall fireplace and windows overlooking the pond. Joyful memories of Christmases past invaded her musings. The house belonged to her aunt and uncle. When she took over the bakery and they moved away, they insisted she live in the house. It was meant for a large family, but now held only a woman and her dog. Oreo enjoyed the run of the yard and the sixteen acres surrounding the house. The four bedrooms, a finished basement, a huge shop with a separate barn, and a gleaming modern kitchen no longer teemed with activity. The house was thirty-five years old, same as Ellie, and both were a bit worn. Each time Ellie baked at home she was thankful her aunt had elected to update the kitchen and bathrooms ten years ago.

The house was quiet and empty without her aunt and uncle. Ellie spent most of her time working and when she found herself alone, she tricked her brain into believing they'd be home soon. She had considered getting a smaller place in town, but thought she'd be lonelier there than in the home that possessed such strong memories of the fun life they had given her. The money she saved on rent helped her make the monthly payment on the bakery, especially during the winter.

Ellie cleaned up the kitchen and stored her leftovers, clicked off the remote, and plodded to her bedroom. She eyed her stack of adult coloring books and assorted markers and pencils. She had taken to coloring years ago with Aunt Ginny and still used it to relieve stress. Oreo followed and jumped up to claim her side of the bed. Ellie snuggled under the comforter, making sure her alarm was set for three o'clock. As she fluffed her pillow, she fought the urge to call Aunt Ginny.

She had talked to her yesterday and Uncle Bob was still in the hospital, but doing better after a heart attack. She knew they were both fine, surrounded by their loving children, but she still felt a tug to be near them. She always considered them her parents; it was easier. She hadn't seen or spoken to her real parents in twenty years. Not since the day she boarded the ferry to live with her dad's brother and his family on San Juan Island.

She felt a tear trickle down her face and heard the soft plop of it on her pillow. Once she knew Nicole could manage the bakery on her own for a few days, she'd make the trip to the mainland and visit, but it would be at least a few weeks. Oreo scrunched closer and placed her head on Ellie's shoulder. Ellie wiped her tears away and petted the silky fur, thankful for the comfort of her faithful friend.

Two

After a busy Saturday at the bakery and making dozens of cupcakes for the party, Ellie was grateful she was closed on Sundays during the winter. She relished sleeping in and lounging around the house like a normal human being. Conditioned to rise early, she had a hard time staying awake in the evenings. A late night movie kept her up, and she was in a deep sleep until six in the morning. Oreo was snuggled against her and sprang to life as soon as Ellie's eyes cracked open.

The two of them spent the morning taking down the tree and storing all the Christmas decorations in the basement. After breakfast and a shower she put in a call to Aunt Ginny. As she inquired about Uncle Bob, she stroked Oreo's head. She learned Uncle Bob would be released and coming home by the end of the day. He had orders to follow up with a cardiologist for a new diet and exercise regimen.

Her aunt steered the conversation away from Bob's medical issues and asked about the bakery and Ellie's social life. "It was a busy Christmas and I'm looking forward to Nicole taking some of the work load, so I can have a life," said Ellie, with a chuckle. "I always have help in the summer, but finally decided I need help all the time."

She promised to be in touch in the next few weeks with her travel plans for a visit and hung up. She let out a sigh as some of the tension in her neck and shoulders loosened. "Uncle Bob's going home today," she said to Oreo. The dog's fluffy tail thumped against the floor.

She pulled a coloring book from her stack and began shading the intricate designs with a pencil. This page was mostly leaves and trees with a few wildlife creatures peeking out from the foliage. She toiled with a variety of green pencils until she was satisfied with the look. She glanced at the clock and rushed to stow her art supplies.

Ellie rifled her closet for something to wear. She wore jeans and t-shirts to work. It was always warm in the bakery, so her selection of cool weather shirts was scarce. She unearthed an emerald green blouse and paired it with black pants. As she zipped up the slacks she vowed to stop sampling so much at work. The biting waistband served as an uncomfortable reminder she needed to lose a few pounds. The muffin top drooping over her pants was a direct result of too many of her sweet treats.

She never wore much makeup and fiddled with items from her drawer to outline her gray eyes, adding a touch of eye shadow. She vetoed her signature ponytail and plugged in the curling iron. Jen always cut her hair and curled it for her, but Ellie never took the time to fix it. She mimicked Jen's movements with the curling iron and after checking the back of her head in the mirror, decided it was done. Her golden honey hair shined and the soft curls accentuated her face.

She left some lights on in the house, knowing she wouldn't be home until after dark. She carted the pink boxes of cupcakes to her car. She searched the closet for a suitable coat and pulled out her old camel wool coat. She used her hand to brush it off, deciding it would look better than her usual hoodie. The leather bag responsible for snaring her foot Friday night was in the way again. She grabbed it and flung it to the base of the stairs. "Damn bag anyway."

She stuffed the parcel of homemade dog treats in her purse and motioned for Oreo to follow. Regi had included Oreo in the invitation and the dog zigged and zagged with excitement, as she darted to the car. Ellie lived near the middle of San Juan Island, which meant she was never more than a few minutes from anything. She pulled into the driveway behind Linda and Max. Oreo and Linda's dog, Lucy, began running around the yard. Linda juggled a salad and Max insisted on helping Ellie carry her boxes as the dogs ran to the front door.

Nate opened the door and the dogs shot through it. He laughed and took Linda's bowl. "Zoe, Bailey, and Murphy are in the back. We'll toss these two hooligans out there with them." He hugged Linda and Ellie and told them they'd find Regi in the kitchen.

Nate and Regi's home was one of the older homes situated on the waterfront. It had been remodeled recently and featured stunning views with multiple decks on the top level. The beautiful patio area leading to a sloping lawn that met the beach would be put to use as soon as the weather was warmer. Ellie marveled at the gorgeous kitchen, filled with stainless and granite, as she placed her boxes on the island countertop.

Regi was busy arranging appetizers, but her eyes lit up when she saw Ellie. "I'm so glad you could come. And not just because you make the best treats." She laughed as she moved to hug Ellie.

"Your house is fabulous. Oreo is so excited to play."

Regi's eyes twinkled as she smiled. "The dogs are in heaven. There's a huge fenced area for them to play and romp."

Nate embraced Ellie in a hug and handed her an iced tea. "I can't believe you guys have this place so put together. You just got married a week ago."

"We've been busy," he said. "We wanted to have the party before Cam and Gianna left, since Cam was kind enough to give us the house as a wedding gift." He shook his head. "It's surreal. More so for Regi."

"I'm glad they reconnected after so long. It's wonderful Molly is able to have a relationship with her dad after never knowing him." She took a sip of her tea. "It's inspiring."

Nate nodded and looked up to find his parents. "Hey, Mom and Dad."

Ellie turned and smiled at Lulu and Jack, noticing an unfamiliar man behind them. "We brought along Friday Harbor's newest resident, Blake Griffin. We wrapped up the sale of the winery and this is Blake's first day on the island," said Jack.

Nate gripped the newcomer's hand. "Welcome, nice to meet you. I'm Nate, Jack's son, and this is my new bride, Regi." She joined him and extended her hand to Blake.

He presented her with a bag filled with several bottles of wine. "Congratulations on your new home. I brought along something to help you celebrate."

"How thoughtful of you. I'll open a couple now," said Regi, toting the bag across the kitchen.

"This is our lovely friend and purveyor of all things sweet and delicious, Ellie Carlson. She owns Sweet Treats by the harbor," said Nate.

Blake extended his hand and his clear blue eyes met Ellie's. She sucked in a breath as she took in his wavy dark hair and kind smile above a slight cleft in his chin, but was drawn back to his gorgeous eyes. Patrick Dempsey's couldn't hold a candle to them. She felt his hand in hers, noticing he was missing half of a finger on his right hand, and was nudged from her trance when he said, "Oh, I'm so glad to meet you. I have a weakness for baked goods, so I'm sure I'll be seeing way too much of you."

She kept smiling as she gripped her glass of tea. "Welcome to Friday Harbor, Blake. I'd love you...I mean I'd love to have you stop in the bakery," she stammered and removed her hand from his.

Regi took in Ellie's reaction and added, "Ellie, would you take Blake around and introduce him? You know everyone."

"Uh, sure, not a problem." She stashed her glass on the counter and ushered Blake out of the kitchen. She made her way through the dining room and the great room. He met Linda and Max along with Jeff and Sam. Jen and Sean arrived while she was making the rounds. Lou came through the door bearing a platter of his famous crab cakes. Kyle and his grandmother were seated by the fireplace, enjoying the warmth. Megan and Molly were nearby, where Molly was regaling the group with tales of her trip to Italy.

Ellie answered the door as the bell chimed. Cam and Gianna came through the entry, hidden behind a huge bouquet of flowers. "Cam, Gianna, so glad you're still in town. I'd like to introduce Blake Griffin. He's new to Friday Harbor and purchased Island Winery," said Ellie. "If memory serves Gianna owns a winery in Italy, right?"

Gianna beamed. "Yes, this is true. We must discuss," she said, accepting Blake's hand.

"I'm giving Blake a tour, but I'll make sure he connects with you later," said Ellie. "Regi's in the kitchen." Cam jostled the flowers and shook Blake's hand before guiding Gianna to the kitchen.

As soon as they were out of earshot, Ellie motioned Blake closer and lowered her voice. "Cam and Regi grew up together. They came here to Friday Harbor for a high school graduation trip, where they made a pact to meet up on their fortieth birthdays, if they were still available. She ended up pregnant with Molly," she pointed to the young woman with hair the color of cinnamon, "and didn't tell him. He was rich and she wasn't. So, for the last twenty years she waited for him and came to the island last year. He never showed, but they ended up meeting each other in the waiting room of a doctor's office after poor Molly was attacked at college in Seattle."

Blake's eyes widened as she continued. "I know it's crazy. Anyway, Cam lost his young daughter in a car accident and his wife was at fault. The wife ended up committing suicide, leaving him all alone. Regi and Cam have reconnected as friends and he has a great relationship with Molly. His family is in the hotel business and he now spends his time in Italy at a new property, where he met charming Gianna. Molly spent last semester with them in Italy. Regi and Nate were married before Christmas and Cam gave them this house as a gift." She took a deep breath. "That's it."

"Wow, what a story. I have a feeling there's much more to it, but you did a great job condensing it in," he glanced at his watch, "under two minutes."

"I'll fill in the gaps later, but wanted you to understand the relationship at play. And I still haven't told you about Sam and Jeff or Linda and Max." They wandered to the bank of windows overlooking the deck and the sea beyond. As he took in the view, Ellie stole another look at him and detected a scar running from the outside of his eye up to his hairline.

Ellie pointed out the dogs, naming them all and linking them with their owners. Kate and Spence joined them as they took a seat at the dining room table. "Kate owns a new antique and art gallery down the street from me. Spence is a retired police detective from Seattle and Kate's best friend," said Ellie.

Blake shook hands with both of them as Nate arrived with glasses of wine. "Blake was kind enough to bring some wines from his new winery. Help yourselves," he said, offering the tray. They each took a glass and continued visiting.

"How'd you come to buy the winery?" asked Spence.

"I've grown up working with wine. My family has a vineyard and winery in the Yakima Valley and the Island Winery has used our grapes in some of their wines for years. When it came up for sale, we decided to buy it and I volunteered to move here and run it, since I needed a new challenge."

Kate took a sip. "Lovely, and what a fun adventure for you. I know you'll fall in love with the island. I'm relatively new in town and have found such wonderful friends here."

"I'm looking forward to it," said Blake. "The winery is closed from now until March, so I have some time to get acclimated and organized. I know summer and fall will be busy."

"It's a gorgeous property. I've been there a few times delivering wedding cakes and it's breathtaking," added Ellie. "Is there still a home on the land?"

Blake took a sip of his wine and nodded. "Yes, it's an older home, and needs some remodeling. It's been vacant for years. I'm actually living on my boat in the marina, until I have the time to fix the house up. Once I get organized, I'll invite you all out for a tour. The entire property is around twenty acres, with only five planted. I'm hoping to expand the planting area next year."

"We haven't been there yet, so it sounds like fun," said Kate. Spence nodded and helped himself to a skewer of a chicken appetizer from the platter on the table.

"I'm hoping to add more events. The previous owners were winding down in their career and I'd like to get more locals out during the off season and host a few more community gatherings. I know it's busy with tourists after Memorial Day."

Ellie bobbed her head in agreement. "It's crazy once the season hits until after Labor Day."

Regi announced the food was ready and set up buffet style. She invited everyone to make their way to the kitchen island and load up their plates. Ellie's cupcakes were arranged on a tiered serving piece on the side table in the dining room.

After retrieving mountains of food, the foursome found themselves seated together at one end of the table. They visited and educated Blake about the island, highlighting Cooper Hardware, owned by Jeff and his son, Charlie. Ellie filled him in on the local market, drugstore, and eateries. Spence took a forkful of crab cake and said, "Lou has the best crab on the island. I'm also partial to Big Tony's for pizza and Dottie's Deli for sandwiches."

"I'm not planning to do much cooking aboard the boat, so I'll be sampling the local restaurants," said Blake.

Kate added, "I get take-out from Soup D'Jour often and the Jade Garden has terrific Chinese."

"Back to some of the people here," Ellie gestured with her hand. "Jeff and his sister, Jen, grew up on the island, but his wife, Sam, is a newbie. They met when she bought Harbor Coffee and Books. They're both terrific and her best friend from childhood is Max. He's a doctor and moved here after Sam and Jeff were married."

"Max is married to Linda, who is a native and owns Buds and Blooms floral shop in town and a gorgeous nursery not far from here. The four of them are quite close and live nearby," said Kate, eyeing the cupcakes they had taken from the dessert table. "I can't decide which flavor to have, Ellie. They all look delicious."

"We could cut them in half and sample more of them," said Ellie with a grin. "I love the chocolate with the salted caramel and the coconut lime is refreshing and makes me think of summer."

"I've got to try the strawberry mini cheesecake and the one with the marshmallow and graham cracker," said Spence. "Do you want to split those with me?" he asked Kate.

In answer, she slid the plate closer and cut them both in half. "Delicious," she said, popping a bite of the cheesecake in her mouth. "Jen started dating Dr. Sean, one of Max's friends. Max convinced him to move here and manage the emergency room at our new hospital. Jen's daughter, Megan, is a sweet girl and works at Sam's coffee shop."

Ellie cut the other two in half and offered Blake his choice. He deposited half of the salted caramel in his mouth and wiggled his brows at Ellie. "I understand why it's your favorite." He took a sip of water before finishing off the coconut lime. "It tastes like sunshine."

"Well, thank you, I'm glad you like them," she said.

Sam visited the table with a carafe of coffee. "Jeff and I were just saying we haven't had a chance to visit with Blake. We'd love to host a dinner and have you over, along with a few friends and family and get to know you."

"That sounds great," said Blake. "You've all been so welcoming."

"How about a Sunday? Then Ellie won't be working and can join us," said Sam, pouring the last cup.

"Works for me," said Blake. The others nodded their agreement.

"Let us know what we can bring," offered Kate.

"I'll be in touch as soon as we get it organized," she said, continuing around the table to offer coffee.

Laughter and visiting filled the evening and at ten o'clock, Ellie attempted to stifle another yawn. She sighed, hating to go, but knew she'd be too tired in the morning if she delayed. She thanked Nate and Regi, getting hugs from both of them. Nate offered to retrieve Oreo and loaded her in Ellie's car.

Ellie made her way through the house and said her goodbyes. Blake was in a conversation with Jeff, discussing remodeling options, when she interrupted to say good night. "Great to meet you, Blake."

He stood and said, "I'll see you tomorrow. After eating your cupcakes, I've decided to make you my first stop every morning. I can walk over from the marina for exercise."

She grinned. "All of two blocks. What kind of exercise program is that?"

"It's my own system." He laughed and took her hand in his. "I'll be there in the morning, Ellie."

"She's always there by four, so if you can't sleep, you can wander over and watch her bake," suggested Jeff. "Ellie and I have bonded over many early morning cinnamon rolls."

"I'll keep it in mind," said Blake, squeezing her hand.

She waved goodbye traipsing down the walkway to her car. She hopped in and noticed Blake still waving from the steps. She backed out and turned onto the road and took one more look in the rearview mirror, wondering if she'd see him tomorrow.

Three

Tuesday morning while it was still dark outside, Ellie loaded another pan of cupcakes into the oven. She needed to bake a few more batches to complete the order for thirty-six dozen. She propped the back door open and the cool air wafted over her. She poured herself an iced tea, slumped onto her stool, and took a long sip. Tapping on the door startled her and she hollered out, "Hello."

She saw the door open and held her breath. Blake stuck his head through the opening. "Good morning," he said. She let out a sigh and he noticed her hand shake when she set her glass down. "I didn't mean to scare you. Saw the door open and thought I'd stop by early today."

"No problem, I didn't expect anyone so early. I was engrossed in this project and it was getting warm in here."

"Yesterday when I came by for a turnover you were so busy, I barely had time to say hello." He stepped past the storeroom and into the main kitchen. "Wow," he said, noticing every available surface was covered with the mini confections. "What's all this for?"

"Tomorrow night's New Year's Eve party. The firemen put it on every year and I'm doing cupcakes."

"Jeff mentioned the party and told me I should plan to come. Are you going?"

She nodded. "Yeah, it's a fun time and I'm closed the next day."

"I can't believe you do this all by yourself." He looked at his watch. "It's only four-thirty and it looks like you've been here all day."

"I got an early start this morning for this monster order. I've got muffins and fresh cinnamon rolls ready to come out in fifteen minutes, if you're interested."

He smiled. "I'm definitely interested."

"I usually have a pot of coffee going by now, but haven't made it yet. I'm having iced tea. What would you like to drink?"

"I'll make the coffee. Point me in the right direction."

She showed him the cupboard above the coffee maker and started on the frosting process. She filled a pastry bag and with deft movements swirled the cream colored frosting in a ruffled peak atop a sea of cupcakes. By the time he started the coffee and returned to the work table, she was sprinkling colored beads on the soft mounds of buttercream.

The timer sounded on the oven and she removed several pans of freshly baked cupcakes and put them on racks to cool. She opened another oven and slid the muffins and cinnamon rolls out.

The rich aroma of fresh baked cinnamon mixed with pumpkin and banana muffins tickled their noses. "These need to cool a bit and then I'll ice the cinnamon rolls."

"I'm in no hurry. I enjoy watching you work."

She boxed the decorated cupcakes and cleared the work table. She plucked another pastry bag from her supply and filled it with chocolate frosting and with quick precise movements embellished the cakes with a design resembling several small flowers.

Blake stood and watched her movements, mesmerized by her graceful dance. The coffee maker beeped, jolting him from his trance. "How do you take yours?"

"Real sugar and cream. It's in the fridge," she said, sprinkling iridescent sugar atop the frosting. She loaded the empty pans with fresh batter and slid them into the oven.

When he returned with their coffees she had the work table cleared again and the decorated cupcakes stored. She retrieved a bowl of cream cheese icing from the walk in refrigerator and applied it to the tops of the cinnamon rolls, making sure she left a healthy layer of topping on each roll.

When she was done, she plated one of them and presented it to Blake.

He forked a bite into his mouth and moaned. "This is the best thing I've ever tasted."

She smiled and her grey eyes twinkled with delight. "I'm glad you like them." She plopped the muffins into baskets and placed them in the display case. She glanced at the clock and hurried to the kitchen.

After a long gulp of coffee she slid the cooled cupcakes onto the work table and twirled lemon icing over them, sprinkling them with chunky sugar, leaving a shimmer across the surface. Another timer rang out and she retrieved loaves of freshly baked bread and glided them onto racks to cool.

Blake sniffed the air and said, "I'm going to have to take a loaf of bread with me. It will make great sandwiches for lunch."

"They need to cool a bit first. I'm a bit behind this morning," she said, wiping the sheen of sweat from her brow.

"I can't believe how much you've done. You're a whirlwind."

"Once I open at six, it's hard to work in the kitchen, so it's a necessity. I'll have some help starting Friday." She hefted another batch of cupcakes to the table. "Not a day too soon."

"If I knew the first thing about any of this, I'd be happy to help, but I'm not much of a baker." He stuffed the rest of the cinnamon roll into his mouth. "I'm more of an eater."

Her eyes brightened. "I know something you could do that would be a huge help. I need a bag of flour opened and poured into the bins. They weight fifty pounds, so your help would be fabulous."

Blake puffed his chest out and clenched his fists. "No problem. I can handle fifty pounds." He grinned and laughed as he exaggerated a caveman-like walk to the storage room. She showed him the bins and pointed out the bags of flour stacked on a shelf. With ease he pulled down the bag, but when he opened it, a poof of flour escaped and dusted his hair, face, and shirt. He wrestled the bag into the bins, but the end result left white streaks in his dark hair.

She broke into a laugh and forced the last of the salted caramel frosting out of the pastry bag. "Check yourself out in the mirror. You make quite the distinguished looking older gentleman." She snickered as she went back to her cupcakes. "There are towels on the shelf behind you. Dust it all off first and then wash your hands." She eyed him brushing away the powder from his face and hair. "How's it going at the winery? I don't know anything about wine, so speak slowly."

"I'm getting the lay of the land right now." He inspected himself in the mirror above the sink. "Jeff and I have been discussing remodeling the old house. He gave me some great ideas. It sounded like he'd be open to helping me, but told me he can't do as much since his accident."

"Yeah, he's made huge strides. He's working at the hardware store, but has cut way back on his handyman business. Sam worries if he's on a job alone, especially if he has to be on a ladder. His balance still isn't one hundred percent."

"I told him I could do the brunt of the work, but I need his expertise. I can figure out most things, but I know remodels can bring all sorts of surprises and value his experience." He emerged from the storeroom, with only a few specks of white dotting his shirt.

"He's the best and well respected on the island. Sam's a wonderful person. You'll get to know them at the dinner they're hosting on Sunday. She called you, right?"

He nodded his head. "I told her I'd bring the wine and I hope you're bringing dessert."

"I'll whip something up." She grinned and blew her bangs out of her face as she finished off the cupcakes. "Would you mind unlocking the front door and turning the open sign around?"

A few minutes later the door chimed while she was in the middle of loading dishes into the dishwasher. She dried her hands and hurried to the front counter. When the early birds had been served, Blake stuck his head around the corner. "I did what I could back here. I'm going to take off."

She stuffed a fresh loaf of bread in a bag and boxed up some cupcakes and shoved them both in his arms. "Thanks for your help. Sorry about the flour, I should have warned you."

He admired his stash of bakery goods. "I'd say it was worth it for all this. Are you sure I can't pay you for these and my cinnamon roll?"

She shook her head. "Consider them a welcome to the island gift." The bells on the door rang out. "I'll see you later."

"Tomorrow night for the party, right?" He smiled and gave her a nod before she disappeared to serve the new arrivals.

* * *

Gray clouds hung in the sky, threatening rain on New Year's Day. Ellie snuggled under her comforter, savoring the warmth of Oreo huddled next to her. The exhaustion of the holiday season, coupled with staying up to view the midnight fireworks over the harbor had caught up with her. The fog of sleep was lifting, but she resisted waking, preferring to stay in the haze between a dream and her memories of last night's party.

She had chosen to close the bakery early and Jen had dragged her down the street to her salon for a hairdo. After fixing her hair, she loaned her a gorgeous sheath in dark champagne covered with lace and dotted with sequins. To her delight the shirring on the dress hid her ever-growing waistline. Kate added a pair of her shoes that matched the dress. Sam contributed a gorgeous wrap and Linda provided a beautiful necklace and earrings. The color of the dress with her blond hair, which Jen had made look terrific, was perfect. She hadn't dressed up in years, opting for her best jeans and a blouse or sweater for the annual party, but admitted she looked attractive, maybe even happy.

The twelve of them had taken up two of the round tables at the firehouse. They laughed and visited, while they ate the delicious buffet. Despite her firm protests, Nate hauled her to the dance floor. She hadn't danced since high school and her whole body tensed as she attempted to keep up with Nate. "Ellie, you need to relax," he said, as he tried to budge her rigid hand.

"I'm not a dancer and feel like everyone's watching me and laughing." Her voice cracked. "Plus these are borrowed heels."

"Ah, come on. I could tell Blake was going to ask you to dance, so I thought I'd grab you and get you loosened up."

"You think?"

"Uh, yeah. He can't keep his eyes off you."

"I can't dance with him."

"Yes, you can. Loosen your arms and shoulders. Just let me guide you."

She took a breath. "I should've stayed home this year."

"He's a great guy. Successful. From all appearances, normal. And you never date anyone." He steered them across the dance floor. "Could be because there aren't many eligible men in Friday Harbor."

"I'm busy with work. I don't have time for a man."

"Maybe you should make time. I've known you for twenty years, Ellie. All you do is work. Take it from me, there's more to life," he said, glancing across the room and catching the eye of his new bride.

Tears stung her eyes as she concentrated on moving her feet without catching the loaned heels and falling. "It's easier to work than think about things."

"Don't think so much. Song's almost over and then I bet you a cinnamon roll, Blake will sprint over here to dance with you."

Her eyes widened with panic. "I don't think I can do it." The prickle of perspiration dampened her chest.

The last notes of the song played and he said, "Yes, you can." He released her hand and when they turned, Blake was standing next to them.

"How about a dance, Ellie?" he asked.

"I'll be by Friday for my cinnamon roll," said Nate, laughing as he walked to the table and met Regi.

"I'm not a skilled dancer. I haven't danced in decades," she said, feeling sweat form on her upper lip and the scratchiness of lace against her chest.

"Lucky for you, I'm a great dancer," he said, wrapping his arm around her waist.

She shut her eyes tighter not wanting the memories swarming in her head to escape. She smiled as she rested in her bed, savoring the feeling of Blake's hands and the smell of his neck. She inhaled and sighed. The scent of sage and tobacco with a hint of citrus still lingered. She scrunched her toes into the sheets, feeling the soreness on the balls of her feet. It wasn't a dream. The pain she suffered from dancing for hours was all too real.

Lavender slivers of light filtered into the room, tugging at her eyes. She resisted and kept them shut, content to stay lost in her memories of the party.

Everyone shared her magnificent cupcakes and sipped champagne while they visited. Max and Linda invited the group to their house for a New Year's brunch. The evening ended at the harbor. The fireworks over the water were always a thrill, but last night they had been magical.

It was cold, but the colors heated up the sky. Blake put his arm around her to keep her warm. She came close to kissing him at midnight. The other ten in the group were couples and kissed each other as soon as "Happy New Year" was shouted by the crowd. Blake leaned in, testing the waters, but she panicked and said something about the fireworks. Jeff engulfed her in a hug and planted a kiss on her cheek, saving her from stretching the awkward moment out any longer. Blake walked her to her car and suggested he treat her to a tour of the winery after brunch.

Her eyes fluttered and thoughts of last night receded as she focused on the clock. It was after eight. She nuzzled Oreo and threw the covers back. "Time to get going," she said, petting the dog's head. "I think I've got a date today."

Four

She put together the dough for her caramel sticky buns and jumped in the shower. When she walked past the stairs, she saw the brown satchel. She picked it up and the feel of the supple leather, albeit blemished and marred, carried her back twenty years. It had belonged to her father.

She remembered the sting of the bag when her mother had thrown it at her. She demanded Ellie fill it with her things and barked at her to get ready for their drive to the coast. Her parents were delivering her to catch the ferry to Friday Harbor. Her mother, Caroline, had been threatening to send her away for as long as she could remember and today she was finally getting her wish.

On that day, Ellie had stomped to her room, which had been an afterthought addition in the garage. It was easy to keep clean, since the twin bed took up most of the space and left room only for a small bookcase and closet. Even though her older sister was out of the house, Ellie hadn't been allowed to take up residence in the old room she had shared with Ceci when they were young. When her younger brother, Teddy had gotten old enough for a room, her dad had added onto the house. Teddy's room was palatial, outfitted with a queen sized bed, a flat screen television, fancy computer gaming boxes, and new furniture.

Through hot tears, she had crammed her meager supply of clothes and toiletries, one pair of shoes, and a small stuffed animal from her twin bed in the brown duffle. She cried when she said goodbye to her dog, Freckles. She pleaded with her parents to allow the dog to accompany her, but her mother had refused. Her brother, who her parents called "Baby Bear", was holding the dog when they pulled away from the house.

The drive she had made with her parents was the happiest she remembered them in years. It was the first time she witnessed them not fighting with each other. She sat in the backseat, gripping the leather bag, not saying a word on the four hour drive.

When they had finally reached the dock, her mother sat in the car, glaring at her as her father lugged the bag and walked her to the ticket counter. Caroline hollered out the window, "Teddy, hurry up. I don't want to leave Baby Bear too long."

He handed Ellie the ticket, put the leather strap on her shoulder, and hugged her. "Please be good for Uncle Bob and Aunt Ginny. If it weren't for them, I don't know where you'd go."

Her throat had constricted when he put his strong arms around her. She wanted him to say *I love you, Ellie.* She nodded her head on his shoulder, but he hadn't said anything else and neither had she. He plucked a wad of bills from his wallet and stuffed them in her hand. "Take care of yourself." He gave a wave and trudged back to the car, shoulders sagging and head hanging. She had seen her mother's mouth moving, shouting something, but the glass doors of the terminal had shut, saving her from the words.

Ellie put the money in her wallet and plodded through the crowd of passengers boarding the ferry. She bought a soft drink and sat by a window. Lulled by the slow motion and the lush swells of tree covered masses through which the ferry traveled, she relaxed. She hadn't seen her dad's brother and his wife since she was young, soon after her baby brother, Teddy, had been born.

As they neared Friday Harbor, her leg bounced and vibrated. She tried to stop it from shaking, but when she was nervous, it always shook. *What will they think of me?* The only thing she remembered from her visit with them at six years old was the bakery where her aunt made sure she had her fill of warm cookies.

She knew they still had the bakery and her mother took delight in telling her she would be expected to work there. The sting of her words was still fresh. "You'll finally have to get off your ass and have some responsibility. You expect us to cater to you. Now you'll have to work for your keep. I don't even know why your dad called Uncle Bob. We should have shipped you off to a reform school. You're never going to amount to anything anyway."

The harshness of her mother was a stark contrast to the welcome she received at the Friday Harbor end of her journey. Uncle Bob and Aunt Ginny were waiting and waving when she disembarked onto the landing. They rushed to her, which was helpful, since she wouldn't have recognized them. Uncle Bob was in his fifties and had become gray and rounder. Aunt Ginny's stunning red hair was now dull and streaked with white, but her golden brown eyes still sparkled. They both hugged her and kissed her on the cheek. Her aunt linked her arm in Ellie's and Uncle Bob took the leather duffle.

Ellie wiped fresh tears from her cheeks and nuzzled Oreo. She caressed the leather one more time and gently put it in the closet, stuffing the strap inside.

* * *

Linda and Max still had their Christmas decorations up for brunch. Linda was known for her amazing ability to deck the halls and she always chose a gorgeous tree. Ellie enjoyed visiting them, especially since they included Oreo in the invitation, who loved to play with all her dog friends.

Blake pulled into the driveway behind Ellie and offered to tote the box of sticky buns along with his wine, while she deposited Oreo in the doggie play area in the backyard.

Linda was in the kitchen retrieving pans from the oven. Ellie arranged her sticky buns on a platter and finished slicing some fruit. Kate and Spence had been the first to arrive and were helping arrange the food on the dining room table.

Sam and Jeff came up the walkway, followed by Sam's silky golden retriever, Zoe, and Jeff's chocolate lab, Bailey. Sam balanced two pie plates, while Jeff led the canine parade to the backyard. Nate and Regi came through the door with Murphy, who being a puppy, was always revved and ready to play. Nate wrestled her to the deck and sent her to terrorize the other dogs.

Blake stood at the glass doors off the great room and watched the dogs tumble over each other. "I guess I better get a dog if I want to be part of this group, huh?"

Jeff swiped a carrot from the veggie tray and nodded. "Yeah, we all love our dogs. Sam moved here with Zoe, who became great friends with my dog Bailey. Until we met each other, they were our only companions." He munched another carrot. "Last year Sam and I got that terror of a golden puppy, Murphy, for Regi's birthday gift. Linda's black lab, Lucy, and Oreo go way back."

Max made mimosas and poured them along with their non-alcoholic counterpart into champagne flutes. Sean and Jen rang the bell and Jeff led them to the great room. Sean had a late night call and was due back at the hospital in the afternoon, so he opted for the orange juice. Linda herded the group into the dining room and directed the twelve of them to their seats around the festive table.

Blake and Ellie were seated across from each other, flanking Linda at her end of the table. Max had a gift for toasts and he invited them all to join him in welcoming the New Year. "I'm so thankful for my life with my lovely wife, Linda. I'm blessed to live down the road from my best friend, Sam, and her incredible Jeff. Jeff's sister, Jen has made me feel like her own brother and has put a smile on Sean's face. Ellie is as sweet as her awesome treats. Nate and Regi are embarking on their new life together as husband and wife. Kate is someone we all admire and not just for her sense of style. She's introduced us to her best friend, Spence, who fits right in with our gang. Last, but definitely not least, we are lucky enough to be in the presence of a man who has unlimited access to wine. Welcome to Friday Harbor, Blake. To the New Year."

Max raised his mimosa and amid kisses and cheers, they all clinked glasses. The group spent several hours passing plates of delicious food around the table and indulging in Sam's wonderful pies and bottles of wine. Linda set a pot of coffee to brew and heated water for tea. The men cleared the table before sacking out on the couches in the great room in front of Max's larger than life television.

Once the ladies tidied the kitchen, Sam and Ellie carried trays of hot beverages to the great room and the women joined the men. Blake and Jeff had ventured outside to play with the pack of wild animals. Laughter and happy barks masked the chatter of the television football announcers. Ellie slipped the bag of dog cookies from her purse and stepped onto the patio.

She caught Blake's eye and tossed him the bag. Upon his successful catch he was instantly elevated to the most popular human on the planet. The dogs, with the exception of Murphy, who couldn't yet control her enthusiasm, all sat at Blake's feet. Zoe stood on her hind legs, motioning with her paws for a cookie. Bailey followed with a roll over and Lucy raised a paw, as if to offer a high-five. Oreo sat without moving, staring at the bag, intent on Blake's hands.

Once he dispensed all the dog bone shaped cookies, the lineup scattered and went back to bouncing around the yard. Jeff and Blake made their way up to the patio and came through the door, bringing a draft of cool air with them. Sam saw them rubbing their hands together. "We've got hot coffee and tea ready for you."

Jeff took a cup of coffee and deposited a kiss on his wife's lips. "Thank you, sweetie. Blake tamed the wild beasts with cookies and now they're back at it."

Blake took his coffee and sat on the couch next to Spence and Kate. Kate tapped her spoon against her cup and captured the attention of the group. "I know Dr. Sean needs to get back to the hospital soon, so before the party breaks up, we have a bit of news to share." She cast her whiskey eyes at Spence and set her cup on the table. She grasped his hand. "Spence has officially decided to move to the island. He's moving out of his apartment this week and will be living with me."

Smiles filled the faces of the group of friends gathered around the fireplace. Spence added, "Kate has been my best friend for more than forty-five years and means the world to me." His blue eyes twinkled as he squeezed her hand. "I asked Kate to be my wife, but after a lot of discussion," he glanced her way again, "we decided to live together."

"You all mean so much to us," she said, looking around the room at the people who had welcomed her and had become her family. "We don't want you to think less of us for this choice and if Spence had his way, we'd be married tomorrow." The group chuckled along with Kate. "We've both had disastrous marriages in the past and I'm reluctant to ruin the best relationship I've ever had with a man, so you'll have to forgive us."

Spence put his arm around her and pulled her close. "I told Katie you all would understand." He paused and kissed her. "Her son, Mitch, gave us his approval before he left."

"And so do we," said Regi. "We couldn't be happier and support you in whatever you decide." She got up and gave them both a hug. "Kate's like the mom I wish I'd had and now I get the bonus of you, Spence."

Nate followed and gripped Spence by the shoulder while pumping his hand. "I'm thrilled to have a fishing buddy full time."

Sam hugged Kate. "You're the best big sister I never had. I couldn't be happier for both of you." Spence engulfed her in a bear hug and she kissed him on the cheek. "You're one lucky man."

"It's apparent how happy you make each other, so I think it's wonderful," said Ellie.

Spence and Kate hugged each of their precious friends more than once before Sean and Jen left. Jeff and Max offered their help in getting Spence packed and moved and made a plan for a trip to Seattle in the coming week. Nate had to work but volunteered the use of his truck.

Linda sent everyone home with leftover care packages and Sam reminded the group about Sunday dinner. The dogs were retrieved by their owners and soon only Blake and Ellie were left.

"I promised Ellie a quick tour of the winery today, so we should probably head out," he said. Ellie called Oreo from the back gate and she came running. Linda coerced Lucy into the house, while Blake toted their leftovers to the cars.

Ellie led the way to the winery and when she opened the car door Oreo jumped out, eager to explore Blake's property. With only an hour of daylight left, they began the tour outdoors. They strolled through the vines and he explained the two types of grapes grown on the estate. "Both of these are used to make white wine. We grow the Madeleine Angevine, which originated in France, and the Siegerrebe, which is from Germany. The Madeleine Angevine is quite popular in Washington and is perfect with seafood. It's a dry, crisp wine with a hint of peach and apple."

She fingered the vines. "So you grew up around wine and learned by experience? My extensive wine knowledge consists of knowing there's white and then there's red."

He laughed. "Yeah, my dad taught me and I spent lots of time with our winemakers over the years. My degree is in business, but I went to California for a winemaking program. I was lucky enough to mentor under some famous winemakers."

They continued through the orderly rows and came upon the large covered pavilion. "This always makes a great spot for weddings," she said, taking in the view across the acreage and the quaint white church on the property.

"Do you have time to check out the tasting room?"

She nodded and motioned for Oreo to follow. They took the winding path to the white sided old schoolhouse. He opened the door and held it for her. "This was built in the 1890's and remodeled about a hundred years later. It's served as the tasting room ever since."

Inside the large space, Ellie found blackboards mounted along the walls and a large granite counter, atop a striking wooden floor. The blackboard was chalked with the wine offerings and prices. Displays held bottles and wine accessories. There was a small commercial kitchen in the back with a door leading outside to the pavilion. What she guessed had been a supply room or cloak room had been transformed into a small private room set up for tastings.

"It's the perfect blend. I love the blackboards mingled with the modern additions."

"I like it, with the exception of the lack of a real office." He showed her the tiny space, no bigger than a linen closet. "I've got to figure out a better space for my office."

"There's not much choice, is there?"

"I'm toying with the idea of making the private room into an office. I've got lots of ideas, but need to work through them."

"I'm sure you'll figure it all out. It's a peaceful place to spend your days."

"I can't wait for the first event of the season. The pavilion is the perfect spot for outdoor events. It's in great shape and has everything we need to host a buffet and bar. Not to mention a band and dancing. It's idyllic."

As they glanced outside, Ellie noticed how dark it was. "I better get home. Back to the grind tomorrow."

"Oh, I wanted to offer you a tasting while you're here."

"How about a raincheck? I'm not much of a wine drinker and it's too late with my drive home."

'I'll hold you to it. It'll be my chance to explain wine and show you there's more than white or red." He walked her to her car and helped her load Oreo in the passenger seat. She glanced in the rearview mirror and saw his silhouette in the porch light.

"Maybe I need to broaden my interests and learn more about wine," she said to Oreo. The dog titled her head to the side and gave her a quizzical look.

Five

Ellie bounced out of bed Friday, anxious to work with Nicole and get her up to speed. As soon as Ellie deposited her things in the office, she heard her young apprentice. Ellie hollered out "Good morning." She smiled as she sighed, filled with relief.

Ellie spent the early hours concentrating on breads and pastries. She showed Nicole the techniques and then watched as her new helper made the next batches. Once the bakery opened for business they both worked the counter. The cash register was set up with the pricing, so as long as Nicole hit the right buttons it would be a breeze.

Ellie offered bottled juices and waters, plain old coffee and iced tea, but left the fancy coffees and drinks to Sam's shop. With all the baking responsibilities, she didn't have the time to dedicate to the coffee business. She always referred customers to Harbor Coffee and Books if they were looking for such a beverage. Sam supported Ellie by carrying a small selection of her pastries, in addition to her own delicious pies and brownies.

Once they had dispensed with the early customers, Ellie watched over her protégé as she retrieved hot pans from the oven and slid them onto the cooling racks. "Tomorrow we'll make donuts and then next week I'll have you do most of the baking. I want to get you comfortable before I take a quick trip to visit my family."

"When do you need to go?" Nicole asked as she maneuvered a fresh pan of cinnamon rolls in the oven and set the timer.

"I'm shooting for the end of the month, or sooner if it works out." Ellie plucked the recipe for the icing from the book on the counter. "Go ahead and work on this," she said, handing it to Nicole.

Ellie perched on her stool and finished her weekly supply order, keeping an eye out for customers. As she completed the spreadsheet and checked her stock, she mulled over the idea of teaching Nicole the process, but discarded it. Instead, she would make sure and stock up before the trip, so there would be no worries while she was away.

Once the baking was done, Nicole turned her attention to cleaning all the equipment and pans they had dirtied during their morning frenzy. Ellie fixed Nicole a large iced tea before she left the kitchen to cover the front.

Foot traffic by the window diminished after the early afternoon ferry left the harbor. Families who had united for Christmas were saying goodbye and vacationers were heading back to the mainland. The holiday rush was over. Experience taught Ellie there would be a lull until Valentine's Day. Parties and weddings would boost business and then it would be slow again until summer.

She looked up from straightening the display case, surprised to find the same thin young girl from several days ago. "Good morning…I mean afternoon. You're back?"

The girl nodded. "Yeah, I was hoping uh, to ask you, uh…"

"Are you looking for a job?" Ellie scrunched her forehead, trying to decipher what the girl wanted. "I don't have any openings right now. It's our slow time, but could use help this summer. I didn't catch your name."

The girl's eyes widened. "Oh, yeah, summer would be great. I'm Danielle."

"I'll get you an application to fill out. Go ahead and have a seat, Danielle." She gestured to a table and dashed to retrieve the paperwork from her office.

Ellie returned, adding a pumpkin muffin swirled with cream cheese frosting to the table. She slid it and the paperwork in front of the young woman and handed her a pen. "Give a yell when you've got it filled out and I'll be back with you."

Ellie made her way to the kitchen and admired the gleaming stainless surfaces. She turned and saw Nicole, her face pink with perspiration and her wilted hair hanging limp across her face. "Wow, you did a great job. Let's call in lunch and take a break. We'll be closing soon."

Nicole volunteered to walk to Soup D'Jour and pick up their lunch. Ellie made sure all the tables were wiped and ready for customers. She used the opportunity to steal a glance at the job application. Only the name block had been completed. Danielle had eaten a few bites of the muffin, but was staring across the shop, fixated on the window.

"You doing okay, Danielle?"

The girl flinched and looked down at the table. "Yeah, I'm almost done."

Nicole came through the door toting a bag and the wonderful aroma of chicken noodle soup filled the shop. "We're taking our lunch break. Would you care for some soup, Danielle?" The girl's sunken cheeks and bony arms screamed for food.

"Oh, uh, I'm sorry. I don't want to interrupt you."

"Not to worry. We have plenty, how about a bowl?"

She shrugged. "Uh, okay, it smells good."

Ellie returned with soup and a slice of her homemade bread. After Nicole finished her lunch, Ellie suggested she take off early. "See you tomorrow. You did a great job today."

The hint of morning sun had disappeared beneath a blanket of gloomy clouds the color of smeared pencil lead. The dark sky brought a dimness that made it seem much later in the day. Ellie tallied the cash register as the first sprinkling of rain peppered the sidewalk in front of the bakery. She flipped the closed sign around and made her way to Danielle's table.

"Let's take a look at what you've got down so far."

Danielle lifted her blonde head. "I'm not here for a job. I'm here to ask you a question."

Ellie's eyebrows arched. "Okay, go ahead."

"This is going to sound weird." A long sigh followed and Danielle continued. "I was adopted nineteen years ago. I think you're my birth mother. Your real name is Elaine Carlson."

Ellie's throat tightened and her mouth went dry. She opened her mouth to speak, but had no words. The only sound was the pelting of the rain against the window.

"My mom and dad helped me find you." She pulled a folded paper out of her jacket. "Here are my DNA results for you to compare to yours. I'm sick. I've been sick for a long time and I'm getting worse. I have a rare kidney disease and need a transplant." She swallowed hard. "I should say another transplant. I've been dealing with chronic rejection."

Ellie's eyes clouded with confusion and she shook her head. "I'm, I'm so sorry." Tears formed in her eyes and sweat sprang from her pores. "I didn't know." She studied the girl. Her hazel eyes stared back at Ellie. Ellie sucked in a breath, recognizing the brown flecks in the green eyes. She hadn't seen those eyes in twenty years. When she made the mistake of thinking they held the answer to her problems.

"So, I know this is a shock for you, but I've known I was adopted a long time. I would've never bothered to look for you except I need a kidney. I had a transplant a few years ago. From the list. But, now the doctors say I'd have a better chance if I could get a donor from a blood relative. So, that's why I'm here. I need to ask you to get tested and see if you're a candidate." Danielle let out a breath and stared at Ellie.

"Wow, that's a lot of information to take in." She sighed and stared at the DNA results.

"Don't you believe me? You had a baby nineteen years ago, right? Here in Friday Harbor. The adoption was handled by the Law Offices of Brooks and McBride." Her eyes bored into Ellie's.

"It's not that I don't believe you. All of it is…is correct. This is all just so…unexpected." Ellie's leg began to shake under the table. "Are you staying on the island?"

"We leave tomorrow. I start dialysis on Monday." Danielle reached into her pocket and pulled out a card. "Here's my doctor's information. He said to have your doctor get in touch and he would explain everything."

Ellie took the card and saw the logo from the University of Washington Medical Center. "Do you live in Seattle?"

"We do now. Once I started having problems, we needed to be closer to the specialists. We live in Lake Forest Park."

"Danielle, I'm so sorry you're ill." Tears snaked down Ellie's cheeks. "I regret a lot of things in my past. I was only sixteen and definitely not prepared to be a mother."

The young girl shrugged her shoulders. "Is there any history of kidney problems in your family?"

Ellie wiped her eyes. "Not that I know of, but I'll check." She fiddled with the application. "How do I get in touch with you?"

Danielle dug a cell phone out of her pocket. "Give me your number and I'll text you."

Ellie rattled it off and seconds later she heard her phone chirp. "I'll talk with my doctor next week. I'm not sure what to say at this point. I need to know more information."

"The way the doctors talk, this is my last chance. I've done everything else and I'm getting worse. The plan is to do dialysis at home at night, but until things stabilize I won't be able to travel." Danielle finished her juice in one gulp. "I was going to talk to you the other day, but chickened out."

Ellie nodded. "I can understand why. I'm overwhelmed right now."

"Are you married with other kids?"

Ellie shook her head. "No, it's just me and my dog."

"There's no father listed in the records. Do you know who my father is?"

Ellie felt her breathing quicken and her heart thudded. "I do know, but the whole situation was complicated. I didn't list him and haven't talked to him since. He doesn't know I had a baby."

"Do you know how to get in touch with him?"

Ellie shook her head, feeling a tear leak out of her eye. She reached under the table to put a hand on her offending leg.

"If it doesn't work out with you, I'll need to find him next."

"I grew up in Sunnyside and that's the last place I saw him. I have no idea if he still lives there."

"What's his name?"

"Lance, Lance Franklin."

Danielle slid out of her chair. "Let me know once you talk to your doctor and what you decide."

As the girl put her hand on the door, Ellie blurted, "What are your parents' names?"

"Dan and April Lawson. They're terrific parents and wanted to be here, but I needed to meet you alone."

"I'm sorry, Danielle, I truly am."

She tilted her head, staring at the floor. "It's Dani. I go by Dani and it's the way it is." She turned the handle on the door. "I'll talk to you next week."

Ellie nodded and said, "Bye, Dani."

As soon as the door shut, Ellie rushed to lock it. She turned off the lights and flopped into a chair. Her head drooped and fell onto her arms atop the table. The racking sobs shook the table as her chest heaved with grief. All the memories she had worked so hard to forget were rushing over her like a raging river, sucking the breath from her.

Six

When Ellie got up she spotted the disarray on the counter from last night. Coloring books were strewn across the surface and pens, pencils, and markers were scattered about the area. She shook her head with disgust, recalling the funk she'd been in and the comfort of the distraction she'd mastered as a teenager. She picked up the implements, grouping them by type and color and restacked her books.

Ellie plodded through Saturday on automatic pilot. She and Nicole made the dough for donuts and while letting it rise, she whipped together the glazes. During the winter, she only made donuts on Saturdays. They were popular, but time consuming. Once they were fried, she showed Nicole how to dip them in glaze. Ellie left the decorating up to her, giving her a basket of sprinkles and a glass shaker of cinnamon and sugar.

While Nicole finished, she went to work on the cake for Sam's dinner party tomorrow. Nobody could resist her salted caramel chocolate cake and the recipe was like an old friend. She didn't have to think. Muscle memory took over when she baked. She had the cake layers in the oven by the time Nicole finished the donuts.

By the end of the day, they had sold all the donuts, plus the rest of the pastries, except for one lonely cinnamon roll. She packed it to take home. Nicole cleaned the display cases, while Ellie put the finishing touches on the cake and boxed it.

She gave Nicole a wave and wished her a pleasant weekend. The thick gray skies had lingered and a light rain persisted on the drive home. Each time the wipers swept across the windshield Ellie flinched, jarred from the weight of her foggy daze. Alarm gripped her when she pulled into the garage and realized she had no memory of her drive home.

Oreo's happy face greeted her from the door. She hung her coat and caught a glimpse of the leather duffel. She slammed the door on the wounded bag that stowed her heartaches and failures. She sidled up to her computer. After researching kidney transplant information for a solid hour, she succumbed to Oreo's nose nudging and took her outside.

Oreo bounced through the meadow and Ellie trudged along, lost in thought. She ambled after the dog in the light drizzle. Her next steps darted through her mind. She had to get tested. If she was a match, she'd have to figure out how to be off work for several weeks. She'd have a ten pound lifting limit for at least a month. The recovery was going to complicate her ability to earn a living. Winter on the island was not a lucrative time. She might have to part with some of her savings, if surgery was in her future.

She longed to talk to her aunt and uncle, but didn't want to burden them with anything more. It was dusk when she and Oreo returned to the house. Ellie took out some leftovers to heat and made sure Oreo's bowl was filled. As she stirred her soup, she shouted, "Max." Oreo stopped eating and gave her a sideways glance. "It's okay, Oreo. I figured out the best person to talk to about this."

She picked up the phone and dialed Linda and Max. He answered and when she explained she had a medical issue she needed to discuss, he made plans to meet her on Sunday morning at his office in the hospital.

She let out the breath she had been holding when she hung up the phone. She ate her soup and the cinnamon roll. Her brain continued to race with thoughts of Dani and the hardships she had endured. She colored until she was too sleepy to focus on the detailed patterns.

She wandered to her bed while various scenarios tumbled across the movie screen in her mind. Sleep eluded her, replaced by anxiety and panic. She feared being a match as much as being rejected terrified her. Each time she was on the brink of sleep, she sprang up gasping for breath. Her heart knocked and her pulse throbbed at her temple and her throat. She was slick with sweat and shivering. After tossing and turning, exhaustion prevailed and extinguished the emotional firestorm for a few hours.

* * *

Ellie felt Oreo's tongue on her arm. She forced open a slit in her eye and saw the soft purple light of dawn filling her bedroom. She pressed the tips of her fingers into the sides of her head. "Ah," she moaned. Her head pounded. "Great, I have a hangover headache without the fun of drinking."

She tried to keep her head steady as she sloughed the covers off and swung her legs over the edge of the bed. She shuffled to the kitchen and started a pot of coffee, before seeking relief in a scalding shower. She emerged with her hair wrapped in a towel and poured coffee into her largest cup. She added a healthy splash of cream and scooped in sugar.

The enticing aroma delighted her nose as she took her first sip. She combed out her wet hair and tucked the fluffy robe around her neck. She cradled the cup of healing liquid in her hands and snuggled into her recliner, distracting herself with an old episode of *Murder, She Wrote*.

Oreo rested her head against the chair and Ellie ruffled the dog's shiny fur. The motion and the comfort of Oreo's warmth calmed Ellie. After the episode ended, she took the time to blow her hair dry and curl it. She skipped makeup, planning to apply it before the dinner party.

She donned a jacket and took Oreo outside to play ball until she had to drive into town to meet Max. There was a chill in the air and the fresh scent of rain, but it was dry at the moment. The dog verged on fanaticism when it came to her ball. She never tired and Ellie's arm gave out long before Oreo was ready to call it quits. She rewarded her loyal friend with a dog cookie before she left for town.

She followed Max's directions and came through his private entrance. She found him at his desk and he offered her a latte. "I stopped by Sam's place on the way and decided I'd treat us to a drink."

She took the cup and he gestured for her to have a seat. He perched on the edge of his desk. "I appreciate you making time for me today, Max." She dug the paperwork out of her purse and took a deep breath. She explained the events as they had unfolded yesterday in the bakery. Ellie hung her head when she admitted giving up her baby for adoption when she was sixteen.

"Dani gave me her DNA results and the card for her doctor. I need to get tested and have my doctor talk with hers. I know you're a cardiac surgeon, but I trust you and was hoping you could do the testing for me and help me figure this out." Her voice cracked and her throat was parched, despite several sips of the creamy coffee.

"I'm happy to help you, Ellie." Max put his glasses on and perused the paperwork. "Let's start with some simple blood tests and go from there. I can run a DNA workup in addition to the bloodwork we'll need to determine if you're a match for Dani."

Ellie sniffed and nodded. He handed her a box of tissues from the other side of the desk. "I believe her. She has Lance's eyes. Plus, who would make this up?"

"If we determine you're a viable donor, there will be more extensive tests and questionnaires for you to answer. Then you'll have to figure out if you're mentally prepared to do this, Ellie. It's not to be taken lightly."

"I know. I've been worried about being able to work. I'm barely able to afford extra help and couldn't possibly pay for more hours." She shook her head. "I can't believe this is happening."

Max gripped her hand. "Let's not get ahead of ourselves. One step at a time, okay?" She swallowed a sob and squeezed his hand. "I can draw your blood myself right here and we should have results by Tuesday. Then we'll go over them and figure out the next step."

He excused himself to gather supplies and she rolled up her sleeve. He distracted her by talking about Sam's party and asked her what she made for dessert. He was rewarded with a hint of a smile.

"One of your favorites. The salted caramel chocolate cake."

"It's definitely irresistible. I have a horrible time avoiding treats, between your cakes and Sam's pies."

"I need to cut back on my sampling. I've gained weight over the last year."

He finished collecting the last vial and applied pressure to her arm. "All done. I'll wrap this and no lifting today with that arm. I don't want any bruising."

He wrapped her in a bear hug before she left. "We'll figure this out, Ellie. Worrying about it isn't going to help. We'll know more on Tuesday. Stop by after you close the bakery and we'll go over everything. I'll have talked to Dani's doctor by then and we'll have all the information."

She nodded her head against his shoulder and was reminded of the last time her dad had hugged her. "Thanks, Max. For everything."

He walked her to the exit and promised to see her in a few hours, waving as he turned for the laboratory.

* * *

Sam's party was a useful distraction. Even though Ellie considered staying home, she knew brooding about Dani would only make things worse. She had fun playing with the dogs in the backyard and focusing on them kept her worrisome thoughts at bay.

She sat next to Kate at the table and more than once the perceptive woman asked her if she was feeling well. "You don't seem yourself tonight. Are you sure you're okay?" she asked, when dessert was being served.

"I'm just tired. I didn't sleep well."

"You ought to close on Mondays and take a bit more time for yourself, Ellie. Life goes by too fast."

"Mondays are my slowest day."

"Probably because so many stores are closed. A lot of people don't bother coming into town on Mondays. I haven't had any complaints about it," said Kate.

"It's something to consider. I'm still training Nicole this week and hoping she'll be okay to manage alone soon."

"How's your uncle?"

"About the same. Aunt Ginny said he's not too happy with his new diet and exercise plan. He's always had a sweet tooth." She took a plate with a sliver of the cake and Sam's berry cheesecake pie. She noticed Spence take

Kate's hand in his. "It's obvious Spence is happy to be moving here."

Kate beamed as she forked a bite of cake. "He's so excited. I think the move will be easy. His apartment is small, so the guys think they can use the two pickups and do it in one trip."

"Is he going to continue his consulting work with the police in Seattle?"

"He plans to do it, but not full-time. He's excited about fishing more and wants to get back into golf. He and Max already have plans for tee times." She slid her plate to Spence with half the slice of cake. She eyed his plate and saw only a nibble of pie left. She took another forkful of cake and stole the plate with the pie. She shook her head and said, "We had a deal to split these."

Ellie laughed. "Maybe you should cut them in half before he starts."

"You'd think I could trust a highly decorated police detective, huh?" Kate popped the small bite of pie in her mouth. "Spence is going to help me out at the store when he isn't busy. Nate's mom is still working part-time, so between the two of them, I'll get a break."

"Maybe I'll put him to work at the bakery."

"I think he'd eat all your profits. The good news is he'll work for food."

They both laughed and when he tore himself away from chatting with Blake and looked at them with stern brows, they both erupted into hysterics. "What are you girls up to?"

"Oh, not much, just getting some jobs lined up for you once you get settled in," said Kate, her eyes twinkling with mischief.

"Now don't get me a job too quickly. Blake and I are organizing a salmon fishing trip for the weekend. We're going to take his boat out. Max, Sean, Jeff, and Nate are all in, so it'll be a manly weekend."

"Well then, maybe the ladies need to have a weekend. What fun could we plan?" asked Kate, glancing around the table.

"How about we take the ferry over to Orcas Island and do a spa package at the Rosario? We could do movies and a sleepover here. And with all the dogs," suggested Sam.

Linda hurried from the table. "I think I've got some two-for-one deals from the Rosario." She came back clutching her purse and smiling. She held the coupons high above her head. I've got three, so we're set."

"When are you boys leaving town?" asked Kate.

Blake said, "We're going to take off Friday afternoon and we'll be home Sunday night. They only allow salmon fishing on Fridays, Saturdays, and Sundays now, so we need to take advantage of the weekend."

"I could close on Saturday unless Lulu is free and wants to work. Do you think you could leave Nicole alone for the day, Ellie?" asked Kate.

"I think so. It would be an easy way to find out how she does."

"Do you have any appointments scheduled Saturday, Jen?" asked Linda.

She thumbed the screen of her smart phone. "Only one and I can move her, so I'm in," Jen said with a grin.

"Okay, I think it's settled," said Kate. "It'll be fun to have a mini getaway."

"I'll make the reservations at the Rosario," offered Linda.

"We can take my SUV and I'll handle the ferry," said Sam.

Blake cleared his throat. "Uh, Ellie, we were hoping you'd make us some stuff to take on the trip. Will you have time to squeeze us in?"

"Sure, not a problem. I'll set you guys up." She pulled away from the table. "I need to catch Oreo and hit the road. I've got an early morning."

Blake hollered at Oreo and she came at full speed. He walked Ellie to her car and opened the door for Oreo. "Your cake was the best. Sam's going to let me take some of it and her pie home."

"Score for you," she said, climbing behind the wheel. "I'll have all your goodies ready for you on Friday."

"I'll stop by before then. I'm glad you came tonight. Are you okay?"

"Just tired."

"You seemed quiet. Get some rest. I'll check on you in the morning." He winked and shut the door on Oreo, waving through the window.

* * *

Ellie couldn't wait for Monday and Tuesday to be over. She distracted herself with batch after batch of muffins, turnovers, croissants, cupcakes, and cinnamon rolls. The display cases were loaded and she stored a stack of muffins and unfrosted cupcakes in the freezer.

Nicole mastered the end of day procedures and Ellie was confident she could leave her for a day. To make Saturday easier, they decided to make donuts on Friday instead. She put a sign in the window, so her regulars would know they'd have to get their donut fix on Friday.

She locked the doors and drove the few blocks to the hospital. Max was waiting for her. "Come on in, Ellie." He motioned her to one of the chairs in front of his desk and he took the other.

"Did you get the results?"

He pulled a file from the top of the desk. "Right here, I've got everything we need."

Ellie let out a sigh. "Okay, I'm ready."

"First off, Dani is your daughter. The DNA is conclusive." Ellie licked her lips and nodded.

"I spoke to her doctor and he shared more about her condition. She did get set up for dialysis at home, which is a better option and much more convenient. She can do it at night while she sleeps."

"How long can she do dialysis?"

"Indefinitely or until things progress. She's doing well and it's taking the place of a fully functional kidney, but ideally she needs a new one."

"So, am I a match?"

Max took his glasses off and said, "This is where it gets tricky. Your blood tests indicate you're not a viable candidate. Have you had blood work done recently?"

She shook her head. "No, it's been several years."

"Okay, well your bloodwork shows you're diabetic. I want to run some more tests while you're fasting, but I'm not happy with these. It's going to take some work on your part to get this under control. You'll need to exercise and watch your diet. You mentioned you've put on some weight?"

"Yeah, over the last year maybe two, I've noticed much more of a muffin top," said Ellie.

"Let me take your blood pressure. It will probably be high with this stress, but I'll give you a machine to take home and I want you to record it each day. Your cholesterol is too high, so we need to get it under control."

"So, I'm too unhealthy to donate a kidney?"

"Basically, yes. People who are diabetic or pre-diabetic are not suitable candidates." He finished and released the pressure on the blood pressure cuff. "It's high, but let's monitor it for a few weeks and evaluate it when you're not dealing with this pressure."

"I don't exercise at all. I don't have any spare time and I know I eat too much junk at the bakery," Ellie said, tears burning her eyes. "I didn't want to let her down. I gave her away so she'd have a better life. Poor Dani. I'm going to have to look into finding Lance and convince him to help her."

"Let's concentrate on your health right now. I already talked to Dani's doctor and explained you're not a donor candidate. He'll let her know today. You have too many risk factors for having your own health problems, so you can't chance giving up an organ you may need in the future. Diabetics can suffer from kidney problems."

"But if I can reverse it, maybe I can donate."

He shook his head. "I don't think so, Ellie. You may need medication to get this under control and once you're a diabetic, you can't donate. Like I said, I need more tests to determine the extent. We need to get your health under control. Your numbers are too high. I know it doesn't seem like it, but having this test was a gift."

She couldn't control the tears cascading down her cheeks that plopped onto her shirt. "What about Dani? She's going to hate me now."

"All she's going to know is you're not a candidate. You mentioned her father. Is he an option? Or do you have siblings?"

"I have two siblings, but I haven't talked to either of them in twenty years. I'll have to find Lance before I know if he's willing." She wiped her eyes. "What a mess I've made of my life. Our lives."

Max took her hands in his. "You need to calm down and focus on getting healthy or you won't be helping anyone. I want you to fast starting tonight and come in tomorrow morning for a blood test. I'm going to order a more extensive test. Here's a lab slip for it," he said, handing her the white paper. "I'll call you when I have the results. In the meantime, go ahead and read these materials on diabetes. Check over the foods listed and make some meal plans."

She took the stack of brochures and pamphlets and stuffed them in her bag. "This is all just too much, Max."

"I have another homework assignment for you," he smiled. "You need to talk to someone and share some of this. You'll be with your friends this weekend, tell them. Let them help you with this burden."

"It's so awful and embarrassing. You don't even know everything."

"I know you're a wonderful and talented person. You're always helping other people, let them help you."

She nodded and shrugged. "I'll think about it." She picked up her bag and stood. "I need to call Dani tonight."

"My advice would be not to say too much. You can share how sorry you are without getting into the specifics. It won't help the situation and might make things worse for you."

She nodded and gave him a hug. "You're a kind and wise man, Max. Thank you."

"I'll talk to you no later than Thursday. Take care, Ellie."

She lumbered down the hallway in a fog. She tossed her bag in the passenger seat and turned the key in the ignition. She kept switching on the wipers until she realized her vision wasn't blurred from rain, but with tears.

Seven

Stretched out on her bed with Oreo, she stroked the dog to calm down before making the call to Dani. She fell asleep and woke up a few hours later, filled with dread. She rearranged the pillows and propped herself against them. When she tapped the button for Dani, her pulse quickened.

"Hi Dani. It's Ellie Carlson."

"If you're calling to tell me you can't donate, I already know. I talked to my doctor this afternoon."

"Oh, well yes, I, uh…wanted to let you know. I found out today from my doctor and wanted to tell how sorry I am."

"Well, that's the way it goes. I wasn't sure you'd do it anyway, even if you could."

Ellie's head throbbed. "I would have done it, Dani."

Dani's voice on the other end of the phone bit back. "I'm sure you care about a kid you didn't even bother to keep. Whatever."

Ellie took a deep breath to keep her voice from shattering. "I'll try to find Lance and determine if he'll agree to be tested."

"Right. He'll be so excited to know he has a sick kid he never knew about. I'm sure your plan will work out." Dani's voice dripped with sarcasm.

"Dani, I'm truly sorry this is happening. I'll let you know if I have any luck with Lance."

"I won't hold my breath." Her frozen tone stung.

Ellie gripped her temple. "I'll be in touch as soon as I can."

"Yeah, whatever. Just go back to your own life and forget about it." The phone disconnected.

Ellie hands were shaking when she hit the red button. She tugged the blanket to her chin and wept.

* * *

Sleep came in short bursts. Erratic dreams woke her with a start several times during the night. The shrill sound of her alarm jolted her awake. She disengaged the tangled sheets and shuffled to the shower. Hunger pangs wrenched her stomach, reminding her she had a lab appointment and couldn't eat anything.

The throbbing in her head had turned into a dull ache. She longed for a cup of coffee to lift the fog settled in her brain. Nicole's car was parked behind the bakery when Ellie arrived. The aroma of the fresh brew she craved teased her when she opened the back door.

After depositing her things in her office, she grabbed an apron and a large glass of water. They finished the morning baking and Ellie took a break, choosing to walk to the hospital, intent on getting some exercise. She was one of the first in line and was finished within minutes. On her way back, she treated herself to a non-fat latte at Harbor Coffee and Books. She resisted the temptation of fresh brownies and opted for a carrot muffin sans frosting back at the bakery.

She knew her choices weren't the healthiest, but they beat her usual fare. The concept of planning diabetic meals was depressing, not to mention she lacked the energy to deal with it after her conversation with Dani. She kept busy and tried to shake off the rebuff Dani had delivered, but the conversation kept replaying in her head.

Lunch consisted of a stingy garden salad with dressing on the side. She skipped her usual slice of crusty French bread. One thing was certain— this new eating plan was making her cranky. She volunteered to handle the cleanup and slammed the pans with gusto as she thought more about Dani.

Her stomach rumbled as they were closing. Dinner was a few hours away, but she had nothing prepared. Her normal routine was under attack.

Between the stress of meeting Dani and her new "Living Well with Diabetes" homework, she felt like the donkey in *Shrek*—on the edge. After Nicole left for the day, she pulled out the diabetic literature and penned a grocery list.

Carbs had always been her favorite food. Soothing when things went wrong or a piece of deliciousness for celebrating—they were her go-to food group. That was all about to change. The things she liked most and the staples in her diet were off limits. It was all non-fat, low sodium, fresh fruits and vegetables, and lean meats. Not much room for anything she baked.

She stopped at the market and began her quest for permitted foods. She plopped a rotisserie chicken in her basket, knowing it would make an easy dinner. Light salad dressings, low sodium ingredients for soups, and fresh produce rounded out her provisions. She added non-fat half and half and a natural sweetener, since she wouldn't be giving up her coffee.

She vowed to add walking to her daily routine and took Oreo for a jaunt around the property before dinner. She made a salad and doctored it up with the pre-cooked chicken and a light balsamic dressing. She missed her crusty bread and butter, but the apple she sliced satisfied her craving for sweets.

Her plan to research Lance Franklin online dissolved in exhaustion after she tidied the kitchen and changed into her pajamas. She lacked the strength to dedicate to surfing the web or coloring. She fell into bed and was asleep before she could worry about Dani or her diabetes.

* * *

Blake stopped in for an early cinnamon roll on Thursday. He helped himself to a cup of coffee and offered to make hers. "Use the non-fat half and half and the green sugar stuff in mine," she said, as she scraped icing from a bowl.

He frowned. "What's with that?"

"Doctor's orders. I had some bloodwork done and found out I need to cut back on all the foods I love."

He handed her the concoction. "It seems to happen when we creep up on forty. Sorry to hear it."

"Yeah, it doesn't make it easy to work here. I'm so used to popping something in my mouth to test it or just because. It's going to be a hard adjustment."

"It's a mental game, more than anything." He wiped the remaining icing off his plate with his last bite. "I'm not sure I could do it working here though. Your stuff is delicious."

He put some money on the counter and promised to stop by in the morning to pick up the order for the weekend fishing trip. "I've got to get to work since I'm taking off a few days. Thanks for breakfast."

Max called before noon and reminded Ellie to stop by after she closed. She and Nicole prepped for the donut making in the morning and Nicole assured her again she would be fine on Saturday.

"If you sell out of stuff early, just close the place. I'll see you in the morning and we'll get those donuts made."

Ellie finished some bookkeeping and then walked to Max's office. He took her blood pressure log and his eyebrows arched as he assessed the numbers. "These are high, Ellie."

"I know. I'm not sure if it's related to stress or always high. I read through the stuff you gave me and it sounds like the diet plan will help with cholesterol, blood pressure, and blood sugar."

He nodded. "Exactly, a healthier diet plus exercise will do wonders. I'll hold off on a blood pressure medication for now, but I want to look at your log every two weeks. I reviewed your blood work and I want to get you started on an oral treatment. Then after a few months, we'll test you again and check your numbers. If you're doing well with your new diet and exercise plan, we'll hope to avoid insulin injections." He gave her several packets of samples and a prescription.

He handed her a blood glucose monitor and showed her how to use it. He included a chart with her target ranges for different times of the day. You can also download the results to a computer." He went to the cabinet and retrieved a box. "One last gift for you today," he said, handing her the container. "This is a fitness monitor. I get a few of these to pass out to special patients. It counts your steps and mileage. It's an easy way to know how you're doing with your exercise goals."

"Wow, there's a lot to this. I was already depressed with my new food choices. I sort of forgot about the blood testing part." She looked over the mound of boxes on the desk in front of her. "Is there a chance I can get this under control and quit doing all this someday?"

He gave her a copy of the results and pursed his lips. "Let's give this a chance to work. It all depends how your body responds and how you do managing it. It's not easy to reverse and we want to make sure your organ systems stay healthy."

She nodded and stashed the boxes in her bag. "It's hard to be at the bakery. It's the worst part of all this. The one place that has brought me the most comfort and security has betrayed me. I need to think about something else to do."

His head bobbed in agreement. "I'm not sure I could resist being surrounded by all the goodies you bake. It might be something to consider."

"I'm not sure I can deal with more change right now."

"One more thing I want to say. I'm not an endocrinologist, so diabetes is not my specialty. I'm a heart guy and happy to treat you, but I want you to feel free to seek out another doctor. I can recommend a few if you'd feel better with one of them."

She shook her head, "No, no, I trust you completely. If you're willing to treat me I want to stay with you."

"Okay, then we're partners in this." He put an arm around her shoulder as she stood to leave. "Remember, talk to your friends. Those ladies you hang out with are all smart and think very highly of you. I know they'll help you through this."

She nodded and her lips quivered. "I miss Aunt Ginny and Uncle Bob right now. They've always been there to help me with the important stuff."

"Your friends are here now. You'll navigate this detour, I promise," he said, squeezing her shoulder.

* * *

She prepared another boring meal and was about to eat, when she remembered the meter. She pulled out the paperwork and the new gizmos Max had supplied. She opted to take her blood from her arm and was surprised when she didn't feel any pain. She checked the result and saw it was a bit higher than the goal range.

She spent the evening reviewing her results and after looking up a few things online, understood why Max had been reluctant to promise anything. Her numbers were way outside of the normal range. She set up her fitness tracker and linked it with an app to use on her phone to log her food. She integrated her glucose monitor with it and had a complete package for tracking her food and exercise.

A sense of accomplishment washed away some of her fear. The numbers had made her condition real and scary. A fresh battery and a thorough cleaning revived her bathroom scale. She learned about the complications many diabetics faced and knew she didn't want any of them. Everything she read advised patients to eliminate food temptations and focus on surrounding themselves with only healthy options. For the woman who owned and loved her bakery, it made for a colossal dilemma.

Eight

Friday Blake stopped by during lunch and picked up his order of muffins, cinnamon rolls, cupcakes, and bread for the fishermen. He also snagged the last three donuts in the shop. "Are you ready for your spa-cation?" he asked.

She smiled as she bagged his donuts. "I'm definitely looking forward to a massage and being away for the day."

"I'm stoked to fish in the ocean. I was hoping to hook up with some guys who knew about fishing the islands and it seems I've hit the jackpot."

"Nate loves fishing and before he met Regi I think he spent every spare minute on the water. I remember Jeff always fishing too."

"Spence is addicted and we may turn Max and Sean into fishermen, but they're gonna be my golfing buddies for sure." Blake vibrated with excitement as he talked about their weekend plans.

They were interrupted by another customer and Blake grabbed the boxes. "I need to get to the market and get the rest of our groceries. You girls have a great weekend. I'll catch up with you Sunday when we get home."

* * *

As she ladled up her low sodium chicken tortilla soup, she decided it was dull, but simpler to eat the same thing each day. Boring might be helpful, she reasoned, and take the excitement out of food. If she didn't look forward to eating, maybe it would be easier.

She searched online for diabetic-friendly recipes and made a loaf of whole wheat cinnamon raisin bread she liked. A slice, without butter, would serve as breakfast. She planned fruit and yogurt for snacks. Takeout salad or soup for lunch would be easy. Dinner would consist of one of her slow cooker creations, adjusted to make it low in fat and sodium. She resolved she could pick up a chicken from the market if she didn't feel like making dinner.

She bookmarked a few other recipes that didn't sound horrible before settling into bed with her laptop. She cruised the web perusing her favorite baking blogs and tagged some things to try. She typed in Lance's name in the search engine and it delivered pages of information about an Australian athlete. She kept searching and found nobody who resembled the Lance she grew up with in Sunnyside, Washington.

She tried social media and came up empty. There were several Lance Franklins online, many without pictures or information. Those who included a photo didn't look like Lance. This was going to be harder than she'd hoped.

* * *

Saturday morning she stowed a box of muffins she had made for the ferry ride, along with a change of clothes and her new glucose monitor. She stuffed an apple in her jacket pocket as she left. The urge to peek in the door of the bakery was intense, but she parked her car and hustled down the street to meet her friends.

Sam was waiting in line with each of their favorite coffee drinks. Ellie waved at Linda in the passenger seat and Regi in the back. Ellie took the caramel latte, topped with whipped cream and a drizzle of golden sweetness. "Oh, how thoughtful, thanks," she said. "I have a box of muffins for the trip, once we get settled at a table." Kate and Jen appeared behind Sam's SUV as the line began to move forward. They crammed in long enough to park the car and then the group went upstairs.

Ellie opened the box of muffins and passed it around the table, being careful to choose the special diabetic banana muffin she had included in the assortment. Not wanting to hurt Sam's feelings, or dampen the mood with her medical drama, she sipped her latte, savoring the sweetness she missed.

With the crossing less than an hour, they had to hurry and gobble their muffins before the announcement came to return to their vehicle. Ellie's hand hovered over the trash receptacle. She longed to drink the latte down, but knew it was on the forbidden list. It was all she could do to let over half of the perfect drink fall from her fingers into the trash.

Sam drove the thirty minutes from the dock to the Rosario. Linda had arranged a full day of activities, including massages, facials, hand and foot treatments, and time in the therapeutic pool. They were set up for lunch in a private alcove, where they could relax and enjoy a leisurely meal.

Ellie and Kate were paired for their treatments. After changing into soft white robes they were shown to a waiting room with an ocean view. They kicked off the day with facials that left their skin smooth and moisturized. Their hands and feet were pampered with soothing scrubs and coated in warm paraffin, wrapped, and placed into heated mittens and socks. The technicians followed with manicures and pedicures.

They crossed paths with Sam and Regi when they were waiting for their massages and were treated to refreshing herbal teas. Sam and Regi were fresh from their own massages and awaiting their manicures and pedicures. "I think I could live here," said Regi.

"It's gorgeous. I hope we have time to check out the museum," said Kate. "I love the style of the mansion and would appreciate viewing some of the antiques."

"We have plenty of time. We all end up in the pool after lunch and we can spend as much or as little time as we like. We need to be at the dock around five," said Sam.

Ellie and Kate were whisked away to the massage room, where they were treated to ninety minutes of complete respite. A hint of mandarin filled the room and a small fountain bubbled in the corner. She and Kate were shown to luxurious tables and covered in smooth sheets. Ellie's head rested in a soft cradle through which she glimpsed the glittery toes of her therapist, Rhonda.

Ellie concentrated on the sounds of water trickling over rocks interspersed with soft piano music. She inhaled the soothing scent of jasmine and vanilla she had chosen for her massage oil. Using her fingertips, Rhonda worked coconut oil into Ellie's scalp, using small circular motions over her head. She finished with rapid finger movements and ran her thumbs down the sides of her head and to her neck.

The weight of Ellie's burdens had burrowed into the muscles in her neck and shoulders. The massage therapist's strong fingers dug into the tight tissue and the tension gave way. Ellie sighed and let some of the angst of the past weeks float away with the breath she exhaled.

Rhonda continued massaging until Ellie's body, drained of tension, lay limp on the table. She finished with a reflexology massage of Ellie's feet, mixing in a bit of peppermint oil. The therapists left the room and told Ellie and Kate to take their time getting up and relax with some fresh cucumber water in the adjoining room.

"Wow, I've never felt this calm," said Ellie.

"It's been a long time since I've indulged in a massage and this one was wonderful," said Kate, from her table. "I could stay here and take a nap."

Ellie giggled. "I was thinking the same thing. I should take my blood pressure now."

"I'm not sure I have any blood pressure." Kate laughed and then added. "Are you having trouble with yours?"

"It's probably stress."

"This is a perfect fix for stress," said Kate. "I better get up or I will fall asleep." Ellie heard the sheets rustle as Kate moved and slipped into her robe. "I'll meet you out there." The door shut with a soft click.

She relished the warmth of the heated table and the sensation of utter abandon. Uncle Bob, Dani, Lance, or diabetes hadn't invaded her thoughts for the last two hours. She longed to stay in the warm cocoon, comforted by the peaceful sounds, but let out a deep breath and swung her legs off the table.

She found Kate in the waiting room, sipping a glass of water. "What's next on our agenda?"

"We're supposed to meet up with the others for lunch in a few minutes," said Kate. "I'm hungry. Considering I've done nothing, it makes no sense."

"I'll be right back," said Ellie, walking to the locker room entrance. She hurried to the wooden locker and rummaged in her bag for her monitor. After she pricked her arm she eyed the reading, disappointment reflected in her posture.

She didn't hear Kate behind her. "You doing okay?" she asked.

The meter slipped out of her hand and landed on the bench with a clatter. Kate bent and picked it up. "Here you go. I didn't know you were a diabetic."

Ellie slumped to the bench, her cheeks rosy with embarrassment. "I just found out. I haven't told anyone. Max is helping me with it."

"It's nothing to be ashamed of. I had a friend in the city who had it. I know it's a struggle."

Ellie's chin quivered. Kate sat beside her and put her arm around her. "I'm, uh, I'm feeling overwhelmed right now."

"I'm so sorry, Ellie, but you can get through this."

Ellie nodded her head as tears rolled down her cheeks and plopped onto the collar of her robe. "It's been a bad couple of weeks."

Sam walked into the room and saw the two huddled together. "What's wrong?"

She slid next to Ellie, concern contorting her face.

Ellie's head was resting on her friend's shoulder. Kate twisted her neck to look Ellie in the eyes with her eyebrows raised in question. Ellie nodded. "Tell her. It's okay."

Kate related Ellie's illness to Sam. Sam patted her blond head. "Sweetie, try not to worry. Max will take excellent care of you. He's the best."

"I know. It's more than the diabetes." Ellie sat up and rested against the bank of lockers. "This is such a long story and it began over twenty years ago."

Sam smiled. "I know all about long stories. We'll listen and help you." Kate gripped Ellie's hand.

The other three women passed by the row of lockers. They heard Regi's voice announcing lunch was ready. "What's going on?" asked Linda.

Ellie took a breath. "Max diagnosed me with diabetes." The newest arrivals gasped and sat on the bench across from the others. "That's the tip of the iceberg," added Ellie. "I don't want to ruin our lunch."

"Nonsense, take your time," said Kate and the others nodded in agreement.

Ellie began, "I found out I was diabetic because I asked Max to test me to be a kidney donor." She paused and her voice cracked. "For my daughter."

Surprise swept across the faces of her closest friends. Jen and Linda had known Ellie since she had moved to the island. "Your daughter?" they both said at the same time.

Ellie sighed. "Yeah, I got pregnant in high school. That's how I ended up in Friday Harbor. My parents shipped me off to live with my dad's brother, Uncle Bob. I had the baby and gave her up for adoption when I was sixteen." Kate gripped her hand tighter and Sam rested a hand on Ellie's knee.

She relayed the visit from Dani and the subsequent request for a kidney. Regi's eyes widened as Ellie told them she couldn't donate because of the diabetes along with high blood pressure and cholesterol. She replayed the painful conversation with Dani and saw Regi's eyes fill with tears.

Linda asked, "Have you talked to your aunt and uncle about all this?"

Ellie shook her head. "No, with Uncle Bob still recovering from his heart attack, I didn't want to worry them. I'm planning a trip in a week or two to visit them." Ellie saw the concern in Linda's eyes. "I take it Max didn't tell you any of this?"

"No, not a peep. He takes the doctor-patient privilege seriously. He would never betray your trust in him. I'm so sorry, Ellie."

"So, now I need to find Lance. Dani's father."

"I bet Spence could help you," Kate said. "He decided to get his private detective license in addition to his consulting work. He's got access to databases that could help you locate him."

"I tried to find Lance online last night, but didn't have any luck."

"Let me know if you want Spence to check it out for you."

Ellie nodded, "Yeah, I think I do. It would take a load off my plate." She rearranged her legs. "I've still got to figure out what to say to Lance when I find him, but locating him would help."

"What else can we do?" asked Sam.

Ellie shook her head. "I'm worried I'm going to have to get rid of the bakery. I don't think I can be around all those things and stay on track with my new eating plan. There are too many temptations."

"Nate's dad could try and find a buyer for you," said Regi.

"But what would I do? I don't have any skills other than baking and didn't go to college." She wiped at her eye with the sleeve of the robe. "It's been my…my everything."

"It's your safe place, right?" asked Sam. Ellie smiled and nodded through the tears.

"I bet we can come up with something," said Sam, nodding her head at the others. "Let's think about some options."

"I'm sorry we didn't know about this before, when you moved here," said Jen. "Linda and I are older than you, so we didn't know you from school. We met you through the bakery. We never asked much about you back then. Bob and Ginny told us you were their niece. They never said a word."

"They were wonderful to me and helped me out of a dark place. My parents, oh, my parents. That's a whole story in itself."

"We've got all day, sweetie," said Sam.

Ellie let a laugh escape. "How about we have our lunch and then I'll tell you about them."

The group gathered around Ellie with hugs and words of encouragement before they strolled into their private nook for lunch. They enjoyed a selection of salads, cheeses, olives, nuts, and flatbreads. In deference to Ellie, they skipped the dessert selections.

While they sat on comfy cushions, ensconced in their warm robes, sipping tea, Ellie shared the story of her beginnings. "My sister Cecilia, or Ceci, is four years older than me. We were always close growing up until I was about ten. My brother, Teddy Jr., is five years younger. My mother, Caroline, developed a genuine hatred for me after he was born."

The circle of women stopped sipping and focused their attention on Ellie. "Both of my parents were enamored with their new son. They called him 'Baby Bear' since my mom called Dad 'Teddy Bear'—sickening, I know. Dad went by Teddy, so it got confusing." Ellie rolled her eyes. "By the time I was ten, Ceci had her own life and wasn't around the house much. She played sports and was popular. Dad got her a summer job. If she showed me any kindness, Mom would berate her, so Ceci learned to shun me to get along."

"Where was your father in all of this?" asked Kate.

"He's the principal at the high school and involved in the community. He also coached. He wasn't home much and I think he didn't like being around Mom. All they did was fight when they were home together. She doted on Teddy and he could do no wrong. Anytime he was upset, it was my fault, no matter what."

Ellie took a sip from the delicate tea cup. "To be fair, I rebelled in a big way. I wanted to be noticed by them. It was like I was invisible. So, I did some bad stuff, but nothing made them pay attention. They doled out more punishment, usually in the form of not being allowed to go with them. I spent lots of time alone at home. The four of them would go places and pawn me off on one of my dad's friends. My mom told me she hated me every chance she got. She used to do it only when my dad wasn't around, but as I got older it got worse."

Regi set her cup down with enough force to rattle it against the saucer. "Sorry, but as a mother that pisses me off. What a horrible thing to say to a child."

Kate nodded. "I agree, it's despicable."

Jen's eyes filled with tears. "I can't imagine saying that to Megan, ever."

"What did your mom do for a living?" asked Sam.

"She was an elementary school teacher."

"You've got to be kidding me," yelled Regi. She popped a hand over her mouth when she realized her volume.

The group of women shook their heads with disdain. "Unfreakinbelievable," said Jen.

"Like I said, I wasn't an easy child. I figured out how to push her buttons and I pushed them every chance I got. It was my way of fighting back. She'd scream constantly and hit me. She even tossed my dog against the wall one night. My dad used to break up the fighting, but he wore down eventually. I used to feel like he was on my side. I'd even hear him tell her she needed to get help. I'm not sure if she was mean or actually mentally ill. Dad took us to counseling, but when I opened up about Mom's actions, she decided the doctor was a quack."

Ellie looked down at the tablecloth bunched in her hand. "Dad sort of did what Ceci did and figured out his life was easier if he went along with Mom. I became the object of everyone's loathing. Everything I did was wrong, so punishment didn't mean much. I failed most of my classes and all that did was embarrass them." Ellie smirked. "Looking back I think humiliating them was my goal."

"They pretended to be this happy family with the perfect life. My mom decorated for every stupid holiday and on the outside we looked normal. But even some of her colleagues figured out she didn't like me. When Teddy and I were at the same school, it was apparent to the other teachers and some parents. She couldn't confine her hatred of me to our private gatherings anymore."

"Did that cause anything to change?" asked Linda.

Ellie shook her head. "Not really. I reported her slapping me to her boss at the time I was going to her school. The principal had to call child services, but nothing happened. Mom was beyond embarrassed though. She had me transferred to another school and told me how horrible I was."

"When I went to high school, Dad's school, it was better at first. He tried a few things, but all the other kids at school were more important and he did everything he could to stay away from home. I started experimenting with drugs and alcohol. Not crazy, but enough to make me forget what was going on sometimes. My mom spent money to the point of breaking them and Dad would raise holy hell. But he never did anything. He was a master yeller and complainer, but took no action."

"One day I told her I couldn't figure out why Dad stayed with her and he'd be better off divorced."

"Ballsy choice," said Regi, smirking.

"Yeah, he told me he felt sorry for her. I think that's why he stayed. And, of course for Teddy. Anyway, the last straw was me getting pregnant. My parents warned me about Lance and looking back on it now, he wasn't a wise choice. But, at the time he was the perfect fit to irritate them and he made me feel special. So, I ended up pregnant and refused to tell them who the father was. I had been dating a few guys. They basically let me run around doing whatever I wanted. I think it was easier than dealing with me. So, they weren't sure who to blame. I never told Lance either. Nobody knew."

Fresh pots of hot water were delivered and the group brewed more tea. "So, one day in late May, my mother threw a bag at me and told me to pack. The bump was beginning to show. We lived in a small town and I know they were humiliated and didn't want anyone to know. They drove me to the coast and told me I was going to live with Uncle Bob and Aunt Ginny. I think my dad was sad when he hugged me goodbye. My mom never even got out of the car or said goodbye. I've never talked to either of them since that day."

Spoons were silenced and cups were held in midair. "You've not had any contact with your brother or sister either?" asked Kate.

"Not a word. My aunt and uncle let me hang out at their house until I had the baby in August. They got me into counseling and helped me find a program at the school to make up the classes I had failed. Turns out I wasn't stupid, so I was able to do the extra work and finish school here and graduate on time."

"Probably because they gave a shit about you," said Regi.

"Yeah, they sat with me each night and went over my homework. After working at the bakery, I'm not sure how they had the energy." Ellie held her hands around the warm cup in front of her. "My parents would never sit with me and do anything. They yelled and belittled me, insisting I should know how to do my work. They would go on vacations and leave me with a friend or home alone."

"Show of hands," said Jen, "who else despises Caroline and Ted?" In answer, five hands went up around the table.

In a choked voice and with tears falling, Ellie said, "All I ever wanted was for them to love me like I was." Kate tucked an arm around her and held her close.

"I'm speechless," said Sam. "I can't believe parents, and teachers no less, could do this to their child. I'm so thankful your aunt and uncle were here to help you and give you a home. I think you were much better off with them."

"You must have missed your family, though. I understand you would have mixed emotions," said Linda.

"I think the therapeutic pool sounds perfect right now," said Kate. "Are you up for a soak, Ellie?"

Reassuring words echoed around the table and soon the group was back in the locker room donning swimsuits. They eased into the pool, languishing in the water. Ellie floated in the warm liquid, closing her eyes letting herself bob across the pool. With her burden shared, she felt lighter, letting the healing waters lap over her.

Nine

The teasing aroma of bacon and coffee stirred Ellie from sleep Sunday morning. She opened her eyes, disoriented for a moment until she realized she was in one of Sam's guest rooms. She padded downstairs and saw the others, several still in their pajamas, gathered around the kitchen island.

"How about some eggs, Ellie?" asked Sam, as she worked at the cooktop.

Ellie placed her order and perched on a stool with the others. "I can't believe I slept in so late."

Linda added the fruit she had sliced to a bowl and mixed it together. "I'm sure you needed the extra rest."

"Not to mention how late we stayed up watching movies last night," said Kate, taking a pan from the oven.

Jen poured glasses of juice and retrieved mugs from the cupboard. "I haven't had this relaxing of a weekend in a long time. The spa at the Rosario was the best."

Ellie fixed herself a cup of coffee. Regi put cream and non-fat half and half on the counter, along with sugar and sugar substitutes. Ellie glanced at Sam, who gave her a conspiratorial wink.

"The spa was absolutely wonderful, but the best part of my weekend was unloading my problems on all of you." Ellie stirred her coffee until the rich roast was the perfect shade of beige. "Max told me I needed to talk with you guys and he was right. I feel better and not quite so alone. So, thank you." She raised her mug in a toast.

The women raised their mugs and glasses. "Let's eat up while everything is nice and warm," said Sam. The women swarmed the counter and filled their plates. They gathered in the breakfast nook and relived their favorite spa treatments.

The conversation turned to the next steps for Ellie. Kate suggested they brainstorm, allowing all ideas to be shared and then Ellie could choose those things that made sense to her. Always ready to make a list, Sam poised her pen over a pad, as the women made suggestions.

When the dishes were empty and all the coffee had been drained, Sam cleared her throat to read the list. "I tried to group these together, but I'm not sure it's organized. Under bakery we have—sell it, lease it, hire a baker, hire a manager. For Ellie's career options—coffee shop, hardware store, school district, nursery or flower shop, antique store, and go back to school and pursue something you enjoy. Then for the Dani and Lance issue we came up with—use Spence to find Lance, take someone with you and visit Lance, your siblings, Lance's siblings, tell your aunt and uncle."

Ellie's eyes widened. "It's a great start and gives me lots of things to consider." She glanced at Kate. "Spence is a definite yes. If he finds Lance, I like the idea of having someone go with me. I'm going to tell Aunt Ginny and Uncle Bob when I visit them. Lance didn't have siblings."

Linda and Jen began clearing the dishes. "The bakery doesn't make enough money to support me and hire a baker. I think I'd be better off selling it than adding more stress by increasing my overhead. I guess I could talk to Nate's dad and find out what he thinks. I have a loan I would need to pay off with the proceeds." She stared down at the paper napkin she had shredded, wrapped around her finger. "I need to talk to Aunt Ginny and Uncle Bob. They gave me such a deal on the business. I would hate to disappoint them."

Kate placed her hand across Ellie's back. "They'll understand when you explain about your recent diagnosis. From what I know, they think of you as their own child and would only want what is best for your health."

Ellie blinked to discourage the tears she felt forming in her eyes and nodded. "You're right, but I hate to let them down. I can't fail again."

"Life changes as we travel down the road. We don't always know what's going to happen—good or bad. What I've come to realize is, it's not what happens to you, but how you react that defines your path. Sometimes what seems horrible at first is a change for the better," said Sam.

"I agree," said Kate. "We sometimes endure horrific losses, from which we'll never fully recover or forget. But we all have to move on at some point and barring the tragedies, the other things are small bumps. Our challenge is to overcome and find the best solution and sometimes those choices lead us to better things. A change in direction doesn't mean you fail."

Ellie wiped her eyes with the torn napkin and Linda handed her another. "I've hidden on this island for the last twenty years. I came here broken and a complete mess. My aunt and uncle helped repair some of the damage. I wanted everything to stay the same." She sniffed and took a sip of water. "It sounds immature when I say it out loud. I know Kate and Sam have endured such loss in their lives. This is small in comparison, but I feel so lost and afraid."

"You've made progress today with the bakery and Lance. Think about the other ideas and keep talking about things with us. We'll listen and," Regi looked around the circle smiling, "always give you advice, whether you want it or not."

The women's laughter pierced the balloon of tension in the air. Ellie looked out the windows and saw all the dogs lined up on the deck, waiting to be invited inside. "Let me help you clean up the kitchen, Sam. Then I'm going to hit the shower and get home. I've played hooky long enough," said Ellie.

"The guys will be home this afternoon. How about we grill the salmon I hope they caught and have an easy dinner together at our place tonight?" asked Linda.

"On one condition," said Ellie. "No talk about me or my problems tonight."

"Deal," said Linda and the others nodded in agreement.

They put together a dinner menu and split up the duties. Linda sent Max a text with the evening's details to pass on to the fishermen. The women helped Sam return her house to its normal state before the dogs were paired with their owners and they left for their own homes.

***

Spence stopped by the bakery Tuesday afternoon as Ellie was closing. "I've got some information for you on Lance."

"Wow, you do quick work. Have a seat," she gestured to a table.

Spence produced a file folder. "Lance still lives in Sunnyside. He's had a few brushes with the law. He's employed at the cheese factory and is currently living with his mother."

Ellie studied the report. "So, he's been in jail?"

"I'm afraid so. His record shows a history of drinking, drugs, and assault. Looks like he had a cocaine problem. No arrests in the last year. He's on probation, so he's got to check in and keep a job."

Ellie blew out a breath that fluttered her bangs. "I guess I need to make plans for a road trip back to Sunnyside."

"I'm happy to go with you. From what Blake was saying Sunday night he's planning a trip that way soon. You could always hitch a ride with him. I think you need to make sure you don't go alone."

Like hot cocoa on a cold morning, his desire to protect her filled her with warmth. She smiled and put her hand on top of his. "Thanks, Spence. I appreciate your help and your offer. I won't go alone, I promise."

"Good girl." He scanned the display case. "How about you pay me in cupcakes?"

Ellie laughed and stood. She intended to give him a quick hug but found herself held tight in strong arms. Memories of her dad flooded her mind. She felt the rough stubble on Spence's cheek and squeezed her eyes tight. He loosened his grip and she whispered in his ear. "Thank you."

She loaded one of her signature pink boxes full of muffins and cupcakes and flipped the lock behind him.

***

Ellie made plans to visit Mt. Vernon in late January to check on her aunt and uncle before dealing with a possible trip to find Lance. Nicole had proven to be responsible and capable. Ellie had been letting her do more of the early baking, even coming in late a few mornings.

Friday morning Ellie stopped by Harbor Coffee and Books to treat herself to a non-fat latte. Sam was working and joined her at a table. "Are you set for your trip?"

"I think so. Oreo and I are booked on the early ferry tomorrow. I won't be gone too long. We're coming home on Thursday."

"My offer still stands. If Nicole gets in a bind, I can go over and help or send a helper from the store."

Ellie took a sip of her warm drink. "That's so kind of you. I gave Nicole your cell number and told her to call you with any problems. She's been doing great. This time of year is slow, so I think she'll do fine."

"Did you talk to Nate's dad about selling yet?"

Ellie nodded. "Jack came by last week and is working on some comparisons to give me an idea of what the market would bring for the business. He agreed to keep it quiet until I give him the green light."

"Jeff and I talked about what you could do if you sold it. He said you would always have a job at the hardware store, if you need it."

Ellie blinked away tears. "He's the best, isn't he?"

Sam grinned over her mug of tea. "I think so." She set the cup on the table. "I'm happy to have you work here, but I think the temptation would still be high. We don't carry a lot of healthy treats."

"I agree. It would help not to have to bake so much, but you still have too many enticing goodies. Nobody can resist your pies."

"Did you hear Blake talking about having to hire help at the winery?"

"Yeah, but I don't know a thing about wine." She chuckled and added, "I wouldn't be tempted much there. I'm not much of a wine drinker."

"I'm sure he could teach you what you need to know and you've got great experience managing a business. You ought to talk to him about it."

Ellie sighed. "I'm not sure I want him to know so much about me."

"You don't have to share everything. Tell him you're trying to get healthier and need to step away from Sweet Treats. That's all you need to share, until you're comfortable."

Ellie drained the last of her latte. "I'll think about it." She stood to leave. "Tell Jeff thanks for keeping an eye on the house while I'm away. I appreciate you guys so much." She hugged Sam and waved goodbye as she walked by the window.

She spent the rest of the day making sure things were set for the next week. She went over the schedule with Nicole and reminded her about the order that would be delivered while she was away. She made sure she left all her contact numbers, along with Sam's, and the number at her aunt's house.

"I'll be fine. Enjoy your time with your family," said Nicole. "I'll call you with any problems, I promise."

"I know you will. It's my first time leaving the bakery. I'm a touch nervous."

"It'll be great. It's less than a week."

Ellie checked over things one more time before she locked the back door. She pilfered a few of her healthy muffins for the trip. They were even catching on with her regular customers.

* * *

Saturday morning's ferry bore a sparse number of passengers and the journey across the water proved to be relaxing. Ellie and Oreo sat outside on a bench and shared a muffin. The drive from Anacortes to Mt. Vernon took less than an hour. When she pulled up to the house, Aunt Ginny was in the driveway waving and smiling.

Oreo bounded out of the car and bolted for the woman. Ellie followed and engulfed her in a hug. "I'm so glad to see you. Oreo is too." Ellie felt the slightness of her aunt. She noticed the woman she thought of as her mother walked slower and looked tinier than she remembered. Her eyes still sparkled, but the face surrounding them was weary.

Aunt Ginny laughed and bent to pet the sweet dog. "You two come in. We'll put your bags away and I'll get lunch on the table."

They had downsized when they moved to the mainland. The house was modern and bright. Uncle Bob treasured his pond at the old place and this house was situated near Otter Pond, with a view from the deck.

Ellie lugged her suitcase inside and put it in the guest room. She smiled when she saw a new coloring book and a fresh pack of colored pencils on her pillow. Aunt Ginny was the best. She wandered to the great room and found Uncle Bob sitting in his recliner. She rushed to him, surprised at the sight of the frail man gazing out the window. "Uncle Bob, I've missed you. How are you?"

"Doing okay, I guess. I'm not near as feisty these days."

Ellie sat on the hearth next to the fire. Oreo followed Ginny to the kitchen. "I love this open space. It's wonderful to have the kitchen open so the cook doesn't miss anything." He gave her a slow smile and continued to stare through the glass.

Aunt Ginny gathered dishes and slid pans out of the oven. "We love it and it's so much less for us to take care of than the island house. As you know, it's a lot to do between the house and the acreage."

"Uncle Bob still has a great view of a beautiful pond. Do you spend a lot of time outside on the deck?" asked Ellie.

"Yes, when it's warm outside we love to sit out there," he said.

"Lunch is ready you two," said Aunt Ginny, carrying a pitcher to the table.

After feasting on chicken stew with homemade rolls, Aunt Ginny helped Uncle Bob to the bedroom for a nap. When she returned Ellie had all the dishes done and the leftovers stored.

Oreo was snoozing by the fire. Ginny put on the kettle for tea and she arranged some of her famous chocolate chip cookies on a plate. She poured the tea and sat across from Ellie.

"Uncle Bob looks so weak. How's he doing?"

Ginny's smile faded. "He's tired all the time. The doctors think it might be his medications." She took a cookie. "I baked these last night, for you."

Ellie looked at the perfectly formed cookies with longing. Her aunt lifted the plate and the sweet smell tickled Ellie's nose. Her mouth watered, yearning for a bite. "I can't," she said. "I've got some news to share."

Fortified with a sip of wild orange tea, Ellie plunged in and told her aunt about Dani's visit that led to the discovery of her diabetes. Aunt Ginny cradled the teacup, listening with wide eyes. She reached across the table as soon as Ellie finished and gripped her niece's hand. "I'm so sorry you had to tackle this on your own."

Ellie couldn't stop the flow of tears down her face. "I'm okay." She sniffed and her aunt produced a box of tissues. "I've got wonderful friends. Linda's new husband, Max, is a doctor and he's treating me."

"Are you going to go back to Sunnyside and find Lance?"

Ellie shrugged. "It's all I can think to do." She refilled her cup. "There's something else. I don't think I can keep working in the bakery with this disease. I'm having a hard time resisting foods I shouldn't eat and being surrounded by them all day isn't going to work. I feel horrible since you guys sold me the bakery at such a deal, knowing it would be in the family."

"Oh, sweetheart, you don't need to worry. You need to take care of yourself and do whatever you need to do. You work too hard anyway. Sometimes the unexpected path is a gift."

"You really think so?"

"I do. You were unexpected in our lives and turned out to be a wonderful gift."

Ellie smiled and touched her aunt's hand. "I feel so guilty selling it. I'm not sure what I can get for it, but I can give you some of it to make up for the deal you gave me."

"Nonsense. We don't need money and we did it because we knew you loved it so. None of our other kids wanted anything to do with it. You treasured it like we did. But, it's just a bakery. It did its job and helped you find a purpose when you came to live with us."

Ellie wiped her eyes. "How come you let me come live with you?"

"Because we knew you were worth it." Ginny took a cookie. "I hate to eat this in front of you, but I need one."

Ellie smiled. "It's okay, go ahead."

"Uncle Bob and I couldn't bear the thought of you being sent away to some horrible place. We also couldn't stand the way your parents treated you or talked about you. It broke our hearts." She took a sip from her cup. "We always blamed your mother, but as time wore on, we got more frustrated with Ted. Bob talked to him about divorcing Caroline and taking the kids. We told him he and the kids could move to the island and we would help. When we would talk he sounded like he knew the life they were giving you kids was not normal, but then he'd be right back defending her. Bob always checked in with Ted each week and as things progressed we had discussed offering to have you live with us. Then when you got pregnant, we knew we had to step in and do something."

"When's the last time you heard from my dad?"

Ginny shook her head in disgust. "Not since about a year after you came to live with us. Bob continued to call and update him on your progress each week. The good news we shared about you upset Ted. One week when Bob called, Caroline answered. She told him they had their perfect family now with you gone and they didn't need to be bothered with further updates. She told him to stop calling and making Ted feel guilty. She didn't want to hear from us anymore."

Ellie's heart pounded as anger bubbled to the surface. "Why does she hate me so much?"

"I don't know, honey. After that conversation, Bob called Ted on his cell phone when he knew he'd be at work. Ted told him it would be easier if we didn't call the house and promised to call us when he could." She paused and shook her head. "I guess he never found the time."

"Do they still live in Sunnyside?"

Ginny shrugged her shoulders. "I think so, but wouldn't know for sure."

Ellie took both of her aunt's hands in hers. "I'm so thankful you and Uncle Bob were in my life when I needed you the most. I'm still sad and can't figure out why my dad would discard me. I don't think about my mom much, but I always hoped my dad would come back for me."

"We did too. It broke Bob's heart and he lost all respect for Ted. We never had much respect for Caroline, but we loved Ted and were so saddened by the way he acted."

"Do you think Uncle Bob can handle all my news about the bakery and Dani?"

"I'll tell him in the morning. He's usually best early in the day. He'll be fine with it."

"You look tired. Are you doing okay? Do you need some help around here?"

Tears flashed across her golden eyes. "I'm okay. The kids haven't been by as much as I'd hoped. They're busy, I know."

"Have you considered asking them?"

"I was hoping not to have to ask," she said, looking down at her cup.

"Let's make a list of what you need help with and come up with some ideas." Ellie retrieved a notepad and pen and over the next hour they talked about meals, cleaning, and yardwork. Two of her cousins lived within thirty miles and one lived in Portland.

On a trip to town for coffees, Ellie stopped by her aunt's church and talked to the pastor about their needs. He promised to put them on the youth group's list. They did odd jobs for seniors in the congregation and could handle helping with the yard. He told her about a handyman who did work for a reduced rate for the elderly. She pocketed the number and he assured Ellie he would check in more and make sure they were treated to meals a few times a month.

Over the next week, Ginny didn't have to lift a finger. Ellie cooked all their meals and made extras for the freezer. She cleaned the house and completed some chores that were difficult for her aunt, like scrubbing all the baseboards. While she was there the youth group coordinator stopped by and offered to set up a chore schedule.

The two cousins near Mt. Vernon agreed to come once a month. Ellie set up video chat software on her aunt's computer and showed her how she could use it to talk to her on the island. Between help from the church and the new agreement with her cousins, Ellie was confident her aunt and uncle would get some well-deserved rest.

Aunt Ginny and Uncle Bob insisted on treating Ellie to lunch on her last day. Over delicious homemade fare at a local cafe her uncle said, "We want you to know how much we appreciate your visit. And, we're absolutely fine with you selling the bakery. We want you to be happy and healthy."

"Plus, maybe with a different career you'll have more time to visit us," said Ginny, smiling and looked more rested than she had when Ellie had arrived.

"I would love to spend more time with you. I hadn't considered anything positive, only the sadness of not being at the bakery each day."

"You'll have a new adventure, honey. You're young enough to do something different and exciting."

"I hope things work out with Lance, for Dani's sake. You do what your friends say and take someone with you," said Bob, sounding more like a concerned father.

"I will, Uncle Bob. I'll keep you two posted on what happens."

After Uncle Bob paid the bill they went home and spent the rest of the day reminiscing and playing with Oreo. The dog had attached herself to Uncle Bob like a string to a tetherball. She took naps with him and rested at his feet wherever he sat.

Tears were shed when Ellie and Oreo loaded the car in the morning. She made a batch of healthy muffins and took a few with her, assuring her uncle they were almost as yummy as the others. They hugged her goodbye and waved until she turned the corner.

When they were out of sight, Oreo whined and pawed at the window and Ellie wiped her eyes. She craved the warmth and comfort of family and fought the urge to turn around and rush back to them. The time spent with them had been a lavish gift and she didn't want it to end.

Ten

The bakery was still standing when Ellie returned. She popped in when she drove off the ferry and found everything in order. The display cases sparkled, the kitchen was clean, all the daily reports were in order, and Nicole had made the bank deposits.

Dusk was settling in as she locked the back door. Oreo's friendly bark made her turn. "I was on my way to dinner and saw your car," said Blake.

"We got in a few minutes ago and I was checking on things."

"Care to join me for pizza?"

Excuses tumbled through her mind like clothes in a dryer. "Uh, I need to get home and catch up on things. I've got an early day tomorrow." She saw regret flash through his eyes. "How about a raincheck?"

"That's twice, you know? I'm beginning to think it's me." He held the door for her while she got behind the wheel. "I'll be by tomorrow for breakfast. See you then."

"It's not you, honest. I'll be here. Have a good night." She turned the key and put the car in gear. Reaching across the console she nuzzled Oreo. "I don't need him to know how messed up my life is. I need to get all of this figured out before I add anything else to my plate."

Oreo looked at her and gave a quick yip.

She went around the block and made a detour to the market to pick up groceries and dinner fixings. She was careful to stay away from the harbor and Big Tony's, so she wouldn't run into Blake. She enjoyed the time she had spent with him, but the risk of him finding out about her past was one she didn't want to take.

* * *

The next week Nicole started working the early shift and Ellie dedicated her free mornings to the sale of the bakery. Ellie met with Jack and signed the listing agreement. The sales price he recommended was higher than she anticipated. The idea of being out from under the responsibility brought a glimmer of excitement.

Her mornings were spent perched in front of her computer taking career and personality quizzes or at the library rifling through their collection of career handbooks. Employment opportunities on the island were sparse. Seasonal positions were plentiful in the summer, but permanent posts were hard to find. She scanned the list Sam had made for her the night of the slumber party and highlighted a few.

Creativity stood out on all the tests she took. She was accustomed to the autonomy of being her own boss and wasn't sure she'd like working for someone else. One thing was clear—between all her friends, she'd have a job working for one of them. She'd be able to support herself, but she wanted to find something she loved doing.

She stuffed her notes in her bag and stopped by the antiques store on her way to the bakery. Kate was waiting on a customer and gestured upstairs to her office. Ellie found Spence on the sofa, engrossed in a book. "Hey, Ellie, what brings you by?"

She slid next to him. "I decided to take you up on your offer to go with me to find Lance. Are you available this weekend?"

"Sure, works for me."

"I thought we could take the ferry over Friday and drive to Ellensburg or Yakima. Then Saturday morning, we'd only be an hour or so from Sunnyside. If all goes well, we can head back on the late ferry Saturday night."

"I'm all yours and I vote for Ellensburg. My son lives there and I'd love to visit him."

She noticed the sparkle in his eyes. "Sounds like a plan."

"How about I drive? We can take my car. You'll have enough on your mind without worrying about driving."

"That would be wonderful, Spence. I'll buy gas and pack us some snacks for the ride." She stood and checked the time. "I need to get going, but I'll meet you at the ferry terminal on Friday."

He rose from the sofa and wrapped her in a hug. "It's going to be fine." He used his fingers to prop her chin and saw worry in her eyes. "We'll get this figured out, you'll see."

* * *

Linda and Max agreed to keep Oreo and Jeff offered to check on the house while she was away. Feeling less apprehensive about leaving Nicole in charge, she shifted her worry to the upcoming encounter with Lance.

According to Spence's research, Lance's mother lived in an apartment about ten miles from the cheese factory. From what she saw online, it looked like a low income complex. A phone call Thursday morning interrupted her pondering.

She answered, "Hi, Max."

"Hey, Ellie. We received some bad news about Linda's mom. Linda's brother called early this morning and said Peggy passed away in her sleep last night. He found her this morning in her bed."

"Oh, no. I'm so sorry. How's Linda?"

"She's upset, but coping. She's packing some things. We're going to take the afternoon ferry so we can get to her brother's late tonight. She wanted you to know about her mom, but I wanted to let you know we made arrangements for the dogs."

"Oh, I can find someone to watch Oreo and Lucy. You shouldn't have to deal with them on top of everything else."

"It's handled. I called Blake and he's going to come and stay at the house and watch both dogs. He was happy to do it, so don't worry about Oreo. Go ahead and drop her off tonight like you planned."

"Are you sure? I can talk to Sam and Jeff, I'm sure they'd take her."

"She'll have fun with Lucy. It's no problem. I think Blake's happy to get off his boat for a few nights."

"Is there anything I can do for you guys?"

"Thanks, but I don't think so. You have a safe trip and we'll catch up with you when we get back. I expect we'll be gone at least a week."

"Tell Linda I'm thinking of her. Take good care of her." She hung up, Lance now forgotten. Concern for Linda creased her forehead, followed by the fear Max may have told Blake why she was going to be gone for a few days. Her pulse quickened and she noticed she was late.

She hustled to the bakery and found it quiet and organized, with Nicole eating an early lunch. They reviewed the upcoming orders for the next few days and Ellie made sure Nicole had the phone number of her hotel in Ellensburg.

After she closed for the day she put in a batch of cupcakes and some diabetic friendly pumpkin muffins. While they were baking she put together her peanut butter dog cookies. With the fresh treats cooling, she dashed down the street to pick up a light dinner at Soup D'Jour.

She boxed up the cupcakes and muffins for the road trip and bagged the cookies. She prepared a separate box of the dark chocolate cupcakes with peanut butter frosting and put a ribbon around the box. After toting the loot to the car, she locked the door and steered for home.

After feeding Oreo, she loaded her dog bed, food, and a few toys into the car. Oreo leapt through the open door, excited for an adventure. When she turned for Linda's house, Oreo panted and whined. Her enthusiasm for a visit with Lucy obvious, as she pivoted her head between Ellie and the windshield.

Oreo bolted for the front door while Ellie attempted to cart the dog paraphernalia. Instead of ringing the bell, Oreo barked. Blake answered the door and Oreo dashed by him, intent on finding her friend.

He laughed and stepped onto the walkway. "I was hoping she didn't run over here by herself." He scrambled to help Ellie and seized the dog bed and food from her.

"She's anxious for her sleepover date." Ellie returned to the car and removed the bakery box with the ribbon and the bag of cookies. She stepped through the open door and heard Blake in the kitchen.

The dogs were snuggled together on Lucy's bed and Blake flopped

Oreo's down next to them. He eyed the fancy box when he returned from putting the dog food in the mud room. "What could this be?"

"A token for taking care of my girl. Are you sure you're okay with both of these scoundrels?"

"Sure, it'll be fun. Max said he thought your trip would be quick."

"Yeah, I should be back no later than Sunday night. If anything changes, I'll give you a call."

He popped open the top on the box. "Oh, these look delicious."

"Chocolate with peanut butter, plus some homemade cookies for the dogs. They love them."

"How about some coffee? I'm going to have one of these bad boys right now."

She looked at the clock. "I still need to pack."

"Aww, one cup, come on."

She sighed and slid onto a chair. "Okay, one cup." Oreo and Lucy surrounded her, leaning against her legs. She used both hands to stroke them at the same time.

"So, where are you off to on your trip?"

The cup was poised at her lips. "Uh, just a trip to take care of some family business."

"I've got to make a trip home soon myself. My parents live in Richland."

"Oh, I grew up in Sunnyside." She cringed as the words escaped her mouth. If only she could pull them back. She took another sip of coffee. *Why did I say that?*

"Really? I thought you grew up here?"

"Oh, yeah, I did. I lived in Sunnyside before I moved here."

"Is that where your aunt and uncle live now? I got the impression they were closer to Seattle."

"No, they live in Mt. Vernon. I had a great visit with them."

"Do you have a large family?"

"I have one brother and one sister." She took another gulp of coffee. "I haven't seen them in a long time."

"Since moving here, this is the longest I've gone without visiting my family. I have a whole herd of sisters."

"Well, I better hit the road. I need to get some things done. Thanks again for watching Oreo." She turned her head and saw both of the dogs sacked out on their beds. "She's quite comfortable here." She stood and slipped into her jacket and bent to nuzzle Oreo behind her ears.

"They'll keep each other company." He followed her to the door. "Have a safe trip."

She hurried down the walkway to her car, anxious to escape more questions and keep herself from blurting out the details of her messy life.

* * *

Spence met her at the ferry and loaded the car. They chose a table and enjoyed the view from the large windows. Spence opened a file folder while they sipped their drinks. "I called the cheese factory and found out Lance's shift. He works the night shift and gets off early Saturday morning. I've also got a current photo." He slid the blowup of his picture across the table.

Ellie gazed at the picture of his license. "Wow, he looks different." She squinted and added, "I recognize his eyes, but he looks old and unkempt."

"I think we should hang out at the factory and try to catch him when he gets off work. I talked to his probation officer and it sounds like he uses his mom's car, so we'll know what to look for in the parking lot."

"I'm glad you're on my side," she said with a chuckle.

"If we miss him, we can always go to the apartment."

"Sounds like a plan. That will give us the whole day to find him."

Knowing Spence had a plan and details helped calm her nerves. She opted to put in an audio book for the drive. It helped keep her mind occupied. They stopped a few times along the way for snacks. Spence devoured several cupcakes, while Ellie stuck to her new diet and munched on healthy snacks.

They pulled up to the hotel in the early afternoon. Spence hauled her bag to the desk and waited while she checked in with the clerk. "You get settled and I'll pick you up in a few hours for dinner. I want to spend some time with Kevin."

Ellie unpacked and set her coloring books and supplies on the desk, hoping she brought enough to stem the anxious feeling deep in her chest. She took advantage of the free time and colored while she watched television. When she grew sleepy, she pulled the blackout blinds closed. After setting the alarm on her cell phone, she snuggled into the comfy oversize bed and fell asleep.

* * *

Spence treated them to a wonderful Italian dinner. Kevin and Spence carried the dinner conversation, catching up on Kevin's new job and loft apartment. He was working for a graphic design firm and radiated excitement when he explained his projects. Ellie was content to listen and watch the father and son interact. Kevin never asked any questions about her reason for being in Ellensburg. He was satisfied when Spence said he was working a case and helping a friend.

Ellie waited with Kevin while Spence took care of the tab. "I hope you'll be able to come for a visit to the island someday soon."

"I can't take time off for at least six months, but Dad told me I need to plan a trip."

"It's busy during summer, but after Labor Day is lovely."

Spence joined them. "Are you thinking about a visit in September?"

"Ellie pitched the same idea. I could make it work."

They wandered to the car and Spence dropped Ellie at the lobby entrance with a promise to meet at six the next morning. Ellie stuck her head through the driver's window. "Wonderful to meet you Kevin. Congratulations on the new job and I hope you come and visit us later this year." She straightened and added, "I'll meet you here in the morning, Spence." She gave a quick wave before disappearing through the door.

* * *

The next morning, after stopping for coffee, they drove to the cheese factory in the dark. Spence cruised the parking lot and scanned the cars for a 1998 Toyota Camry. They found it in the first row and parked in the space behind it.

Lance was due to get off work in a few minutes and Spence kept his eyes glued to the employee entrance. He propped a blow up of Lance's photo on the steering wheel. Movement at the employee door triggered Spence to lean forward. A stream of workers left the building. "There he is, third in the last group. The one with the cigarette."

Spence grabbed the third cup of coffee they had picked up in Sunnyside. He eased out of the car and Ellie followed his lead, but hung back. Spence met Lance at the fender of the Camry. "Hey, Lance."

The scrawny man with greasy hair cast his red rimmed eyes at Spence. "Yeah, who are you?" A billow of strong smelling smoke wafted in Spence's direction.

"Spence Chandler. I'm a private investigator and a friend of Saul, your probation officer."

Lance's eyes darted around the parking lot and he dropped the butt to the ground and crushed it with his dirty boot. "Yeah, well I haven't done nuthin." He scratched one arm and then the other, followed by the back of his head.

"Saul said you've been doing great." He handed him the cup of coffee. "We picked this up for you. Figured you could use it after a long night at work."

Lance fidgeted from foot to foot and with shaky hands seized the cup. He took a sip and sniffed. "So, what do you want with me?" He wiped his nose on his sleeve.

Spence motioned Ellie forward. "This young woman wants to talk with you."

Lance peered at Ellie. She moved under the glow from the light pole. "Hey, Lance." Her glance at the Camry's window revealed litter and filth.

He squinted and shoved a strand of hair out of his eyes. "Is that you, Ellie?"

Eleven

Ellie offered to buy breakfast and the promise of a free meal won over his reluctance to get in Spence's car. Spence drove to a diner a few miles down the road.

"What's it been, like twenty years? Where'd you disappear to anyway?"

Ellie turned in her seat to look at Lance and noticed he was sweating. "I moved to live with my aunt and uncle." She let out a breath, struggling to reconcile the man before her with the boy from her past. The only familiar feature was his eyes. The color hadn't changed but the kindness she remembered had been replaced by hardness. "It's part of a long story and the reason I'm here now."

Spence pulled into the diner and they were shown to a table. Lance removed his jacket, revealing a trail of colorful tattoos down both arms. He ordered the largest breakfast on the menu, coffee, orange juice, and a piece of pie. After the waitress left, Ellie took a deep breath. "So, back when we were dating, my parents sent me away because I was pregnant."

He smirked and took a noisy gulp from his glass. "Busted, huh?" He swiped the sheen from his forehead.

"I never told them or anyone else who the father was, but I had a baby girl that August. I gave her up for adoption and my aunt and uncle helped me straighten out my life." She glanced at Spence and he nodded her encouragement. "Lance, you were the father of the baby."

He scanned the diner and gripped the edge of the table. "You're not gonna come here and try to screw me out of child support after twenty years." He hunched over the table. "This is complete bullshit, Ellie."

She shook her head. "No, it's nothing like that. She was adopted by a family. There's no support issue. The thing is she sought me out a couple of weeks ago. Her name is Danielle and she's nineteen. She's sick and needs a kidney."

"Then give her yours."

"I tried, but I'm not a candidate. I was hoping you would agree to get tested and consider donating one of yours."

The waitress delivered their food with Lance's selections taking up over half of the table. "You want one of my kidneys? Just like that."

"She needs to get a transplant from a blood relative. She had one years ago and it's failing now. You'd be doing a generous thing."

He shoved hash browns in his mouth and used a piece of toast to mop up the runny yolks swirling on the plate. With his mouth full he spat, "It's not gonna happen. I ain't getting any tests or letting some quack slice me up and take my kidney."

Spence cleared his throat. "She's a young girl with her whole life ahead of her. It's a simple blood test."

Lance kept shoveling food in his mouth. "Not my problem."

"She's our own flesh and blood, Lance. Don't you want to help her?"

"Nobody's helped me much." He cleaned the last of the food from his plate and moved to the pie. As he ate he bobbed his head. "Maybe if I got something in return, ya know?"

"What do you mean?" asked Spence.

"I could use some money to get my own place. I'm sick of living with Ma. I need a car. All I've got is this shitty job. Maybe say for ten grand and a new car, I'd think about it." He rested a hand across his stomach and grimaced.

Ellie's body tensed. Spence placed his hand on top on hers and in a stern voice addressed Lance. "You realize what you're proposing is illegal?"

"Illegal, nah. It's just a gift, ya know. You wanna save your girl so bad, you could give old Lance a little something."

Ellie vibrated with anger. "What happened to you Lance? I can't believe you've turned into such a monster."

He sneered. "You didn't used to have a problem with me, did you sweetheart?"

Ellie pictured Dani and her ensuing hatred and disappointment when she'd be forced to tell her Lance wouldn't help. She stiffened her back and sat up straight. "How about you get tested and then if you're a match, we'll talk about a gift."

Spence gave her a questioning look, but remained silent.

"That's more like it. Are you staying in town?"

"No, we're not staying here." Ellie delved into her bag and pulled out a lab slip Max had given her before she left. "Here's an order for the blood tests. The lab at the hospital is open today. The cost of the test is covered."

He fingered the paperwork. In anticipation of Lance agreeing to be tested, Max had provided the necessary order with a request for the results to be forwarded to him and Dani's doctor. Max had agreed to have the charges billed to his account, so there would be no issue of cost. "Okay, Ellie, I'll get the test." He pushed his pie plate away. "When will we know about the gift?"

"I suspect Monday since today is Saturday. You'll hear from Dr. Sullivan or Dr. Jacobs when they get your results. I'll give you a call Monday and we can discuss the next steps."

Lance gave Ellie his cell phone and stuffed the lab order in his pocket, before visiting the restroom. Ellie paid the tab and Spence drove in the opposite direction of the cheese factory. "Where are you taking me?" Lance bellowed from the backseat.

"Making sure you get to the lab today, Lance. It's not far." Spence pulled into the hospital a few miles away, with Lance screaming profanities for the duration of the trip. Spence and Ellie chose not to respond to his ranting. "Here we are. Do you need me to go with you?" asked Spence.

Lance glared at the older man and slammed the door on the car. They watched him swagger to the entrance and disappear inside. Ellie shut her eyes and tried to slow her pulse. "I can't believe I ever even liked him…or had his baby." She shivered with disgust.

"You were a teenager and I suspect he's changed...a bit."

"I'm not going to pay him for a kidney, by the way. It was the only way to get him to agree to the test. Once we know if he's a match, I'll figure out the next move. What kind of a creep sells his kidney anyway?"

"He may have given up cocaine, but he's on something. If he's addicted, he fixated on what the money will get him. Addicts only focus on getting their next hit."

Ellie glanced out the window. "Here he comes."

Lance climbed in the back and banged the door shut. Spence put the car in gear. He took a different route and they passed by Sunnyside High School. Ellie stared out the window, craning her neck long after they had driven past it. They traveled to the cheese factory in silence. Spence stole a look in the rearview mirror and saw Lance was asleep. He parked the car and turned to prod the sleeping man. "We're here."

"I'll talk to you Monday," said Ellie.

They watched Lance stagger to his car. Spence hollered out the window. "Are you okay? Do you want a lift home?"

"I'm fine. Sick of listening to you two when I should have been asleep. Leave me the hell alone."

"I'm going to call his probation officer and tell him my suspicions. I have a feeling he's letting Lance skate because he's working and isn't in trouble."

"Do you know Saul well?"

With a twinkle in his eye, he laughed. "I don't know Saul at all." He put the car in gear. "But Lance doesn't know that."

"I guess we ought to stay until Monday in case I need to pay Lance another visit."

"Fine by me." He came to a main intersection. "Do you want to do anything else while we're here?"

Ellie stared out the window. The light turned green and rather than head to the highway, Spence turned. "Ellie, shall we drive by your old house?"

She turned and he saw tears shining in her eyes. She nodded and told him where to turn. Soon they were in an unremarkable neighborhood. She pointed at a white house in the middle of the block. "There it is."

Spence slowed as they passed by the house. He rolled down the windows so they could get a better look. He looped around to inspect further when a tired looking minivan pulled in the driveway. A short white haired woman, with plastic grocery bags looped around her wrist, got out of the driver's side. A man sat in the passenger seat. The woman hollered, "Get the rest of the groceries, Teddy. We need to get this stuff put away before your dad gets home."

Ellie watched her brother slide the door open and grab dozens of plastic bags. "Hurry up," shouted Caroline. Her mother turned and locked eyes with her as Spence approached the house. Ellie's heart beat faster, fearful her mother would recognize her. Caroline was in her sixties, but in a frumpy long skirt and oversized sweater, she looked older. Her hair had been gray when Ellie last saw her, but now it was white and cut in the same short style that required no effort. She had put on weight and looked shorter and rounder than Ellie remembered. Her mother's eyes, hard as agates, peered at her through glasses, but there was no hint of recognition.

The car was creeping past the house and Ellie continued to stare. She used the button and rolled up the windows. "I guess my younger brother still lives at home. He's thirty now." She shook her head and Spence drove them out of the neighborhood. "I wonder where my sister ended up."

"I could do some digging and find her."

"If it's not too much trouble."

"No trouble, plus we've got to do something to keep busy the rest of the day and tomorrow."

He found an onramp for the highway and when they got to Ellensburg they stopped for a late lunch at the same coffeehouse they enjoyed yesterday. Over fresh sandwiches and soup Ellie told Spence the particulars about Cecilia.

The encounter with Lance had sapped Ellie's energy. Spence dropped her at the hotel and they agreed to meet in the morning. "I should have something on your sister by then. I'll pick you up for breakfast and we'll decide what to do from there."

Ellie carried her non-fat latte to her room and spent the rest of the afternoon watching movies in her pajamas. She sent Max a text and let him know about Lance's test. He texted back to update her on the plans for Peggy's service for the upcoming week and promised to be in touch soon.

She fingered her cell phone and punched the button for Blake. "Hey, Blake. I found out I need to stay in town until Monday, so I won't be there to get Oreo on time. Can she stay there until Monday night?"

"Sure, not a problem. In fact she and Lucy are hanging with me today at the winery. She's a great dog."

"I appreciate it. I'll make it up to you with a batch of whatever you want."

"Is everything okay? You don't sound like your usual cheery self."

Ellie leaned back against the pile of pillows. "It's family stuff." She sighed and added, "I miss Oreo and being home. I'm not a great traveler."

"Don't worry about us. We're fine and we'll see you when you get in Monday night."

"I texted Max today and he said they're working on the service for Linda's mom."

"Yeah, he gave me the same update. Sounds like it wouldn't be until the end of the week. Their place is terrific, so it's no problem to stay there for as long as they need me. It's like a vacation to get off the boat."

"I bet. I love their house, so I understand your willingness to tough it out there." He laughed. "You take care, Ellie. I hope things work out with your family."

She hung up, thankful he didn't pry into her family issues. She found the book she had brought to read and propped the pillows. After half an hour she slammed the book shut and got out of bed.

Cravings for chocolate chip cookies and moist cupcakes dominated Ellie's thoughts. Until she had been forced to alter her diet, she hadn't noticed how much she used food for comfort. She was thankful to be in a hotel room, cut off from her baked goods. She rummaged in the small refrigerator for her healthy snacks and made a meal from them and another muffin. Her blood sugar tests had been better on the trip, which was a step in the right direction.

The television continued to display a movie, but Ellie's mind wandered. She ran through scenarios of what she would say to Ceci, if Spence found her. After she exhausted those possibilities she switched gears and worried about how she would get Lance to donate a kidney, without paying him. She moved to the desk and began coloring a new page.

Her cell phone rang and she saw it was Jeff. He let her know the house was fine, masking his real reason for calling. He and Sam wanted to check on her and make sure she was doing well. She visited for a few minutes and asked about the bakery. Sam had checked on Nicole, but she was handling it like a pro. Ellie enjoyed the distraction and small talk. She was reminded again how much she loved her life in Friday Harbor.

She saw a glimpse of the late news before nodding off to sleep. She missed Oreo cuddling next to her. The television droned on all night and kept her company, while in her dreams she contemplated the choices she would face over the next two days.

* * *

Sunday morning Spence whisked her to a café Kevin recommended for breakfast. He opened another file folder after they ordered. "Your sister lives in Everett. She's married to a teacher and works part-time as a clerk for the city. She's got two children and I've got her phone number and address."

"I'm not sure I'm up to talking with her. I think I'd rather deal with one drama at a time and wait until I know what happens with Lance tomorrow."

"It's up to you." He passed her a summary report from the file. "You hang onto this and if and when you're ready you'll have it."

They went for a drive around the town, visited with Kevin, and found a new movie to watch at the theatre. Kate called to check in and Spence gave her the latest update. They found a frozen yogurt place and Ellie treated herself to a petite non-fat concoction with fresh berries.

After an early dinner with Kevin and a walk around the college campus, Spence dropped her back at her home away from home. She tapped the remote to activate her companion for the night. She got ready for bed and dug out the paper Spence had given her. She read it again. Cecilia Carlson was now Cecilia Barnes, married to Tim. He taught history and coached at a high school. They had a son and a daughter, Tim Jr. and Cynthia.

Ceci's phone number taunted her as she scanned the paper. It was Sunday night, she should be home. Ellie could call and test the waters. Ceci might be excited to hear from her. Then again, she might want nothing to do with Ellie. She wouldn't know unless she was brave enough to risk the call.

She reached for her cell phone and punched in the number. Her finger shook, poised over the green button. As she moved her finger, her phone rang.

Startled, she fumbled with the phone and when she righted it, saw it was Jen. After relaying the eventful meeting with Lance, she felt better. Jen could always make her laugh and appreciate the humor in life. "Be glad you didn't marry the assclown," she said.

"I hadn't thought of that, but you're right. It could always be worse." Ellie laughed as she listened to the island updates courtesy of Jen's patrons at the beauty salon. The ladies who frequented her shop were Friday Harbor's version of the World Wide Web.

As soon as she hung up from Jen, Regi called. "Hey, Ellie. Nate and I wanted to check on you and make sure you were doing okay."

"I'm fine. Jen called before you. She was doing the same thing."

"Aww, well, we all love you. Nate and I had dinner with Blake tonight and he said your business got delayed, so we were worried."

Ellie explained the complication with Lance and why she was waiting until Monday. "Spence found my sister. I've been sitting here working up the courage to call her. She lives in Everett."

"Wow, Spence is pretty handy. What's keeping you from calling her?"

Ellie paused in thought. "Fear, I guess."

"Fear of what?"

"A negative response. She's never tried to make contact with me, so I have to assume she isn't interested in seeing me." Ellie wiped fresh tears from her cheeks. "I've been rejected by her and my parents for so long. I thought I was over it, but I guess I'm not done."

"Why do you want to call her?"

"Well, I guess there's a tiny part of me that wishes we could reconnect. Mom is the one who coerced her into ignoring me. I was hoping now that she's on her own, she'd be like she used to be when we were little."

"I can't tell you what to do, Ellie. But if there's a chance you could have a part of your family back in your life, I think it might be worth the risk. You're a tough lady and I know rejection will hurt you again, but you can survive it. You've got friends in your life to help you. I guess the question is can you survive not knowing?"

Ellie nodded and sniffed. "Thanks, Regi. I'm going to call her tonight."

"If you need me later, call. It doesn't matter when. We love you."

Ellie disconnected and splashed cold water on her face. She fixed a glass of iced water and sat back down on the bed. She tapped in Ceci's number and this time didn't hesitate.

She recognized her sister's voice. "Hi, Ceci. It's Ellie."

"Ellie? How…er…how are you?"

"I'm doing well. I'm actually going to be driving through Everett tomorrow and wondered if I could stop by and visit."

There was a long pause and then she said, "Tomorrow? Um, let me check. I work in the morning, what time are you planning to be here?"

"It'll be in the afternoon. I have to catch the ferry back to Friday Harbor."

"You still live there, huh?"

"Yes. I don't get to the mainland much, but since I haven't seen you in so long, I thought I'd take a chance you'd be around."

"How'd you find me?"

"Through a friend. If you're not available, it's not a problem. We can shoot for another time."

"Um, no, I could make the afternoon work. It needs to be before four o'clock though. I could meet you for coffee."

Ellie let out a breath. "That would be great. I'll give you my cell number. Text me the address and I'll let you know when I get to town."

Ellie recited her number and took Ceci's down on the hotel pad. Ceci gave directions for a coffee place close to her office.

"I'll meet you tomorrow then. Thanks, Ceci."

Ellie hung up and sent Regi a quick text. *She said we could meet tomorrow.*

Regi replied. *Good job. We'll see you when you get home. Sleep well, my friend.*

Twelve

After checking out, Ellie hauled her suitcase to the lobby and met Spence. Over breakfast she shared the news about Ceci. "I was hoping we could make a quick stop to meet her in Everett on our way to the ferry."

"Of course. I'm glad you called her."

"I'll wait until after nine to call Lance. I know Max can't share the results with me, but he said he'd text as soon as he talked to Dr. Jacobs. He put a rush on the results, so I'm hoping I'll hear first thing this morning."

"The last ferry leaves at nine o'clock tonight, so we have plenty of time."

She focused on her phone, checking her messages every few minutes, while she finished her breakfast. To kill some time, they gassed up and picked up some drinks for the road. Her phone chirped as she was walking back to the car.

Max sent a text. *Dr. Jacobs called me, so you should be able to contact Lance. Give me a call when you can.*

Spence found a park nearby and pulled into a space. She raised her brows at him. "Here goes nothing." She punched in his number and waited. Spence went for a walk to give her some privacy.

"Lance, it's Ellie. I wanted to check and find out if you got your results yet."

"Some dude in Seattle called. He told me my kidneys are in bad shape. Along with my liver. He started preaching to me to get help for my drug and alcohol problems and stop smoking. Like I'm gonna do that. He said I'd have to commit to lifestyle changes and get retested each month to see if

I improve before I could donate."

Ellie's bubble of hope deflated. "So, there's a chance it could work down the road?"

"If I have to do all that, it's gonna cost a lot more than ten grand. I don't even know this girl you claim is my daughter."

"She *is* your daughter. Do you think you could stop smoking and the rest of it?"

"Nah, it's not gonna work."

"Could you try?"

"I don't see it happening. If it does, I'll call you. I could use the money."

"You're one selfish…never mind. Good bye, Lance." She disconnected and let the phone fall in her lap. She held her head in her hands and wept.

The look of total despair on her face was all Spence needed. He didn't ask any questions as he started the car and followed the road to the highway. When they reached Snoqualmie Pass she finally spoke. "He can't donate. Drugs, drinking, and smoking have taken their toll and preclude him from being a viable candidate. He's not willing to change and if he did he'd want more money."

"He's a worm, Ellie. After meeting him, I'm not surprised. He's a mess."

"Dani's going to be devastated. I've been thinking maybe I should ask Ceci if she'd consider donating."

Spence's eyes went wide. "Wow, it may be too much for a first meeting."

She stared at her lap and then shifted her gaze out the window. "I know, I think it might be. I feel compelled to try and help Dani."

"She's stable now on dialysis, right?"

Ellie nodded. "So I should calm down, huh?"

Spence put a hand on her arm. "Take it a bit slower and think it through."

"I dread having to call her and tell her Lance can't donate either. She was so angry when I told her I couldn't do it."

"I'm sure her doctor already told her, so it won't be a surprise. You've done more than a lot of people would have." He fiddled with the radio.

"How about we finish the book we started?"

It was noon when they saw the exits for Everett. Spence remembered a restaurant from some time he spent in the area. They found the renovated airplane manufacturing building and settled at a table. While they waited for their meal, Ellie texted Ceci and told her she was in Everett and asked her to pick a time to meet.

The coffee shop was near the library and other city offices. Spence ordered a coffee and told Ellie to text him when she was ready. "I'll wander around while you catch up with your sister."

Ellie sat at a table where she had a view of the entrance. The bouncing of her leg shook the table. She tried to tame her nerves and put a hand on her thigh to quiet the movement. She checked the time on her phone again and looked for a text message. When she looked up she recognized Ceci coming through the door. She was still slim, with an athletic build. Her blond hair was highlighted and styled in a layered bob.

Ellie stood and caught Ceci's eye with a wave. Ellie's throat was dry and her pulse hammered. "Hey, Ellie," said Ceci, putting her jacket on the back of a chair.

Ellie swallowed hard. "You look great, Ceci. I'm so glad you had time to meet."

"I was shocked when you called. I still can't believe it. Do you want a coffee?"

She followed Ceci to the counter and ordered. "How long have you lived in Everett?"

"Tim, my husband, got a job teaching here about seven years ago." They picked up their drinks and made their way to the table. "I've got to pick up Cyndi at four. She's our youngest and is ten. Tim Jr. is thirteen." Ceci flipped through photos on her phone and shared a picture of the two of them.

"What brings you here, Ellie?"

"Uh, well, I had to take care of some business and am heading back to the ferry today. I found out you lived here and took a chance. It's been such a long time."

Ceci took a sip of her drink. "What do you do in Friday Harbor?"

"Aunt Ginny and Uncle Bob moved to Mt. Vernon about five years ago and I stayed and took over their bakery."

"Mmm. I didn't know they left the island. We never visited them after Mom and Dad took you to live with them."

"I always thought that was weird. Aunt Ginny said about a year after I went to live there, Dad quit calling."

"Yeah, I don't know much about it." She looked down at the table and crinkled the napkin in her had. "I asked about you, but Mom said you were gone and it was best we forgot you." She looked up and met Ellie's eyes. "I'm sorry, Ellie. I should have tried harder."

"Why'd you hate me so much when we were growing up?"

Ceci shook her head. "I never hated you, Ellie. It was, you know, easier with Mom. If I stuck up for you, then I'd get punished. When I think about it now, it was horrible. At the time, it was easier for me. I was going to be out of the house and wanted to leave. More than anything."

Ellie nodded. "That's what I thought. What about Teddy? What's he doing?"

"He still lives at home with Mom and Dad. He doesn't have a job right now. Mom did all his homework for him and still he barely graduated. He sits around in front of the television or playing video games all day."

"He's thirty and still lives with them and has no job? And I'm the loser?"

Ceci pursed her lips. "He also got a girl pregnant and has two kids with her. They've never married and he doesn't see the kids often."

Ellie's eyes went wide. It was fortunate the cup was ceramic, otherwise she would have crushed it. "Seriously? They basically discard me because I'm pregnant and he gets a free pass." She shook her head with disgust. "I shouldn't be surprised, Teddy always got away with murder."

Ceci took another drink and stared out the window. "You wouldn't conform, Ellie. Mom likes to control things and you were defiant. You drew attention to her shortcomings."

"Because she's a complete nut job." After she blurted out the words she took a breath. "I know I didn't always behave, but she treated me like garbage. Then when you treated me the same way, it hurt me. I thought we'd always be close."

Ellie saw the glint of tears in her sister's eyes. "I'm sorry, Ellie. I really am sorry. I got out of the house and left the chaos behind. I know Mom had her problems. She had to be the center of attention. I agree she wasn't a great mother to you."

"That's the understatement of the year. After you left it only got worse. Dad always tried to keep us apart, but then he drifted to her side. I was always the one in trouble, no matter what happened." Ellie's tone took on a sarcastic hint. "Baby Bear could do no wrong in her eyes and Mom always made everything my fault when she talked to Dad."

"Well, it didn't get Teddy far in life. He's still at home and spends his time with Mom. He has no friends, no job, nothing."

"How's Dad?"

"He retired several years ago. He keeps busy and doesn't spend much time at home. Remember how he'd always find a summer job? He still seeks out work or goes fishing. I don't think they've been happy for a long time. They used to fight so much. Now they barely speak. Mom's home with Teddy and Dad's always gone."

"I drove by the old house and saw her. She and Teddy had been shopping and were loaded down with bags."

"Did they see you?"

Ellie shook her head. "They didn't act like they recognized me."

Both of them were silent and stared past each other. "Tell me more about what you've been doing," said Ceci.

"The bakery keeps me busy. I've hired a helper, so hope to have a bit more free time."

"Are you married?"

"No, never. I had a serious relationship, but it ended about a year ago. He found somebody online and left."

"How horrible. I would imagine the dating pool on the island is somewhat shallow."

Ellie grinned. "Yeah, I'm not looking. I've got a couple slow months and then the busy season starts and I don't have time to think about anything but work."

"You mentioned being pregnant. What happened to the baby?"

"I gave her up for adoption." Ellie paused and exhaled. "In fact, she got in touch with me right after Christmas. She's nineteen and her name is Danielle. She's sick and needs a kidney transplant."

"Wow, I bet you were shocked. You didn't know anything about her this whole time?"

"Nope. She came by the bakery about a month ago. I found out I can't donate. They did a blood test and I'm diabetic."

"Oh, no, Ellie. You need to take care of yourself. Can she get on the list for a kidney?"

"I'm making some changes, but it's hard. You've always been lucky to be so thin and fit. I wish I had your metabolism, but I'm making some progress. As far as the kidney goes, the doctors are hoping for a blood relative."

"Oh, that makes it difficult." Ceci focused her eyes on the table. "Uh, maybe you could come back again and visit when you have more time?"

Ellie saw the sincerity in Ceci's eyes. "Maybe the next time I get over to visit Uncle Bob and Aunt Ginny. Did you know he had a heart attack?"

"No, I haven't talked with them or even heard about them since you left." She continued to shred the napkin in her hands. "That's on me now. I'm an adult and could have decided to renew a relationship with them. I could have tracked you down too. Mom always speaks so poorly of them. I guess I'm still the weak girl who'd rather go along with her than deal with her wrath."

"They were wonderful to me. Aunt Ginny is a million times the mother Mom could ever be. They gave me a chance and helped me. I can never repay them. I can't believe Dad turned his back on his own brother. I used to think he was such a strong and decent man."

"He helps everyone in town and has a kind heart. He was beloved by his students as a principal and a coach. I think he fell into the same pattern I did. It's easier to give in and do what she wants than deal with the screaming and crying."

"She's a master manipulator and she passed her skills onto Teddy." Ellie took the last gulp from her cup. "I guess I should be glad I was thrown out. At least Uncle Bob and Aunt Ginny care about me."

Ceci checked her watch. "I've gotta run, Ellie. I'm glad we got a chance to visit. I hope we can get together again."

"You're welcome to come to the island anytime that works. I'd like to meet your husband and kids someday."

"I'd like that too, Ellie." Ceci moved closer and gave Ellie a tentative hug. She slipped into her jacket and hoisted her bag on her shoulder. "I'm sorry about the past, Ellie. Maybe we can start over, huh?"

Ellie wiped at the tears on her cheeks. "Yeah, that would be great." She plucked one of her bakery cards out of her purse and shoved it in her sister's hand. "It has my email and work number on it. Give me a call."

Ceci smiled and slipped the card into her bag. "I'll do that."

Thirteen

Spence and Ellie rushed to Anacortes and were one of the last cars permitted to board the six o'clock ferry. She texted Blake to let him know she'd be home in an hour. After thanking Spence for his help, Ellie drove to Max and Linda's.

The growling of her stomach along with a pounding headache reminded Ellie she hadn't eaten since lunch. She was drained from the trip, but the excitement of reuniting with Oreo counteracted the fatigue.

All the outside lights were on when she pulled up to the house. She saw the front door open and Oreo barreled down the walkway. Blake stood on the front step with Lucy not far behind. She kneeled down and Oreo pounced on her, licking her and placing her paws on each side of Ellie's neck.

"I'd say she's happy to see you," said Blake.

"I've missed her." Ellie laughed as the dog tumbled with her on the lawn. Lucy joined the gathering and ran in the midst of the twosome.

"Come on in for a minute. I picked up dinner."

"Oh, you didn't need to do that."

"I eat alone all the time. Come and join me. It'll damage my fragile ego if I get a third raincheck."

She tugged herself loose and tucked her purse under her arm. She followed Blake into the house, with the dogs at her heels. He had a fire going and an enticing aroma filled the air. "Something smells delicious."

"I stopped at the Front Street Café. They had a pork tenderloin special."

He removed the meals from the containers and placed the roasted veggies and warm applesauce next to the meat. He opened the carton of salad and added it to a bowl. Ellie recognized slices of her bread in a basket and saw a bottle of wine on the island.

Ellie's stomach rumbled and the determination she marshalled to pass on the dinner invite dissolved. "Oh, this all looks delicious."

He pulled out a chair, "Have a seat."

She hesitated, remembering she hadn't tested her blood. "I'll be right back."

When she returned from the powder room, she found the two dogs sacked out in the corner and Blake waiting for her at the table. "Sorry, needed to wash my hands."

He pulled out her chair again and she welcomed the tasty meal. She skipped the bread and after some prodding by Blake, tried a sip of wine. "So, how was the trip?"

"Long. I'm worn out."

"Did you get everything done?"

She brought her glass of water to her lips. "Uh, yeah, for the most part." She swallowed a mouthful. "How's the winery progressing?"

"I've been busy this week. I've got a handle on the operations. Jeff came out and put together a materials list for what I want done at the house. I'm hoping to start next week."

He disappeared in the kitchen and returned with a plate of cupcakes. He held the selection in front of her. "I'll give you first pick."

"Oh, I'm stuffed. I don't think I can squeeze in another bite."

He narrowed his eyes. "Okay, what's up? You passed on your delicious bread and now you won't eat a cupcake. Are you boycotting your own food?"

She laughed and weighed the risk of telling him the truth. "No, it's not that. I think I mentioned the doctor told me I needed to make some changes, so I'm trying to behave."

"You are the most obedient patient I've ever met."

"Well…I…uh, I found out I'm diabetic."

"Oh, no. I had no idea. I'm sorry, Ellie." He removed the plate of cupcakes from under her nose and set them on the counter. "How can you work in a bakery and not eat all your stuff?"

"That would be the root of the problem. I put on some pounds over the last few years, but never considered a serious medical condition." She gathered the plates from the table. "I've been upset about it, mostly because I'm not sure I can continue at the bakery. I listed it for sale with Jack."

"I get it. It would be like me being told I can't drink wine. I'd have to remove myself from the constant temptation."

"Yeah, a diabetic owning a bakery is similar to an alcoholic owning a bar, right?"

He laughed and carried the serving dishes into the kitchen. She rinsed the dishes and put them in the dishwasher. "You don't have to clean up. I can do it later."

"It'll only take a minute and then I need to get home and get to bed."

"How about some coffee or tea?"

She saw the hopeful look on his face. She held up a finger. "Okay, one cup of tea."

He fumbled with one of the cups and caught it before it crashed to the floor. "Every once in a while I miss my finger," he said.

"What happened to it?"

"Corking machine. I stuck my finger in it trying to fix it. It was years ago."

"Ouch. That's harsh."

"Yeah, my dad always told me not to put my fingers in there, but I didn't listen."

While she finished cleaning he poured water into a pot and added it to the tray. He touched the scar on his forehead. "This one's from the winery too. Wine barrel incident." He carried the tray into the great room. "I've been accident free for more than a decade now, though." He smiled as he took a seat.

She chose the opposite end of the couch and sunk into the soft leather. As she watched the flames dance and felt the warmth of the cup in her hands, her eyelids struggled to stay open. "Now I'm feeling drowsy."

"You've had a long day." He brought the cup to his lips and then set it on the table. "I've got an idea to run by you."

She raised her brows over the rim of her mug.

"I've been thinking about trying to turn the vineyard into more of a destination, with full service event planning. I'm too busy to handle anything else and would need a manager to handle that side of things. When you said what you did about the bakery, it got me thinking. Would you have an interest in working at the winery?"

Ellie eyes widened, all traces of fatigue dissolved. "Really? I've been trying to figure out what I could do for a job. I'd have to know more and make sure I could do it, but it sounds interesting."

"I want to do more weddings, parties, conferences, any event. I'd like to offer complete packages. I need someone who could manage the entire operation and coordinate with caterers, florists, musicians, entertainment, whatever the client wants."

"Linda would be a great resource. She'd had a lot of experience working events on the island. She knows all the best vendors."

"I talked to Jeff about updating the old barn used for storage. I want to turn it into event space. I think it would make a unique venue for indoor events. Outdoors we have the pavilion."

They continued chatting and making lists of ideas. They finished off two more pots of tea. When Ellie looked at the clock it was after midnight. "Oh, my gosh. I need to get going. I can't believe it's so late."

He gave her a sheepish look. "Sorry, I lost track of time." He gathered Oreo's bed and supplies and carried them to her car. "Stop by when you have some time this week and we'll talk more. Maybe you could play hooky tomorrow. Sleep late and spend the rest of the day at the winery."

"I may sleep in, but I have to check on Nicole tomorrow. I'll give you a call when I figure out what I can make work. Thanks for dinner and for the possible job. You made my week."

* * *

She slept in Tuesday morning and woke to a text from Spence. He'd found Dani's address, as she had asked. She found a striking card at Kate's shop showcasing the coast near Sam's house. With a twinge of guilt, she penned a heartfelt letter and placed it inside the card. Still stinging from her last phone call, she preferred to transmit all her feelings without interruption or rebuff. She wanted Dani to be able to read the letter and not be distracted by disappointment or anger during a phone conversation.

A latte was her reward, after she deposited the card in the mailbox. She found Sam behind the counter at Harbor Coffee. "I'm glad you stopped by. I was going to call you today. Jeff and I decided to go to the service for Linda's mom. It's on Friday, so we're going to take off early Thursday. Jen's going to go with us."

"Oh, I wish I could go, but I've been gone too much lately."

"We were hoping you could take care of the dogs for us. You can stay at the house and bring Oreo, if it's easier." She handed Ellie the cup. "We were going to ask Blake, but I hate to saddle him with three dogs."

"Sure, it's not a problem. I'll stay there with them. It'll be easier for the dogs."

Sam sighed. "Thanks, Ellie. That's a relief." The shop was empty and she fixed herself a chai tea and invited Ellie to sit for a few minutes.

"How's Linda doing? I talked to Max briefly when I was in Sunnyside, but it was all about kidney donations."

"She's doing okay. I think it's hard to lose your mother at any age. I was devastated when I lost my parents, but I was so young."

"I know I'd be overwhelmed if I lost Aunt Ginny or Uncle Bob." Ellie cradled the cup in her hands. "Spence found my sister for me and I met her for coffee on our way home."

"Wow, that's a surprise. How did it go?"

"Okay, actually. We risked talking about the past. She apologized for not trying harder to stay in touch with me. I went off on her about Mom and she listened and agreed with some of it." She filled Sam in on her brother's status.

"Teddy's life certainly confirms your perception of a double standard where he was concerned. Why would a mother do that to her children?"

"I don't know. I've never been able to figure her out, except I know she wasn't happy."

"So, how'd you leave it with your sister?"

"I invited her to come for a visit and she did the same. I told her about Dani, without some of the details. I did tell her I can't donate because of the diabetes." She paused and looked across the street. "I was actually considering asking her to be tested, but Spence talked some sense into me. He convinced me it was too much for our first meeting."

The door chimed and Sam said, "I better get back to work. I'll drop a key by the bakery for you. I think we'll all travel home together and be back by Monday."

"Give Linda a hug for me. When you guys get home, let's all get together."

* * *

Ellie settled in at Sam's with Oreo, Bailey, and Zoe. Oreo was thrilled to have two friends to romp with and the three played in the yard most of the day. Blake stopped by the bakery Thursday morning and Ellie suggested he bring Lucy over in the evenings and join her at Sam's. Not wanting to subject him to one of her boring slow cooker creations, she picked up some meat to grill.

They spent the next three nights going over sketches and plans for Blake's new venture. The elevation views of the barn were incredible and would provide the perfect venue for events. He had been working with his web designer from Yakima and showed Ellie a mockup of the new website. It didn't have all the details, but showcased the property and services they would provide.

Low clouds hung in the sky Saturday and as soon as Ellie arrived at Sam's the dreariness darkened and threatened rain. Blake pulled in and was at the deck door before she had shed her jacket. He offered to start the grill while she worked on a salad. The dogs zipped around the yard, until he whistled at them. They came scuttling onto the deck and through the doors for their own dinner. The chill from the open door prompted him to start a fire in the great room.

Over warm mugs of tea, he proposed a salary far more than Ellie expected or earned at the bakery. "That's quite generous," she said, as she finished the salad and sliced a loaf of bread she nicked from Sweet Treats.

He brought in the grilled chicken and retrieved a bottle of wine. "It's in line with what similar places pay and if it brings in what I'm projecting, you'll get a healthy bonus each year. My parents agree with the idea and want me to move forward. They're my business partners in this venture."

A low rumble of thunder was followed by a drenching downpour. "Wow, looks like we got dinner off the grill in the nick of time." She speared a forkful of salad. "I'm excited about a new focus. I think it'll be tons of fun. With what you've offered, I could probably start now while I'm trying to sell the business. I'd make enough at the bakery to keep Nicole full time, if I weren't relying on it for my salary. She can't do wedding cakes yet, so I'd have to do those, but I think I can make it work." She took a sip of her drink. "I need to get through Valentine's Day. I've got several orders, but after that it'll be slow."

"Sounds terrific. I was hoping you could start soon, but didn't want to pressure you. I know you can't be doing both, but until we get busy, you'd have the freedom to help at the bakery when you need to."

"It would give you a chance to make sure I'm a good fit for the job. I don't want you to hire me because you feel sorry for me."

He scrunched his forehead and shook his head. "You'll be terrific. You're organized and know everyone on the island. I think it'll be great, but we can agree to a trial for a few months to make sure you're happy."

She nodded and her gray eyes danced with excitement. "Deal. Let's give it until the middle of May and if either of us isn't happy, we cut the cord."

"Agreed," he said. "I'm going to give Jeff the go ahead on the barn so we can get it ready for the summer rush."

"Linda should be home Monday. We can pick her brain for ideas. We couldn't host a large indoor event until the barn is done, but we could still offer the coordination services for weddings. The church is perfect for a ceremony and if it's a small party we could make the tasting room work." She began clearing the table. "I never dreamed I'd end up being a wedding planner," she said. Lightning illuminated the sky and thunder growled.

"I think event manager sounds much better." He smiled and helped her clear the dishes. Rain continued to assault the deck, splattering against the glass of the windows. Blake checked on the dogs and found them fast asleep in front of the fire. He wandered to the French doors. "Man, I knew they were predicting rain, but it's like a firehose opened up, plus it's windy now." He lit a few candles in case the power went out.

"It's supposed to clear out tomorrow." Ellie finished tidying the kitchen and brought a tray with tea and dessert. "Before you get too excited, it's a diabetic friendly applesauce cake. I tried a new recipe today."

He helped himself to a slab of the cake and sat on the hearth. Ellie joined him and took a bite. "Mmm, not bad. Not in the same ballpark as my salted caramel and chocolate, but it works."

"It's perfect." He finished his piece and helped himself to another. "How have you been feeling?"

"I'm okay. My blood sugar numbers are improving." A gust of wind rattled the windows and the lights flickered before they were left in darkness. "Good thing you lit candles."

"Yeah, although the fire gives off quite a bit of light." He offered to take their empty plates to the kitchen.

When he returned, he caught her yawning. "Sorry, I'm worn out from the week. Happy to be off tomorrow."

"I should get going."

"I hate to think of you on your boat in this storm. You're welcome to bunk here tonight. They have plenty of bedrooms." She directed her attention to the flames. "I'll probably sleep on one of the couches to keep the fire going. There's a fireplace in the master, but I don't want to mess with it."

"There's plenty of dry wood stacked. Are you sure you wouldn't feel awkward with me here?"

"I'm sure. It's no problem." She took a candle and went down the hall to the master suite. She returned dressed in her pajamas and robe and handed Blake a pair of Jeff's sweats and a long sleeved shirt. "Here you go. I'm going to collect some pillows and blankets."

He changed and then made sure all the doors were locked. She plopped blankets and a pillow on the couch for him and made up the other one with her pillow.

The three dogs lifted their heads to survey the commotion and then went back to sleep in front of the fire. Blake stoked the fire and loaded it with wood before he burrowed under his blankets.

"If it dies down, wake me up."

"Okay," she murmured, hypnotized by the dancing orange flames. She relaxed under the weight of the quilt and her eyes struggled to remain open. "Good night, Blake."

"Sweet dreams, Ellie."

Fourteen

Ellie was the first to wake on Sunday. The logs in the fire, now only chunks of orange embers, provided a faint glow as the first pink light of day filtered through the glass. She stole a glance across the room and saw Blake's mop of dark hair atop a cocoon of blankets.

Ever alert to her mistress's movements, Oreo sprang from her bed and was at Ellie's side. Zoe and Bailey rose with a slow stretch before sitting upright on the floor next to Blake. They both stared at the mound of blankets and sniffed his hair.

Ellie cupped her hand over her mouth to suppress a giggle. She extracted herself from the twist of quilts and padded to the kitchen to start coffee. She looked at the digital clock and calculated the power had been off for over nine hours, which explained why the house was chilly. She tiptoed back into the great room and gritted her teeth while adding wood to the fire, cautious about making noise. Zoe and Bailey were still staring at their overnight guest like he was a suspicious bag left at the airport.

Ellie gave a whisper and the dogs followed her to the mud room for breakfast. She scooped the food with great care to prevent the clatter of bits against the bowls. Once they were engrossed in their morning meal she opened the fridge, intent on finding the makings of a breakfast for humans.

Wisps of fog snaked along the shore and into the trees. She stared through the glass, mesmerized by the tendrils of mist. The coffee maker beeped and she poured herself a large mug. She doctored it and starting mixing the ingredients for a ham and cheese omelet. She heard footsteps and Blake stepped around the corner. "Good morning. Something smells delicious."

"Coffee's ready and I've got an omelet on the stove." She heard the flap of the dog door from the mud room and looked up to find the threesome exploring the yard.

She sliced two chunks of bread from the leftover loaf and slipped them into the toaster. Blake set places at the island counter while she added a bowl of berries to the spread.

They enjoyed the warm breakfast as they watched the morning light shimmer through the fog atop calm waters. The storm had passed and left a crisp morning with the haze already burning off. The sky was the perfect shade of light blue with a faint streak of clouds on their way east.

"What's on your agenda today?" he asked, finishing his second piece of toast.

"With Valentine's Day less than a week away, I need to spend some time making sure I'm on top of all the orders. I've got a wedding that day along with a few parties."

He poured himself another cup of coffee and added more to Ellie's mug. "I think I'm going to start moving stuff out of the old cloak room and repurpose it as an office. It's large enough to allow both of us to have a desk and workspace in there." He took a long sip. "We're going to incorporate a smaller party room in the barn remodel, along with the larger event space."

"The more I think about it, the more excited I get. I'm so glad to have the distraction of a new undertaking. I have always loved the bakery, but it makes it easier to be eager to leave instead of sad." Her phone chirped and she read the text.

"Sam says they're on their way and will be here tonight." She poked in her response and gathered a few of the plates.

"I'll get those. It's the least I can do after you made breakfast." She held the warm mug in her hand, content to watch the dogs and talk more about the winery, as he cleaned the kitchen.

By the time they finished, it was creeping up on ten o'clock. "If you don't mind, I'm going to grab a quick shower and head out. It's the thing I miss the most since living on the boat. A full-sized shower with unlimited water."

"Go right ahead. I've been using their master bedroom and bathroom. It's all set." She led the way down the hall. "Towels are in the cabinet and shampoo is in the shower."

She folded the blankets and collected the pillows from the couches. After tidying up, she powered on her laptop and checked over the upcoming orders, making sure all her supplies would be delivered no later than Wednesday. She added a few extra items and submitted the order.

She checked her email and amid the spam and advertisements for solar rebates and reversing her wrinkles, she saw one from Cecilia Barnes. She clicked the message and her eyes darted across the screen. Her sister wanted to come for a visit over President's Day weekend. She was coming alone and was hoping to stay with Ellie Saturday and Sunday.

Ellie looked at the calendar, confirming it was less than two weeks away. The February rush would be over by then and she felt Nicole could handle another Saturday alone, if necessary. She typed a response and read it several times before hitting the send button. Ellie offered to meet her at the ferry in addition to supplying directions to the bakery.

She was engrossed in the screen and didn't hear Blake behind her. "Hey, wanted to say thanks again. Give me a call when you're done with the wedding and we'll pencil out a schedule that works for you." He was holding wet towels along with Jeff's loaner sweats. "I wasn't sure where to put these."

She hopped off the stool. "I'll take them. I need to clean up and do laundry today anyway." She deposited them on top of the washer and was followed to the kitchen by the trio of dogs.

"Say goodbye to Blake, girls. I'll be in touch after the wedding. Unless you happen to stop in for a pastry." She smiled and laughed, noticing the scruff of dark beard on his face.

"There's a definite chance I'll see you as early as…tomorrow." He gave each of the dogs a through rubbing and waved to Ellie.

* * *

The week flew by with Nicole in charge of all the last minute orders for cupcakes and other party confections. Ellie was putting the finishing touches on a red velvet wedding cake she had to have ready for delivery Saturday morning. The frenzy of activity at the bakery had been a welcome diversion. Not hearing from Dani after she sent the card had been gnawing at her, but the bustle had kept her from focusing on it.

She finished the cake well after the dinner hour on Friday. After storing it in the cooler, she called in an order of soup and salad. Once she arrived home, she wolfed it down and fell into her bed, burned out from her extended hours.

The next morning, after helping Nicole with some festive red, white, and pink glazed donuts, she set about readying the cake for delivery. She stored all her assembly supplies in a soft sided cooler she packed with cold packs. Nicole helped her load the layers in the van in the wooden cradles Jeff had made years ago. The cake top was wrapped in bubble wrap in a box and Linda's staff would be bringing some flowers to put around the cake.

She hopped in the van and flicked the key. The van uttered a low grinding noise followed by several clicks. "Crap, Crap, Crap." She checked the time and knew she wasn't going to make it. She grabbed her cell phone and called the venue to explain she'd be late.

The garage wasn't open on Saturdays. She didn't have time to waste trying to fix it anyway. She had to find someone with a van or SUV. She knew Linda's vans would be busy all morning. She texted Sam to ask if her big SUV was available. As she was mulling over other options, Blake came to the back door.

"What's wrong? You look upset."

"Oh, my damn van won't start and I've got a cake loaded I need to get out to the lodge for a wedding. I'm trying to think of someone with a van or SUV." Her phone chirped. "Sam says she's got hers at the shop and I can borrow it."

Already moving, Blake said, "I'll go get it and be back here in a few minutes."

Ellie slipped back into the bakery and gave Nicole an abbreviated version of her dilemma. "If they call, assure them I'm on my way."

Blake positioned the seats flat in the back of Sam's SUV. He helped Ellie transfer the wooden cradles and cake layers. Once everything was loaded, Ellie jumped in the driver's seat. She drove as fast as she dared and ended up being an hour late.

Blake helped her cart everything into the reception. Linda pitched in and helped them assemble the cake before she placed flowers around it. As she and Blake were stowing the extra icing and tools in her bag, the mother of the bride poked her head into the room. "Oh, Ellie, the cake looks marvelous. It's perfect."

Ellie stopped and chatted with the woman while Blake finished packing. He waited by the door and watched as Ellie visited and wandered around the entire room admiring everything with the woman. The woman pulled Ellie in for a hug and when she was released her eyes darted around in search of Blake.

He gave a quick wave and she hurried to the door. "Sorry, the mother wanted to chat and talk about everything. She's pleased with my work and is a bit giddy." She patted her pocket in search of keys. He held Sam's keyring in front of her. "Thanks for packing everything up and helping me. I'm sure you had better things to do this morning."

He shrugged. "Not really, but you could pay me back with dinner tonight." He paused, waiting for a response that didn't come. "I forgot it's Valentine's Day. You probably have plans."

"Oh, no. I don't have plans. Trying to think of what I could cook."

"We could go out."

"Uh, as you pointed out, it's Valentine's Day." She rolled her eyes, but with a smile.

"Right. Well, I eat anything."

"I'll figure something out. How about six at my place?" She gave him directions and pulled the SUV behind Sam's shop. "I've gotta go, but thanks again. I'll see you tonight."

She returned Sam's keys with a hug and hurried down the street to the bakery. The rack with all the pre-orders was empty, which meant everybody had picked up their treats. Nicole was busy at the counter boxing up some of their festive donuts. Ellie surveyed the display case and snagged four of the decorated red velvet cupcakes and put them in the office.

Nicole hadn't gotten to the dishes yet, so Ellie cleaned up the kitchen while she considered dinner options. It wasn't even noon and she was beat from rushing around all morning with the cake and her stupid van. She'd have to call Jim Monday morning and get him to fix it.

She treated Nicole to an early lunch. While she was munching on her chef's salad she decided she'd get pizza and make a salad for dinner. Blake deserved better, but she didn't have the energy to pull off a gourmet meal.

Nicole left for the day with a box of heart shaped cookies for her family. Ellie added the two cinnamon rolls and a loaf of bread left in the case to her stash. She bagged the few remaining items to drop at the church on her way home. They provided a meal for those in need and she was a regular donor. Her worries were lighter after she tallied the weekly totals and compared them to last year. This Valentine's Day was a bit busier than last and her income reflected it. She ran by the market and picked up fresh salad fixings along with groceries for the coming week.

When she got home she dashed from room to room, cleaning and straightening. Oreo sat on her bed watching Ellie dart around the house, armed with rags and cleaners. When she pulled the vacuum out, Oreo scattered for the outdoors.

She put in a call to Big Tony's for a delivery at six and hopped in the shower to cleanse the dust covered frosting from her skin. After a catnap in her now clean bedroom, she lit a fire and made a salad. Blake and the pizza arrived at the same time. She motioned Blake in while she paid and carried two boxes inside.

"I hope you like pizza. It was either a dirty house and a home cooked meal or a clean house and pizza." She laughed as she led him to the kitchen. "I don't think I've ever met a man who didn't like pizza."

"I love it." When she set the boxes on the counter she noticed he was holding flowers and wine. "For you," he said, presenting her with an armful of pink tulips. "I've never met a woman who didn't like flowers." He grinned, showing off his dimples.

"Wow, those are stunning. Thanks, but you didn't need to bring anything. This is me paying you back, remember?" She took the flowers and placed them in a large vase with water.

"I love your place. It's hard to make out with the sun already down, but it looks like you've got a gorgeous spot in this meadow."

"It's peaceful here. Oreo has the run of the place and there's a cool pond on the property. It belonged to my aunt and uncle and they let me stay here when they moved to Mt. Vernon." She carried the salad and the flowers to the table. He followed with the pizza boxes.

"It's immense for one person, but I like it." She considered the table and asked, "What would you like to drink?"

He smirked. "Wine, of course, and maybe some water."

She took a slice of the thin crust vegetarian pizza she now deemed a special treat. He heaped on slices of the carnivore pizza that had been one of her favorites. Conversation about the barn construction and business plans at the winery dominated the evening. She had two sips of wine to appease Blake, but found it easy to pass up, compared to red velvet cupcakes.

After dinner they found a movie they hadn't watched and relaxed in the recliners near the fire. Her cell phone rang during the first few minutes of the movie. He pushed the pause button and she answered the ring.

"Yes, this is Ellie Carlson." She nodded her head and as she listened the color drained from her face. "Oh, no. What do the doctors say?" She continued to bob her head. "I understand. Please let Dani know I'm thinking of her. If there's anything I can do for you…" She pursed her lips. "Yes, thanks so much, Dan."

She hung up and let out a breath. "What's wrong, Ellie?"

"It's Dani." She winced, realizing her mistake.

"Who's Dani?"

"Uh, oh, hell." She sighed. "She's my daughter I gave up for adoption nineteen years ago." She cradled her warm mug of tea.

Blake's eyes widened. "What's wrong?"

"She's ill. It's serious. That was her adoptive father. She's in the hospital."

"So you guys are close?"

Ellie shook her head. "Not even. I met her right after Christmas. She came to the bakery and asked if I would donate a kidney."

"Wow," he said, taking a sip from his mug. "That's when you found out about your diabetes, huh?"

She nodded and told him the whole sordid tale. It took hours to explain the backstory of her parents and their subsequent abandonment. She revealed what her family business visit had been in Sunnyside and the encounter with Lance. "The upside to all of this is I saw my sister for the first time in twenty years. She's planning a visit here next weekend."

"That's a lot to deal with. No wonder you've been tired and overwhelmed."

"Your idea about working with you has been the lone bright spot in my depressing life."

"Are you going to go and see Dani?"

She felt tears begin to form and shook her head. "No, she didn't even want me to know. Her dad called because he thought I'd want to know. Her parents…they appreciate my help in trying to contact Lance."

"So the only other blood relatives who may be transplant donors are your siblings?"

"Yep. I'm trying to figure out how to ask Ceci when she comes."

"Man, I'm not sure if there's a way to plan it. Probably best to tell her the whole story. She's got children so I'm sure she'll understand your quest to help your daughter."

Ellie wrinkled her nose. "It's not the ideal way to renew an estranged relationship."

"Maybe not. I know I'd do anything to help any of my sisters. She may surprise you."

"Well, I ruined our movie. It's too late now."

"No problem. We'll do it next time." He rose from his chair and retrieved his jacket. "Thanks for dinner and the company."

"Wait a minute," she said, dashing to the kitchen. She handed him a bag from her bakery. "It's a couple loaves of bread and cinnamon rolls."

He grinned and embraced her in a hug. "Come out to the winery this week anytime you're free." He released her and added, "Bring your sister by over the weekend and show her where you'll be working."

"I'd like that. Thanks…for listening."

Fifteen

Sunday Sam hosted an early dinner that served as a quasi-reception to honor Linda's mom. Linda was showered with affection and Max made sure he stuck close to her. She still teared up when she talked about her mom. Jen, Jeff, and Nate shared fond memories they had of Peggy from growing up on the island. "Aunt Ginny and Uncle Bob were so sad to hear about your mom," said Ellie. "They had wonderful memories of her flowers and Christmas trees at the nursery."

Linda smiled through the tears shining in her eyes. "I keep thinking she was lucky to go in her sleep. At the same time, I feel so bad I wasn't there." Max slipped his arm around her.

"She knew how much you adored her," said Kate. "That's what's most important."

The dogs had been outside playing, but Lucy hovered around Linda and she placed her head on Linda's lap. Linda stroked the dog's glossy black fur. "I appreciate all of you so much." She sniffed and said, "I think we need a change of topic. What did we miss while we were gone?"

Blake cleared his throat. "Well, I'd like to announce I've found the perfect event manager for my new expanded venture at the winery. We plan to open the barn as a venue in May. Jeff hooked me up with a crew and they're making great progress."

"That's terrific news. Who's the new manager?" asked Kate.

"Our own Ellie Carlson," said Blake, giving her a wink.

Smiles broke out around the table. Congratulatory wishes peppered

Ellie. "I knew you'd find something you'd love to do," said Sam.

Ellie nodded at Blake. "Blake knows about my diabetes and Dani. Yesterday I found out Dani's back in the hospital. Her adoptive father called. After the debacle with the van yesterday, I was treating Blake to a thank you dinner when I got the call." She looked across the table at him. "So, I broke down and told him the whole sad story about Dani and my parents."

"Her sister is planning to visit this coming weekend, though. That's a positive step," said Blake.

"I hope it goes well. I'm going to tell her more about Dani and determine if she'd be willing to be tested."

"I'll check on Dani and find out what I can from her doctor tomorrow," offered Max.

"She still doesn't want me involved. Dan, her father, called knowing I'd tried to help with Lance. I sent her a card when I got back from Sunnyside and never heard from her."

"You're doing your best, Ellie. It's all you can do," said Spence.

She nodded and shrugged. "It doesn't seem like enough."

"How have you been feeling?" asked Regi.

She smiled at Max. "My numbers have been improving and I've been sticking to the food list. It helps not to be at the bakery as much."

"No bites on the bakery yet?" asked Nate.

She shook her head. "Not yet. I'm closing it on Mondays starting tomorrow." She tipped her glass to Kate. "Thanks for the idea. Nicole is going to handle it until noon each day."

"Maybe we should have a get together next weekend, so you can introduce us to your sister," said Regi. "What do you think, Ellie?"

"I haven't given her visit much thought beyond the Dani situation." She took a drink of water. "I think it's kind of you to consider a dinner. I'd like her to meet all of you."

"Let's plan on Saturday night at our house," said Regi.

Jen suggested she book them both in for pedicures on Saturday. "It'll give you a neutral place to talk and bond."

Ellie gave her a hug in thanks. "Sounds like fun."

Sam brought out a lemon meringue and a chocolate cream pie for dessert. She even prepared a special sugar free pudding parfait. Ellie let the silky chocolate glide down her throat, content to listen to the happy chatter of her family of friends.

* * *

Max kept tabs on Dani's condition throughout the week. She was being treated for a bad infection and making slow progress. Ellie sent flowers to her, but didn't receive a response. Nicole agreed to cover the bakery the entire day on Saturday, so Ellie could spend time with her sister.

Blake kept Ellie entertained and laughing at the winery. They set up the office space with two desks and she organized her workspace and decorated it with a few framed patterns she had colored. She spent some time visiting with Linda, who was happy to share her knowledge of vendors on the island. She also told Ellie she would be willing to offer a discount for events, since Ellie would be the one coordinating, saving Linda time in dealing with the bridal party.

Ellie spent her mornings talking to caterers, restaurants, and musicians to nail down the prices they could offer the winery. She paid a visit to Ben and Sherrie at The Haven and secured special rates for event attendees. She did the same with Bev at the Lighthouse Bed and Breakfast. She knew getting servers for events would be easy, since there were so many on the island during the summer. Between Jeff, Jen, and Linda they knew all the regular servers and she would have her pick of them when they weren't working their normal jobs.

She was willing to give a discount to Blake for wedding cakes from Sweet Treats. She did the same for a couple of other venues for weddings, if they handled the tastings and orders. She hoped these relationships would make her business more attractive to a potential buyer. She made a note to call Jack and find out if there had been any interest in the property.

Friday she organized all the information she had gathered from local vendors and put in a call to Sam. "Hey, Sam, I need to get in touch with your friend who owns the bridal shop in Seattle, Maureen. The island doesn't offer much in the way of tuxedos or wedding gowns and I hope she has an interest in having a satellite store here."

"That's a great idea. I'll give you her number and email. How's it going?"

"It's been a busy week. I've got tons of information and pricing I've collected. Now I need to organize some event packages and get it on our website. The only real hole I have is the gowns and tuxedos, so I'm hoping Maureen and I can work something out."

"Even if she could do something for the high season, I think she could definitely increase her business. She could get by with a small sampling and then ship anything a customer wanted over to the island in a day, if necessary."

"Exactly what I was thinking. We have enough space in the barn to allocate a small room to house some gowns and do the tuxedo measurements. I'll give her a call next week. I've got to get to the bakery soon."

"We'll see you tomorrow night at Regi's. Good luck with your sister."

* * *

Saturday morning butterflies danced in Ellie's stomach and her hands shook as she tried to put on mascara. The house was immaculate and she splurged on fresh flowers from Linda's for Ceci's bedroom and the kitchen. The floors were free of dog hair, for the moment, and every surface shined.

A box of decadent pastries, along with a few diabetic friendly muffins sat on the counter and the fridge was stocked with groceries. Blake gave her a few bottles from the winery to take home, in case she found out Ceci liked wine.

She double checked the house and while pacing the main floor for the hundredth time, realized she couldn't keep still. She drove to town to Sam's for a coffee while she waited for the ferry.

Chatting with Hayley distracted her from checking the time every few minutes. A steady stream of regulars wandered in for coffee and stopped to chat with Ellie on their way. Soon she heard the blast of the ferry horn and scrambled from her chair.

She waited at the dock, checking the walkway for passengers, knowing Ceci had left her car in Anacortes. She spied her head above a navy blue jacket. Ellie waved and caught her sister's eye. A huge smile greeted Ellie.

Ceci wrapped her in a hug. "Thanks for having me, Ellie. It's gorgeous here."

Ellie picked up her suitcase. "I parked by the bakery down the street. Are you hungry?"

"I could eat. I left so early I didn't do breakfast." She gave her a shy smile. "I was too nervous to eat on the ferry."

"I've been edgy all morning myself." Ellie pointed out Lou's and the Front Street Café.

Ceci chose an early lunch of crab cakes, so they deposited her suitcase and poked their heads into the bakery for a few minutes. Ellie introduced Ceci to Nicole and they wandered down the street to Lou's.

"The bakery smells heavenly," said Ceci. "Now I'm hungry."

"I stole a few treats for us and have them back at the house." They were the only ones in the restaurant and Lou greeted Ellie with a hug.

"Hey, Lou. This is my sister, Cecilia. She's visiting from Everett."

"Call me Ceci," she said, shaking his hand.

He led them to a table overlooking the harbor and gave them menus. Ellie steered Ceci to the lobster macaroni and cheese to go with her crab cakes. Ellie selected a salad with hers.

"So, my friend Jen owns a salon and I booked us in for pedicures this afternoon."

"Oh, I haven't had a pedicure in months. It sounds terrific."

Ceci raved about the food and Ellie took a couple bites of the macaroni and cheese, which she had missed since being on her restrictive diet. When they finished lunch, they opted for a stroll around the harbor. Ellie pointed out Sam's shop, Linda's floral business, Kate's antique shop, and Jeff's hardware store. "Actually, you'll be meeting all of them tonight. Another set of friends, Regi and her husband Nate, are hosting a party at their house."

They continued wandering the blocks surrounding the harbor. "Do you think you could call Aunt Ginny and make sure it's okay if I stop by and visit on my way home on Monday?"

Ellie felt her heart lighten. "Of course. She and Uncle Bob would be thrilled to see you."

They spent the remainder of the day window shopping and chatting about the island. After pedicures and visiting with Jen, they headed home. Oreo greeted Ellie with her usual enthusiasm and sniffed Ceci. Ellie showed Ceci her bedroom and gave her a tour of the house.

Her sister stared at the framed colored designs decorating Ellie's bedroom wall. "Those are pretty. Did you do them?"

"Oh, I colored them. It's a hobby. Helps alleviate stress and anxiety."

"This is a charming spot. So peaceful out here."

"That it is. I've been so blessed to be able to live here. Thanks to Uncle Bob and Aunt Ginny. They helped me through a horrible time." Ellie moved to the fridge. "A friend of mine owns a winery. I don't drink much, but he sent me home with a couple bottles. Would you like some?"

"I'd love some." Ellie opened a bottle of the Madeleine Angevine and the light gold liquid filled the glass. Ellie fixed herself a cup of tea. Ceci brought the glass to her lips. "I've thought a lot about what you went through since we saw each other."

Ellie said nothing and took a long drink of tea.

"I wasn't a very good big sister to you and I'm sorry. I let you take the blame for things you didn't even do. I should have done better, especially when I was older."

Tears stung her eyes. She reached across the table and put her hand on Ceci's. "It means a lot. Thanks for saying it."

"I remember when I wasn't living at home and Mom and Dad took Teddy on that trip back east for some school conference. When they got home they accused you of denting Dad's truck. Mom told me the whole thing and launched into her usual spiel about how horrible you were. I finally couldn't take it anymore and confessed to sneaking over and borrowing the truck. A bunch of us wanted to go to the lake and needed the truck. I smacked into a pole and dented the side. I was hoping he wouldn't notice."

Ellie's mouth dropped open. "I told them I didn't know anything about it and they wouldn't listen. Dad was so mad at me."

Tears trailed down Ceci's face. "I know. After I told Mom I did it, she told me to hush up about it and leave it alone. She never told Dad I was the one who did it and you got the punishment."

"I was used to it by then. Nothing mattered."

"I told Tim the story and he couldn't believe a mother would keep me from telling the truth and then continue to punish and blame you—the innocent child. He asked me if I could do that to our children."

Ellie raised her brows in question.

"I told him I could never pit the kids against one another. I love Cynthia and Tim so much and can't imagine treating either of them the way Mom treated you. To this day, I don't understand it."

"I wrote Mom off a long time ago. I have no idea why, but she hates me. Dad is the one I expected to be there for me, but he turned against me."

"Dad is weak. For all the bravado he possessed at work, he was a shell of himself at home. It's clear now, but I didn't pay attention then."

"Do they know you came to visit me?"

Ceci shook her head and panic flashed in her eyes. "No, I didn't want to get in an argument with Mom."

Old anger bubbled to the surface. "That seems to be the never-ending mantra when it comes to her. Why is it nobody's willing to stand up to her or ruffle her feathers? I can be tossed away like an old tire, but if she's upset the world ends."

"I'm sorry, Ellie. I shouldn't have said it like that. I'm not sure why I care." Her voice became softer, "Maybe because I saw how she treated you and I don't want that to happen to me." She shrugged. "I always assumed Dad was staying until Teddy was grown, but honestly I'm not sure why he didn't divorce her long ago. She makes his life miserable. That's why he's never home. He's always golfing, fishing, or finding some odd job to keep busy."

"Well, he's an idiot. There's no reason he should be miserable. There's also no reason he hasn't talked to me or worried about me in twenty years. I'm over it." Ellie slammed her cup on the table.

"I don't blame you. You've always been stronger than me, Ellie. Stronger than Dad. From the looks of it you have a wonderful life here."

"Only because of Aunt Ginny and Uncle Bob. Plus my wonderful friends who've become my family."

"And you. You made your life here."

Ellie nodded. "Speaking of that, I'm selling the bakery. With this whole diabetic thing, I can't handle being surrounded by sugar all day. I landed a new job as the event manager at the winery. I started this week."

Ceci's face brightened. "Wow, it sounds like a fun job."

"I thought we could take a trip around the island tomorrow and I'll take you out to the winery and show you the place."

"I'd love to see it." Ceci splashed a bit more wine in her glass. "The wine is lovely. Very light."

"Blake says it's one of the most popular. He's the owner of the winery. You'll meet him at Regi's tonight."

They passed the rest of the afternoon talking about mundane topics and Ellie's new job. Both of their moods lightened, leaving the dark and heavy subjects of the past to rest.

* * *

When they arrived at Regi's, Nate was busy at the grill and Regi was organizing food in the kitchen. Jeff, Sean, Max, and Spence were all gathered on the patio, supervising the grilling of salmon and steaks. Ellie introduced Ceci to everyone, with the exception of Blake. As Ceci was pouring herself a glass of wine, he arrived. He was wearing a navy jacket over a light blue shirt with blue jeans. His dark hair was still wet from the shower and as he gave Ellie a hug, she shut her eyes and inhaled his hypnotic scent. "Come and meet my sister. She's in the kitchen."

He followed her around the corner and extended his hand to Ceci. "Great to meet you and so happy you could visit Ellie this weekend."

"She told me you're her new boss. Sounds like a great gig," said Ceci. "She treated me to some of your wine and it was delicious."

"Oh, I'm glad you like it. I'll send you home with some." He helped himself to a glass from the counter. "We had a great first week. I'm lucky to have Ellie."

Sam helped Regi in the kitchen while the ladies sat and visited around the granite island. Blake excused himself and made his way to the patio, toting the beer he brought for the guys.

Despite the chill, Ellie and Ceci both wore sandals to show off their fresh pedicures. Ceci chose a bright fuchsia and Ellie's toes were a deep cranberry. Kate and Linda admired them and Ellie thanked Jen for her indulgent gift.

The women gushed about Ellie's baking prowess and asked Ceci questions to get her talking. Ceci flicked through photos on her phone and showed them shots of her children and husband. "You'll have to plan a trip with your family this summer. There are tons of activities they would enjoy," suggested Jen.

"We talked about a visit. I know the kids would love the ocean."

"You're always welcome to stay with us. We all have plenty of room for guests," said Regi, glancing around the group.

"Oh, yes, anytime. In fact my husband's family owns the Harbor Resort with great cabins right on the bay. Kids love the kayaks and paddle boats. It gets busy in the summer, but Jeff is known for pulling strings for important friends," said Sam, sprinkling herbs on top of a salad.

"I can understand why Ellie loves it here so much. You're all terrific and kind. I'm so glad she has all of you." Ceci's voice crackled and she got up and took her glass of wine. "I'm going to check out the patio." She hurried past them to the doors.

Ellie took a sip of her iced tea. "We got into an intense discussion today about the past. Ceci feels bad she wasn't a better sister."

"She should," said Jen, who was the best sister a guy could have. "Sorry," she whispered with a sheepish grin.

"I think we're making progress. I snapped at her when she said she didn't want to get in an argument with Mom and didn't tell her she was coming to visit me."

"I find it ridiculous your mother wields such power over her now," said Kate.

"Well, I'm going to choose to concentrate on the positive point of Ceci coming to visit and hope I can handle asking her about helping Dani without blowing it."

Regi took a look around the kitchen and said, "I think we're ready. I'll go check on Nate." As soon as she reached the doors to the patio, Nate and Max met her carrying platters of salmon and beef fresh off the grill.

They sat around a large table decorated with simple candles and a bouquet from Linda. As usual, the group deferred to Max to offer a toast. He expressed the importance of friends and family. "Raise your glass with me to welcome Ellie's sister to the island. We hope this is the first of many visits to come. To Ceci." The group clinked glasses and dug into the scrumptious meal.

The group chatted about a variety of topics from golf and fishing to antiques and flowers. Conversation flowed as did coffee and tea to accompany Sam's sugar free cheesecake creation topped with raspberries. She had also made thick fudge frosted brownies loaded with sugar and fat.

The group was gathered around the fireplace and Max caught Linda's eye and she gave him a nod. He addressed Ellie and said, "I talked to Dani's doctor. She had a bit of a setback, so she'll be there longer than he expected. Dr. Jacobs said he hopes they can find a blood relative for a donor kidney. Her situation is becoming increasingly difficult to manage."

"Poor Dani," said Ellie, setting down her half eaten cheesecake.

Ceci's eyes indicated her interest. "Have you tried her birth father, Ellie?"

Ellie slouched against the back of her chair and nodded. "Yeah. He's not a candidate. Lance made a complete mess of his life with drugs and drinking. He's too unhealthy and still on drugs. Not to mention he told me he'd only do it for ten thousand dollars."

Ceci gasped. "Lance Franklin? He's the father?"

"I'm not proud of it. He's even more of a loser than Mom and Dad suspected. He doesn't have siblings, so he's a dead end."

Max looked at Ceci. "Ellie's siblings are Dani's last chance. Would you be willing to be tested to find out if you're a viable donor for Dani?"

Her eyes widened with a hint of fear. "Uh, wow, I don't know. I guess so. I'd need to know more about it."

"I can explain most of it and could even do the blood test for you tomorrow, if you're up for it."

Ceci looked around the circle of Ellie's closest friends, all their attention focused on her. She sensed how important this was to all of them. They were tilted forward in their seats waiting on her answer. "Sure, I could do the test tomorrow."

"Ellie could bring you by in the morning. I can meet you anytime that's convenient."

The group let out a collective breath and Max firmed up a time with Ellie and Ceci. Easy conversation began again with Jeff and Blake talking about the barn construction and the electrical needs, as well as plumbing enhancements needed to handle partygoers.

Linda gathered dessert dishes and Ellie jumped out of her chair to help her. When they got to the kitchen Linda whispered, "Max didn't want to upset you, but thought you could use some help approaching Ceci."

"It worked like a charm," said Ellie. "I hope she doesn't feel coerced into it. I was dreading talking to her about it. Tell Max thanks."

Linda gave her a hug and they went about the task of rinsing plates and loading the dishwasher. In the midst of the clank of the dishes they didn't hear Max approach. He slipped his arms around Linda. "Am I in trouble?"

Ellie smiled at him. "No, you're my hero. Thanks for bringing it up."

"It could backfire. She might resent being ambushed."

"Well, she'll get over it. At least we'll know if there's hope. I can't imagine asking Teddy to help. I know that wouldn't work."

"We'll know by Tuesday at the latest."

* * *

Sunday morning Ellie drove Ceci to Max's office early, so she could get her test before breakfast. Max talked with her in his office and explained the process and answered her questions while Ellie waited outside. He went over the surgery and gave her some literature on live kidney donations. After he drew her blood, he promised to call Ceci with the results as soon as he had them. The two sisters then walked down the street to the Front Street Café.

It was another gorgeous sunny day and after a hearty meal Ellie gave Ceci a guided tour of the island. They visited historic sites, the lavender farm, and the alpaca ranch. She also drove through the Harbor Resort so Ceci could get an idea of the accommodations if she planned a family trip. She took her by Sam's house and showed her Linda and Max's house as well as Linda's nursery.

"My goodness, their homes are stunning. Regi's was also gorgeous. I can't get over the views."

"Makes my pond look puny, huh?"

"No, not at all. The water views are just breathtaking."

Ellie saved the winery for their last stop and she saw Blake's truck parked by the barn when she pulled in front of the tasting room. "I'll show you my office first and then we'll head over and check out the barn. Blake will want to show you the vines and explain the grapes."

Ellie showed off her new office space and let Ceci wander around the room, where she checked out the displays and wines. She noticed the photo of Uncle Bob and Aunt Ginny with Ellie and her new puppy atop the desk. They left via the backdoor and followed the sidewalk to the outdoor pavilion and the new path to the barn. They found Blake in the barn, studying the blueprints.

"Hello ladies," he said, looking up from a makeshift bench of plywood and sawhorses. "How's your day?"

"We've been all over the island, but saved the best stop for last," said Ellie, looking up at the rough beams and rafters. "I noticed they've got the new stairs almost done."

"Yeah, we're ahead of schedule." He motioned them to follow. "They've got the restrooms framed in." He continued down the length of the building. "We took down all the old stall walls, except for the large ones at the ends. We'll make them into private rooms for smaller parties." He glanced upstairs. "We're building some linen closets upstairs and another storage area down here for heavier items. We're also going to have a bride's room and groom's room upstairs, plus the small bridal boutique for gowns and tuxedos."

Ceci considered the vast space as she looked across the barn. "This is a huge area."

"Yeah, I think we'll be able to hold even the largest weddings here without a problem. We're lucky all the wooden beams are in terrific shape. We're cleaning it up, but only the floor will need to be replaced."

"I saw you had a bunch of sample books on your desk for flooring and lighting," said Ellie.

"Yeah, I wanted you to look at those tomorrow and get your opinion about the wood for the main floor and tile for the restrooms. I know we talked about a statement chandelier in the middle, with a few smaller ones throughout. We need to make our selections."

"How's the electrical going?" asked Ellie.

"There's a lot to do. The contractor has to install a ton of conduit for all the outlets we want for lighting. So far his guys have been busy with the plumbing. The new septic system is done."

Ellie explained they wanted to be able to decorate the entire upstairs railings and all the upright support beams with twinkle lights in addition to permanent dimmable lighting throughout the space.

"It's going to be gorgeous when you get it done. I'd love to come back and see it," said Ceci, looking up as she walked to the middle. She took several photos with her phone and made Ellie and Blake pose in the midst of the construction.

"Let me close this place up and I'll show you the vineyard," said Blake, hurrying back to the bench. He turned off the work lights and slid the giant doors shut. He led the way and explained the vines to Ceci, as he had on Ellie's first visit.

She gazed across the property and sighed. "What a scenic place to work. You're so lucky, Ellie."

Ellie took in the spectacular view of the greenery and grounds against the white church and tasting room, along with the wooden barn. It looked like a post card. "I'm grateful to be here."

Ceci pointed to the old house. "What's that?"

"I'm working on fixing it up so I can live out here. It hasn't been taken care of and needs some attention."

"Blake lives on his boat in the marina right now."

"Well, you should join us for dinner tonight. Ellie and I are cooking back at her house."

"Oh, I hate to intrude on sister time," he said, shaking his head.

"Come on, you have to eat. Join us for dinner," said Ceci.

"Yeah, you eat out way too much. We're grilling chicken."

"A home cooked meal sounds terrific. I need to clean up and then I'll meet you there."

They walked back to the tasting room and Ellie led the way down the driveway to the main road. When they got home, Oreo was bouncing around the house, begging for a walk. After Ellie doused the chicken breasts in marinade, she invited Ceci to join them for a walk around the property.

As they wandered, Oreo bounded over the tall meadow grass and inspected her usual areas of interest, darting here and there. The two sisters preferred a slow pace and chatted as they walked to the pond. The sun was low in the sky, creating a golden glow on the horizon.

"I'm so proud of you, Ellie. You've created a wonderful life for yourself in a beautiful place to call home."

Ellie glanced at her sister and saw the sincerity in her faraway look as Ceci gazed at the gorgeous vista in front of them. Ellie gripped Ceci's arm. "I'm so happy to have you here and I hope back in my life."

Ceci reached across and squeezed Ellie's hand. "Me too. I shouldn't have let so many years go by."

"I'm thrilled you're going to stop and visit Uncle Bob and Aunt Ginny tomorrow. They're over the moon."

"I knew better than to let the last twenty years evaporate without making an effort to reconnect with them. I'd like Tim and the kids to meet them someday soon."

"You guys should definitely plan a trip this summer. You could spend time with Bob and Ginny on your way. I'd love to talk them into coming for a visit. Uncle Bob looked so fragile in January. Maybe if he's stronger this summer we can talk them into joining you."

The glow on Ceci's face matched the radiance of the setting sun. She leaned her head into Ellie's. "I love the idea."

"I feel bad for Dad sometimes. He's missed out on so much time with his brother and Aunt Ginny. I think he would have been a different person without Mom's influence. So all that loyalty to her and he's left with what? No family connections and it appears he leads a lonely life."

"Yeah, you know he's complained for years none of his friends come by the house. Long ago when I was home for a visit from college I overheard one of his closest friends from work tell another friend he hated to be around Mom, so he avoided Dad."

"She's toxic. I wish he could recognize it."

"I think he does, but he can't bring himself to do anything about it."

Ellie focused on her sister's face. "Thanks for agreeing to be tested for Dani. I appreciate your willingness to help her."

"I'm scared, but I know if I asked you to help Cyndi or Tim you'd do it. It's the least I can do."

Oreo rushed behind them and barked in an attempt to herd them back to the house. Ceci hung their jackets in the closet and saw the old leather duffel stuffed in the corner. She remembered her Dad lugging it around full of athletic gear and ran her hand across the soft material. She tucked it inside further and closed the door.

Blake arrived with bottles of wine for Ceci to take home. He poured two glasses and sat at the counter while the sisters worked together preparing a salad. Ellie sliced up a loaf of her crusty bread from the bakery and tossed green beans and tomatoes with balsamic vinaigrette. She added a bowl of sliced fruit and asked Blake to finish grilling the chicken.

They gathered around a tasty and healthy dinner at a candlelit table, complete with the flowers Ellie had bought from Linda to welcome her sister. Blake insisted on pictures of the two sisters and took several shots at the table and some on the deck.

Ceci had him take pictures on her phone and then made Blake and Ellie pose for a few. As soon as she set her phone down it pinged with a message. She read it and said, "Uh, oh."

"What's wrong?" asked Ellie, as she was plating up leftover desserts courtesy of Sam.

"Tim texted and said Mom called and Cyndi let it slip I was visiting my sister. We didn't tell the kids it was a secret." No sooner did she finish her sentence when her phone rang. She looked at the screen and rolled her eyes. "It's her." She stepped outside on the deck.

Blake and Ellie picked at dessert, trying not to eavesdrop on her conversation. Ceci's volume increased with each response and the two found themselves captivated with the unfolding drama. Ceci's voice splintered as they listened. "Mom, I am not betraying you. Ellie is my sister and I'm going to have a relationship with her." There was a lull and then she yelled, "Quit being so hateful, Mom." She came through the door and slammed it shut.

"Sorry, I'm sure you heard most of it." She flipped the phone onto the table and slid into her chair. "Apparently I'm defying her." She toyed with the fork on her plate. "I'm forty years old and she still thinks she can dictate what I do."

Blake pushed back from the table. "I think I'm going to call it a night. Dinner was wonderful. Thanks, Ellie." He stood. "It was a pleasure to meet you, Ceci. Safe travels home tomorrow."

She looked up and sighed. "I'm sorry to scare you off. I enjoyed meeting you and touring your lovely winery." She extended her hand and shook his. "You and Ellie are going to do great things together."

He glanced at Ellie across the table, her eyes shimmering in the candlelight. "I'm sure we will. She's terrific."

Ellie rose and walked Blake to the door. "I didn't intend to have dinner theatre tonight. Sorry for the fuss. I guess my mother hasn't changed."

"I had a great time. Hearing about your mother makes me appreciate my mom." He winked and surprised her with a quick peck on the cheek. "Have a good night, Ellie. See you tomorrow."

He was out the door before she regained her composure. She put her hand to her cheek, closed her eyes, and savored the sensation.

Sixteen

Upset after the scolding from her mother, Ceci retired early. Since Ellie had shifted her attention away from the bakery she had been trying to stay up later each night. No longer required to wake at three in the morning, she was enjoying her newfound freedom.

She took her time cleaning up the kitchen and tucking away leftovers. She perched at the counter and colored a new page from one of her books before traipsing off to bed.

They had coffee and pastries, albeit diabetic muffins for Ellie, on their last morning together. She made sure Ceci packed up all the wine Blake had left and helped her cart the bags to the car. Ceci retrieved their jackets and said, "I see you have Dad's old duffle."

"Yeah, I used it when they sent me here. I'm not sure why I hang on to it. I never use the thing."

They slipped into their jackets and Ellie drove to the landing. They were early enough to stop for a coffee and visit with Sam for a few minutes. Ellie hugged Ceci before she boarded. "Thanks so much for visiting. Tell Aunt Ginny and Uncle Bob hello from me and call me when you get home."

"I will. I do want to come back soon." Ceci gave Ellie a squeeze. "I love you, Ellie."

Silent tears streaked down Ellie's face. "I love you too." She waved until the ferry lumbered away and she could no longer make out Ceci on the deck.

She picked up another coffee for Blake and drove to the winery. He was in the office on the phone. He mouthed a "thank you" to her when she put the cup in front of him.

She dug into her paperwork she had collected and composed an email to Maureen, so she'd have all the details of her proposal. By lunchtime she had typed up drafts of several wedding packages. She and Blake had gotten in the habit of driving into town for an early lunch before she was due at the bakery.

Over soup and salad, Blake said, "How was the rest of your evening?"

"Uneventful. Ceci went to bed early and we didn't discuss it. She took the early ferry this morning. She's going to stop and spend some time with my aunt and uncle."

The topic shifted to the wedding packages and construction and before long it was time for Ellie to go. When she stood to leave, Blake asked, "You've lost some weight, haven't you?"

Ellie blushed. "Seven pounds as of today."

* * *

Tuesday morning an email arrived from Maureen. She was excited about Ellie's idea and wanted to set up a visit. She planned to call Sam and coordinate a convenient date with the hope of visiting her at the same time.

Ellie had a hard time concentrating, anxious for news about Ceci's blood test. Her sister had sent a text Monday night when she got home and said she'd be in touch soon and had enjoyed her time on the island and in Mt. Vernon.

After her shift at the bakery Ellie took Oreo for a walk, checking her cell phone every few minutes. Once home, she sharpened all her colored pencils and began filling in a pattern she had started earlier. Dinner consisted of leftovers from Sunday night. Her phone remained silent throughout the meal and the cleanup activities.

She relaxed in the recliner, trying to focus on a television show, her leg bouncing up and down. She grabbed her cell and dialed Max. "Hey, I'm sorry to disturb you at home. I haven't heard from Ceci and am getting worried. I know you can't tell me her results, but did you speak with her today?"

"Yeah, I talked with her in the early afternoon." His voice, upbeat and positive, gave credence to the hope she felt. "Why don't you give her a call?"

"I don't want to seem pushy. I'm anxious and worried."

"I understand. I can't share anything with you, but try to relax, okay?"

"Okay. Maybe she's overwhelmed and talking to Tim about things. I don't want to impose." She disconnected after thanking him and checked her email. Nothing new.

She flicked through dozens of channels and found nothing of interest. After finishing a pot of tea, she got ready for bed. It was too late to expect a call, so she finally gave up on checking her phone and went to sleep.

Deceived by the lack of usual morning light due to a thick layer of gray clouds, Ellie woke up late. After a restless night, the gloomy and ominous sky matched her mood. She stomped through the house, hurrying to get to work. Oreo sensed the looming storm and camped out on her bed, instead of her normal observation spot by the bathroom door.

Ellie bound her still wet hair into a ponytail and threw on jeans. She stuffed a muffin in a baggie and zipped up her hoodie. Only two minutes late, she dashed through the door of the office. "Sorry," she said, "bad morning."

"No problem," said Blake. "Everything okay?"

She tossed the muffin on her desk and saw a giftwrapped package on her desk. "Yeah, I haven't heard from Ceci yet, so it's bugging me." She picked up the box, fingering the ribbon. "What's this?"

He shrugged and grinned. "A little something for your new workspace."

She pulled the shimmering ribbon and tore open the paper. "Oh, I love it." She held out the photo of a smiling Ceci and Ellie behind the glow of candles at her dining room table. "I don't remember this one," she added.

"I took it on my phone. I think it's a great shot of the two of you, plus you need a more recent family photo on your desk."

"Thanks, Blake. It means a lot." She placed it next to the one with her aunt and uncle and patted the frame with care.

"I'll be in the barn, if you need me." A cool breeze filtered through the open door when he left and she smelled rain in the air.

She dug into her stack of folders and clicked on her email. A new message from Ceci caught her eye and she opened it. She brought her hand to her mouth and gasped, then moaned. She stared at the screen reading the message again. The screen blurred, as a stream of tears trickled down her face. She grabbed a tissue and blotted her face dry.

"I can't believe this," she whispered.

The ring of the phone jarred her away from the screen. She cleared her throat and answered. She brought up the calendar on her computer as she talked with Maureen and scheduled her visit. Maureen chattered about her excitement for the miniature wedding boutique. Ellie struggled to listen. Her thoughts drifted to Ceci's email and she opened the window to read it again, while Maureen talked.

I'm sorry to tell you I don't think I can go through with the donation to Dani. Suffice it to say I had a surprise visit from Mom Tuesday night. She, of course, continued her outrage that I would dare to visit you. I informed her I planned to continue to have a relationship with you and in my anger I told her about Dani. She was livid and threatened to disown me and my children. I've never seen such hate in her eyes. I'm not sure what to do, but right now I need time. I'm too upset to even make a decision and I've never been strong, like you. Tim's worried about me and I promised Mom I would reconsider. I hope you understand and won't hate me forever. I know I've messed up our do-over. I'm sorry and I love you, Ceci.

Ellie picked up on the tone of Maureen's voice and the cue she was ending the call. "Thanks for calling, Maureen. I look forward to seeing you next week."

Ellie put her elbows on her desk and held her head in her hands. With her upcoming conference call with the web designer, she didn't have time to dwell on the situation with Ceci. She was on the phone with him, providing feedback on the new pages until lunch.

Blake came in ready for the trip to town. Ellie said, "I need to get home so I'll catch up with you tomorrow." She gathered her hoodie from the back of her chair. "Maureen's coming next week, it's on the calendar. The new pages are up for you to look over before they go live."

"Okay, I'll check them out. See you in the morn—"

She was through the door before he could finish. He shook his head and frowned as he watched her get in her car.

She didn't feel like eating, but knew how important it was to keep to her meal schedule. She heated up leftover soup and flopped into the recliner, nuzzling Oreo. She dreaded going to the bakery today and wished she could curl up in bed and sleep the rest of the day away. Once the idea formed, it took only a few minutes for her to call Nicole. She told her she wasn't feeling well and wouldn't make it for her shift. She asked her to close early and wandered to her bedroom where she crawled under the sheets and listened to the pitter-patter of the falling rain.

The doorbell and Oreo's subsequent bark woke her from a haze of sleep, laden with bouts of crying. She huffed as she got out of bed and trudged to the door. She looked through the window and saw Kate standing on the porch.

"Kate, what are you doing out in this weather?"

"Came to check on you." Ellie motioned her inside. She closed her umbrella and shucked off her coat.

"I should start a fire. I've been napping and didn't notice the chill." She busied herself at the hearth and soon had a fire crackling. When she stood and turned, Kate wasn't there.

She found her in the kitchen making a pot of tea. She poured boiling water into mugs and said, "I picked up some takeout on my way." She unearthed two boxes from her tote bag and took out plates.

The aroma of turkey, gravy, and mashed potatoes caused Ellie's stomach to rumble. "It smells delicious." She helped Kate transfer the items and said, "How about we eat by the fire?"

Kate followed her and Ellie set up a tray for her to use and put it by the other recliner. "So, I went by the bakery after lunch and saw you were closed. I gave Blake a call to check if you were at the winery, but he said you left at lunch."

"Yeah, I...uh, I wasn't feeling well and came home."

Kate gave her the look all mothers possess with a raised brow. "Really?" Kate took a bite of her dinner. "Your illness wouldn't have anything to do with an email from your sister would it?"

Ellie's eyes widened. "How do you know about that?" Her tone was snappier than she intended.

Kate held up a hand. "Don't get angry. When I called Blake, he was worried about you and said he'd been sitting there wondering what to do. It seems you left the email open on your screen at work and he read it."

Ellie slammed her fork down. "How dare he?"

"He's concerned about you. He said he knew something was wrong when you left."

"So then he blabs it to you. Nice." She rolled her eyes.

"Ellie, he didn't tell me to gossip. When I called and said you weren't at the bakery, he expressed his concern. He didn't know what to do. I offered to come over after work and check on you." Kate considered her rumpled clothes and messy hair. "I think you could use someone to talk to about this whole situation."

Ellie looked down at her plate. She took a few more bites and then raised her head. "I'm sorry, Kate. I'm so damned mad right now, not to mention embarrassed."

Kate nodded her head and continued to eat. Ellie took a sip of her tea and then enumerated the battles with her mother. Kate had heard most of the story before, but knew Ellie needed to vent. "I'd like to drive to Sunnyside and punch her right in the face."

"You'd have to get in line behind Blake. His plan, before I called, was to do exactly that. He was ready to take the ferry over and make the drive tonight. He was going to call Spence for the address and directions." She watched Ellie's face soften and her mouth form a circle. "We talked him out of it."

"I know he didn't tell you to hurt me. I'm sorry. It's sweet of him to stand up for me. I'm not used to having anyone fight for me."

"He's a good guy. Everyone has been worried about the test and then when you didn't hear from her, we worried more. Max told us he can't discuss patients, but he was shocked Ceci hadn't called you right away. Now we all know why."

"My mother is like a poison. But Ceci needs to grow up. I'm at a complete loss and feel horrible I've let Dani down again." She began eating with gusto.

They finished the meal and Kate offered to clear the dishes. "It was great. I appreciate you bringing me dinner," said Ellie.

"Happy to do it." She made quick work of loading the dishwasher while Ellie sipped her tea. How many times had she sat in this same room wondering why her mother was so hateful? Too many to count.

Kate returned and plopped into the chair. "So, now what? What do you think you're going to do?"

"I contemplated calling Ceci, but I'm too upset."

"Maybe you should respond to the email. Tell her you understand she must feel torn, but you hope she finds it in her heart to do the right thing. If one of her children were in need, what would she do?"

Ellie nodded. "Exactly. I know she wants to do the right thing, but she's been manipulated and controlled by my mother for too long. I keep thinking maybe she should talk to my dad about it." She took a drink and gazed at the fire. "It's a gamble though. He's demonstrated how weak he is when it comes to Mom."

"Do you think there's a chance he doesn't know about this?"

Ellie nodded. "She keeps him in the dark and only feeds him the information she wants him to know." She relayed the story Ceci had shared about denting the truck.

"I don't think it could hurt to have Ceci talk to your father. The worst he'll do is side with your mom and at best maybe he'll grasp how caustic she is and do something."

"For once in his life," said Ellie with disdain.

"My advice is to compose a response tonight and sleep on it. Send it to me and I'll give you my feedback. Spence too, if you want. Then send it on tomorrow morning and see what happens." Kate reached for Ellie's hand. "There's not much more you can do. At some point you need to come to terms with the fact you can't control this situation for Dani. It's not your fault. It's a thoroughly crappy deal for her, but it's beyond you."

Ellie's tears shimmered in the glow of the firelight. She sniffed and said, "I know it in my brain, but not in my heart."

Kate left her with a hug and made her promise not to be upset with Blake. It was still raining and Ellie watched from the porch to make sure Kate was safe in her car and headed to the road.

She spent the rest of the evening composing and rewriting an email to Ceci. As the late news came on television she sent the draft to Kate for her opinion. She went to bed for the second time, this time in pajamas. Being angry proved to be exhausting and she fell asleep as soon as she closed her eyes.

* * *

She was at the winery early the next morning, well before Blake arrived. She'd already made coffee and snagged fresh cinnamon rolls from the bakery. Nicole had instructions to let him know his breakfast had been picked up by Ellie.

Kate and Spence responded to her email late last night with their suggested changes. Their ideas were helpful. Ellie revised the message and hit the send button before she changed her mind.

She was working on a calendar of events when Blake walked through the door. "Hey, Ellie. How's it going?"

"Better today, thanks. Sorry I was in a snit yesterday." She handed him the bakery box. "Breakfast for you, my treat. Kate stopped by last night and we had a long talk."

Blake released his breath. "Whew, that's a relief. I was kicking myself for saying anything to her, but you had me worried. After I saw the email, I freaked out."

She laughed. "You and me both." She unwrapped a carrot muffin and poured Blake a cup of coffee. "I was pissed when I heard you read it, but in the end it was the best thing."

"I wasn't trying to be nosy, it was just there." He stuffed another bite of cinnamon roll in his mouth.

"I know. I shouldn't have left it on the screen and shouldn't even be dealing with it at work."

While they nibbled on pastries, she shared her response to Ceci. It was assertive, but kind. Ellie suggested Ceci share her mother's exploits with her father. She also included a healthy dose of guilt, but wrapped it with a ribbon of understanding and empathy.

"Sounds great to me. I hope it works." He finished the last of the roll and wiped his hands on a napkin.

She steered the conversation back to the winery. The morning passed with a flurry of activity in the office and the barn, interspersed with telephone calls. Ellie resisted the urge to click the refresh button on her email when she found herself in front of the computer. She focused on work and vowed to deal with her personal drama on her own time.

Blake returned to the office in time for their unwritten lunch date. They met at Soup D'Jour and ran into Spence. He was waiting on a takeout order for Kate. He slid into the chair next to Ellie. "Any response?"

She shook her head. "I didn't check. I'm trying to keep myself focused on what I need to do and deal with the whole situation after work. I don't want to get myself so worked up like I did yesterday."

"We'll all be here for you, no matter what happens." Spence rested his hand over the top of hers.

"I'm not sure what I'd do without you." She looked at both of the men and said, "I'm lucky to have all of you in my life."

Seventeen

The rest of the week passed without a word from Ceci. The winery was gearing up to open on the weekends for tastings and events, which kept Ellie busy. Blake's sister, Isabelle, was planning to come and help with the opening. The barn and the house wouldn't be ready until the end of April, so Ellie offered to let her stay at her house.

"Izzy's the oldest and the bossiest, you may want to rethink your offer," said Blake, with a laugh.

"It'll be fun. Plus I might get some dirt on you." She snickered.

"That's what I'm afraid of."

Their banter was interrupted by a call from Jack at the realty office. He had someone interested in the bakery and wanted to meet with Ellie. A twinge of excitement flickered through her. She set up a meeting for later in the afternoon.

"Good news, huh?" he asked.

"Jack has some interest in the bakery. I'm meeting him this afternoon. It would be a load off my mind to be able to sell it."

She finished the work schedule for the tasting room. She slotted herself in on Friday nights and Sundays and Blake hired a former employee of the winery, Ethan, to help on Saturdays. In May, when they were open five days a week and had the event planning in full swing, Blake would have to find more help.

Blake was tied up with the contractor, so Ellie snagged lunch on her own and finished out her day at the bakery. Jack arrived as soon as she was closing and they sat at a table. He helped himself to a cupcake as he opened a folder.

"So, we've had a call from a bakery in the city. They want to expand and like the Friday Harbor location. Problem is they'd rather lease than buy."

He went over the particulars and provided Ellie with a worksheet showing his calculations based on different lease prices. "I was hoping to sell, so I wouldn't have to deal with it again. But, since this is the first nibble we've had in two months, I may have to alter my plans."

"There are some advantages. I think they're willing to do a one year lease and then consider a purchase if things work out for them. They also committed to keeping Nicole on as an employee."

"She's a great worker, so it would be to their benefit. The Flaky Baker has an excellent reputation and produces similar items. I think they'll do well."

"A lease would give you a stable monthly income and when it gets close to the end of the term we could start looking for buyers again. It depends how motivated you are to get out of the business right now."

She wrinkled her nose. "I'd say I'm quite motivated. I like the work at the winery and it's so much easier to adhere to my diet regimen when I'm away from all of this." She waved her hands across the expanse of the display case.

He pointed to a figure at the high end of the monthly lease worksheet and said, "I advise we propose this. It includes the lease of the building and the equipment. You'll make enough to pay for maintenance coverage on the equipment, so the risk to you will be low. It will give you plenty of income and you'd have a year to evaluate how it works. You may end up liking it. The building's in excellent shape, so you shouldn't have to worry about repairs."

She reviewed the income and the list of standard expenses she would still have, being the owner of the building. "Okay, let's go with it and see what happens."

He promised to draw up an agreement and get back to her when he had answers. She sent him home with a few cupcakes to share with Lulu. She closed the bakery and stopped by the market on her way home.

When she got home she checked her email and texts and saw nothing from Ceci. She took a long walk around the acreage with Oreo. As she wandered and followed behind the playful dog, most of her anxiety dissipated. She fixed dinner and relaxed with her coloring books before going to bed. Worry threatened the edges of her mind as she drifted to sleep.

* * *

Ellie spent her weekend at the bakery after giving the house a thorough cleaning. She wanted to make sure things were set for Izzy, who would be arriving Wednesday night to visit and help with the first weekend opening. She also made sure the fridge was well stocked.

She spent her workdays at the winery in the tasting room, cleaning and getting the displays ready for Friday night. Tuesday Maureen arrived to check out the space allocation for the boutique. She was staying at Sam's for a few days and Sam invited Ellie over for a night of looking through wedding gown books. With the help of Linda, Jen, Regi, and Kate, they picked out a selection of gowns and accessories to stock in the new space. Maureen arranged to have mirrors and furnishings shipped so it would be ready for May.

By Wednesday the pantry was filled with crackers and breadsticks and all the glasses cleaned. Linda would be delivering fresh flowers on Friday and Izzy could help put together cheese and fruit platters.

Blake reported the barn was ahead of schedule and he had relegated the work on the house to the back burner. He wanted to make sure they were ready for their grand opening the first week of May and acquiesced to living on the boat a bit longer.

Wednesday morning Ellie and Blake worked in the tasting room. "So, tell me about Izzy," she said as she dusted shelves. "I've got the house ready for her stay, but wanted to know more about her."

"She's fifty-one. Beyond capable and smart. She's been a lawyer for years, but is semi-retired. She takes a lot of time off to spend with my parents and will probably spend time here now too. She's divorced with a grown daughter."

"How many sisters do you have?"

He rolled his eyes. "Four."

"Wow, you're way outnumbered."

"Yeah, I've been bossed around by women my whole life. After Izzy is Esther. She got the short end of the stick in the name department. Izzy was named after Grandma Isabelle on my mom's side. Esther was my dad's grandma. Then there's Lauren and last is Shannon. I'm the youngest."

"They finally got their boy and called it quits."

He shrugged and smiled. "I guess so."

"Who's your favorite?"

"Hmm, that's tough. They all have their good points and a few bad points. Izzy's great at solving problems, but can be authoritative. Esther is a homemaker type, calm, always the peacemaker. She's a lot like my mom. Lauren's the one I've always been closest to growing up. She's fun and full of energy. She'd always play with me and include me. Shannon's a bit spoiled, being the last of the girls. She's an idealist and we're opposites when it comes to politics and world views. She's opinionated and doesn't understand the concept of middle ground."

"Sounds like a diverse group. I bet they terrorized you."

He grinned. "They delighted in terrorism. Izzy's so much older, I wasn't around her as much. Shannon is only two years older and used it against me. Lauren's forty-three now and Esther's forty-six. Esther was always serious and responsible, but kind. She had her moments when they would all gang up on me together, but for the most part she's protective."

"You're fortunate to have such a close family."

"Yeah, never a dull moment at gatherings."

"I missed those relationships growing up. Ceci and I were close for a time, but our relationship disintegrated and I never had one with my brother." Ellie stopped working and fixed her eyes on the window across the room. "We pledged to start over when she was here visiting. Now, I'm not sure."

"She still hasn't responded to your email?"

"Nope. I know she's probably struggling to figure out what to do. I said everything I needed to say. It's up to her."

"I think that's the best way to look at it. I'm sorry it's such a horrible situation for you."

She shifted the conversation to the winery and the weekend. They put the finishing touches on the tasting room and admired their work. "It looks terrific," he said. "I'm going to pick Izzy up soon. How about joining us for dinner in town?"

"I don't want to intrude."

"Don't be silly. It'll give you two a chance to get acquainted before she shows up at the house."

"After the bakery, I'll need to stop at home and shower."

"Me too. Meet us at Lou's at six."

She nodded. "I need to straighten my desk and then I'm out of here."

* * *

Blake and Izzy were already at a table when Ellie arrived. Blake stood and introduced her. "Meet my wise older sister, Izzy." He winked. "This is the best baker on the island and my new event coordinator, Ellie Carlson." The women shook hands.

Izzy had the same dreamy eyes as Blake. Her flawless skin was framed by shoulder length dark hair woven with a few strands of silver. Her stylish black and grey outfit reminded Ellie of Kate. Izzy greeted her with a broad smile. "Blake can't quit talking about you and how lucky he is to have you working with him."

Ellie slid into the chair next to Blake. "His offer has been a godsend." She gave Izzy a brief summary of her health issues and the need for her to find a new career and sell the bakery. "Speaking of the bakery, Jack called and said he has the paperwork for me to look over on the lease."

"You ought to have Izzy take a look. Legal mumbo jumbo is right up her alley."

"Sure," she said. "I'm happy to take a look at the documents and give you my opinion." She took a sip from her wine glass. "Consider it payment for room and board while I'm here."

"That's kind of you," said Ellie. "It's no problem to have you stay. It's an enormous place, so I'd enjoy the company."

"One of these days Blake is going to grow up and get a real house instead of his boat."

"I'm working on it, Izzy. It's not a priority." A trace of defensiveness was evident in his tone.

Lou approached the table and took their orders. Ellie introduced Izzy and Lou charmed her with a free plate of his crab cakes for the table.

"He's a cutie," said Izzy, as she slipped one of his famous creations onto a plate. She took a bite. "And a wonderful cook. These are delicious."

They visited over a relaxing meal. Ellie enjoyed the banter between the brother and sister. Laughter was the elixir she needed and a healthy dose put her in a happy mood.

Lou offered the group dessert menus, but Ellie insisted they have something at her house. She had whipped up her famous chocolate mousse cake at the bakery and brought it home to share.

Blake followed Ellie to her house and carried Izzy's bags for her. He lit a fire while Ellie showed his sister to the guest room and gave her a quick tour of the place. She set a pot of coffee to brew and sliced the cake while Izzy sat at the counter and watched.

Oreo was on her best behavior and after sniffing Izzy and following her to the guest room, plopped on her bed near the hearth. Ellie carried the dessert and coffees on a tray and the threesome gathered in the living room.

Izzy took a bite of the cake and said, "Yum. I love this cake."

Blake tipped his fork in Ellie's direction. "I told you. Best. Baker. Ever."

"I feel horrible eating it in front of you," said Izzy. "Thanks for making it when you can't even enjoy it."

"I like baking. It's relaxing and I get a lot of satisfaction when people enjoy my creations. Since I've been behaving, I don't crave sweets as much as I used to. Only when I'm stressed."

After coffee Blake said, "You girls sleep in tomorrow. Everything is shipshape at the winery, so no need to rush out. You can look over Ellie's papers."

"Sounds good to me. I'm bushed." Izzy rose and collected the plates. "In fact, I'm going to get ready for bed. I'll see you in the morning." She bent and hugged Blake and deposited a loud kiss on his cheek. "Love you." She followed with a hug for Ellie. "Good night."

"I should get a move on. Thanks for letting Izzy stay."

Ellie smiled. "I like her. This will be a fun weekend."

He nuzzled Oreo and gave Ellie a wave before he went through the door. She put the dishes in the dishwasher and readied the coffee pot for the morning. After she climbed into bed, she checked her phone one more time. Nothing from Ceci.

* * *

Ellie was up first and welcomed the day with a cup of coffee. She opened the folder and read the first few pages of the lease agreement and Jack's notes. After monthly expenses, she'd be left with a handsome income. She perused the stack of papers and reviewed the sections she understood. The rest of the gobbledygook she left for Izzy.

She was on her second cup of coffee when Izzy stepped into the kitchen. "Good morning. Did you sleep well?"

Izzy had a long satin robe tied around her and her hair in a makeshift bun. "I did, thanks." She poured coffee into a mug and joined Ellie at the counter.

"Here's the lease agreement, if you're still up for it." Ellie slid the folder to her. "I was going to make egg scrambles this morning."

"Sounds delicious. I'll start reading while you cook." She retrieved a pair of reading glasses and a colored pen and began her review.

Ellie put together eggs, green onions, cheese, tomatoes, and diced ham. She sliced some fruit and cut off chunks of one of her loaves of crusty bread for toast. Within minutes she had plates of steaming food ready and placed them on the counter.

They dug into the eggs and Izzy continued to read and mark a few things while she ate. "It's a fairly standard agreement, but there are a few changes I'd recommend. I can have it finished up in an hour or so."

"Wow, that's perfect. I appreciate this so much. I'd have to hire a lawyer if you weren't so helpful.

"You're happy with the monthly income you'll get?"

Ellie nodded. "Yes, it's more than I ever made at the bakery. I didn't take a large salary for myself."

"Blake told me this house belongs to your uncle. You may want to consider buying a house for the tax benefits."

"I've been thinking about it ever since Jack mentioned the monthly income. It would make it easy to afford a house." She swept her eyes over the kitchen. "This place is full of my best memories, but it's way too much house for me."

"It's worth a look. You'll still get some tax benefits from owning the bakery and the associated expenses, but with this income and your income at the winery, you'll be in a much higher tax bracket."

"Yeah, it makes sense. Plus I need to get a home of my own. My aunt and uncle could sell this place."

Izzy went back to reading while Ellie cleaned up the breakfast dishes and put the kitchen in order. She excused herself to take a shower and when she returned, she found the folder on the counter with a summary sheet of Izzy's changes. She read them over, impressed Izzy was so thorough and quick.

Izzy emerged dressed in a chic outfit of dark jeans, a white blouse, and a cropped black jacket. She ran a hand through her hair. "I need to get my hair done, but ran out of time before I left."

"One of my best friends, Jen, owns a salon. Do you want me to find out if she can get you in?"

Izzy's eyes twinkled with delight. "That would be fantastic."

Ellie made the call as she gathered her things. "You're all set. Jen can do you late in the afternoon today."

"Perfect, thanks." She followed Ellie to the car. "By the way, I wanted to talk to you about a surprise birthday bash for Blake." She went on to explain the family wanted to surprise him the last weekend in April. They were hoping Ellie would help them plan the event. "His birthday is on the twenty-ninth."

Ellie's eyebrows arched. "What about doing it a few days before on Sunday night? We would be done with work before five."

"That works. Mom and Dad and the rest of the family will be there. Sort of congratulations on the winery and birthday celebration combined into one. We were hoping it could be in the new barn."

"It's ahead of schedule and we plan to be open for business May first, so I'm sure we could make it work. It would be an ideal time to test it."

"Terrific. I've got a list of family coming and then we'll rely on you to invite friends from the island. We'll want dinner and a cake, of course. Maybe you could make it?"

"If all goes as planned, I won't have the bakery then, but I could make it at home."

"If it isn't too much trouble. Then we'll need your recommendation for lodging for the group. Probably eight or ten rooms."

"Okay. I'll make some calls. I'll give you my personal email, so there isn't a chance of Blake peeking at our correspondence."

"Mom and Dad will be thrilled. They're excited for him to have his own winery. He's always been a hard worker and done so much for the family." Ellie pulled into a parking spot. Izzy brought her fingers to her lips. "Mum's the word."

Blake was in the barn and after showing Izzy around the tasting room, Ellie got to work. Izzy wandered the property and ended up in the barn. Blake showed her the plans and highlighted the amenities.

Ellie was thrilled to receive their first request for a wedding in mid-May. The couple was from Seattle, but wanted to get married on the island. She sprinted to the barn to share the news. Blake saw her huge smile and said, "What are you so happy about?"

"Our first booking. It's a small wedding, but I think it's the best way to start."

She told him about the event and the package they requested. "So, I'm going to get to work on it." She stomped her feet. "It's so exciting."

She scampered out the door and Blake and Izzy looked at each other and laughed. "She's enthusiastic," said Izzy.

"Yeah, she's a whiz with this stuff. She's worked hard on the web pages and developed all these terrific wedding and event packages. They've only been live a few days, so it's cool to get a booking."

"This is going to be a fabulous venue. It's a perfect location and you seem happy immersed in all this work."

"I am. It's been a challenge, but I like it. Ellie and I make an excellent team. She doesn't drink much wine, but that's her only downside." He laughed. "At least she won't drink the profits."

"Are you going to hire more people soon?"

"As a matter of fact, while you're here I need your help with some job descriptions and all the legal mumbo jumbo. I need to hire attendants for the tasting room. Ellie and I will work during the day and can supervise things, but I'll need some coverage during the busy season, starting in May."

"I'll work on it tonight."

After Blake finished his work with the contractors, he and Izzy followed the path back to the tasting room. Ellie was on the phone arranging things for the wedding. She hung up and checked the time. "I guess we better head for lunch."

Izzy elected to stay in town. She was going to wander around the harbor and meet up with Ellie at the bakery before her hair appointment. Ellie pointed out the flower shop, Sam's coffee shop, and Jeff's hardware store. Izzy left the deli intending to introduce herself to Blake's friends.

Ellie had a slow afternoon and used her free time to update the bride on her requests. She'd have to talk to the new baker about the wedding cake when things were finalized. Jack showed up at closing time to go over the lease changes and Izzy came through the door as soon as he took a seat.

Ellie introduced them and Jack said, "I notice the family resemblance. Ellie tells me you've got some ideas on the lease."

She took a seat and went over each point with Jack. When she was finished, he nodded and said, "Impressive. I'll make the changes and forward it to the folks at the Flaky Baker." Ellie sent him on his way with a couple slices of cake.

"With the weather so gorgeous, how about we grill tonight's dinner?" asked Ellie.

"Sounds great. I should be done by six. I'll ask Blake to pick me up from the salon."

Ellie walked Izzy to the salon and introduced her to Jen. She intended to go back to the bakery and work, but took a seat and commenced visiting. After Jen brushed the color onto Izzy's hair, she persevered in convincing Ellie to let her style her ponytail into something different.

"I need to get home to start dinner," said Ellie.

"I only need a few minutes," said Jen, as she flipped the hair around a curling iron. She gathered her hair and twisted and tucked. She secured it with a few pins and adjusted the bangs. Jen twirled Ellie around to face the mirror. "Voila," she said. "Since you aren't getting up at three in the morning anymore and slaving at the bakery, I think your ponytail needs to go."

Ellie's eyes widened. "I can't believe you did it in just a few minutes. It looks so…elegant." She held a mirror and turned to examine the back of her head. "You need to show me how to do this." Jen spent a few minutes explaining it and showing her how to secure the twist.

The timer dinged for Izzy's color and Ellie scooted out the door with a quick wave. She hurried home and began dinner preparations. She checked her texts and email again, disappointed in Ceci's silence. Once she had the chicken on the grill, she changed clothes and added a touch of makeup, plus some earrings. She looked in the mirror, amazed at what the new hairstyle did for her mood. She flipped the meat and heard the doorbell chime.

Blake took in the new look and gave her an appreciative glance. "Wow, you look…uh, so pretty." Izzy elbowed him in the ribs. "Ouch, what did I do?"

She shook her head. "You're a dufus. Ellie looks lovely."

"Yes, she's right. You are lovely." He motioned to Izzy to step through the open door and followed. He deposited a bottle of wine in the kitchen and said, "Smells yummy."

"Blake, could you finish grilling the chicken while I steam the green beans?"

"Sure." She handed him a platter and he stepped to the deck.

"Your hair looks great. Are you happy with it?"

Izzy smiled. "Yes, Jen does a terrific job. She's a sweetheart and thinks the world of you."

"She's always been a kind friend and a top-notch hair dresser."

Blake brought the platter of chicken in and added it to the table. He poured wine for himself and Izzy and Ellie stuck with her iced tea. They listened to Izzy recount her visit around the harbor while they dined. Blake insisted on doing the dishes while the two women continued chatting.

"My wardrobe needs some serious help," said Ellie. "After Jen did my hair today it got me thinking. I've been dressing in t-shirts and ponytails for most of my life. I need to step it up for the winery."

"They had some cute things at the Bay Boutique today. Even the consignment shop had some attractive outfits."

"I'll have to stop in tomorrow and try to find a few things." She plated two slices of cake and made a pot of coffee to go with dessert. The threesome lingered while they discussed tomorrow's opening.

"I'll bring the cupcakes as soon as I close the bakery and get changed," said Ellie. "Dottie's will have the deli trays ready. I was hoping Izzy could work on making a few fruit and cheese trays to go with them."

She nodded. "Consider it done." She collected the dessert dishes and took them to the kitchen. "I'm going to call it a night. Thanks for dinner, Ellie."

After Izzy left, Blake and Ellie focused on the barn project and wedding. "I almost forgot," he said. "I received another booking for a June wedding after you left today."

"Wow, that's great. I've got a decent start on the other one. I'll contact the new couple tomorrow."

Blake grinned. "I think this new venue and event planning business is going to be great. I couldn't do it without you."

"I never dreamed I'd enjoy anything like the bakery. I can't believe I'm saying this, but I'm looking forward to getting rid of it and working at the winery full time."

He rose and put on his jacket. She followed him to the door. He turned and said, "I told Izzy we make a great team. You and me." He leaned in and kissed her cheek, remaining a bit longer than necessary.

Ellie flipped the lock. *I should have changed my hairstyle a long time ago.* She giggled as she doused the lights.

Eighteen

Friday Ellie found time between her two jobs to pick up a new outfit for the opening night celebration. She talked Kate into going with her and with her help found several pieces to mix and match. As she signed her name to the credit card slip, she hoped the lease of the bakery would go through.

She arrived at the winery with dozens of cupcakes and went about putting them on platters. She heard the door open and came out of the kitchen to find Izzy. "Oh, those look yummy," said Izzy. She admired Ellie's new cropped pants and silk jacket the color of merlot. "I see you had some luck shopping. Love the new outfit and it looks like you mastered Jen's new style for your hair."

Ellie blushed and said, "Do you think it looks okay? I feel a bit awkward." She fiddled with the scarf Kate had helped her tie.

Blake came through the door, "Whoa, you look great, Ellie." He carried a case of bottles behind the counter.

Izzy arched her brows and tilted her head at Ellie. "There's your answer." Izzy proceeded to the kitchen to assemble the food trays. Blake clanked the bottles as he arranged things behind the counter.

Once Ellie finished with the cupcakes she hit the button and instrumental background music filled the room. She turned on the twinkle lights installed around the space and stood at the entrance to admire their work. "Looks great from here."

Blake poked his head up from behind the counter and smiled. "I'm going to run into town and get cleaned up. Izzy will probably want to do the same."

"Sure, I can finish up the trays. Let me get my key to the house, so she can get in."

While they were gone, Linda arrived with a huge bouquet of flowers. "This place and you look absolutely stunning," she said, placing the flowers behind the counter. "Max and I will be back later."

"Oh, terrific. I hope we're busy tonight."

"I'm sure you will be. It's the talk of the town." She left Ellie with a hug and hurried out the door.

The platters were loaded, napkins arranged, and water dispensers filled. Ellie filled up the holders on the tasting counter with plain crackers and long skinny breadsticks. She made sure the dump buckets were placed at convenient intervals along the counter. She transferred cash from the office into the register and made sure the pricing cheat sheet was next to it.

Blake and Izzy came through the door with a bag from Soup D'Jour. "I stopped and grabbed some dinner for us."

"Don't you two look gorgeous?" She studied the blue shirt, the color of his eyes, under a stylish black jacket. Izzy wore black accented with a vibrant purple cardigan.

They perched at a small table and shared the soup and salad. Izzy and Blake were the designated attendants tasked with pouring and suggesting wines. Ellie was charged with mingling and ringing up sales. Ethan offered to come in later in the evening and help, in addition to working Saturday.

"I'm hoping I have time to observe you two pros, so I can learn more about the wines. We haven't had much time to devote to my education."

"The more you're around it, you'll learn what you need to know," he said, gathering the containers from dinner. They cleaned the table and set out a few of the trays when they saw the first cars pull into the lot.

Several locals were the first to arrive and Ellie introduced them to Blake and Izzy. Soon Sam and Jeff arrived with Linda and Max. Ellie kept her eye on the register, while circulating among the guests and pointing out the snacks.

When Jen arrived she gave Ellie a quick hug and thumbs up on her outfit. Regi and Nate came through the door with Jack and Lulu. Jack greeted Ellie with a hug and said, "Got a text and they expect we'll have the lease paperwork back next week. No problems so far."

Ellie breathed a sigh of relief. "That's terrific news. I'm anxious to transition to full time out here." She pointed them in the direction of the counter where Blake and Izzy laughed and chatted with the guests as they poured wines. Kate and Spence arrived and Ellie directed Spence to the cupcakes.

Soon the room was buzzing with conversation and merriment. Ellie was kept busy behind the counter and Ethan relieved Blake. Free to socialize, he meandered through the crowd and visited with friends while being introduced to several islanders he hadn't met.

By the time the last stragglers left it was eleven o'clock. Ethan got to work loading the dishwasher with glasses while Ellie tallied the register. Izzy and Blake focused on scouring the room for stray napkins and glasses. By midnight the place was in order. Ethan wished them goodnight.

Ellie emerged from the office sporting a huge smile and a tape from the adding machine. "Check out the numbers for our first night." Blake and Izzy both looked over her shoulder.

"Not bad, little brother. Not bad at all."

He put his arms around both of them. "It was perfect." He kissed each of them on the cheek. "Now, I need sleep."

They locked up and Izzy rode with Ellie. Blake flicked his lights at them as they made the turn to Ellie's house. Izzy went straight to bed and Ellie sat with Oreo for a few minutes and scrolled through her phone. She saw a new voicemail from Aunt Ginny. She smiled as she listened to her aunt's sweet voice wish her luck on her first big night at the winery.

* * *

Blake came by the house early Monday morning to take Izzy to the ferry. They opted for breakfast at the Front Street Café and tried to persuade Ellie to join them. Instead she gave Izzy a long hug goodbye. "Thanks so much for helping with my lease. It was fun to have a houseguest."

"I appreciate the room and the lovely meals. You make sure Blake brings you to the Yakima winery someday." She hugged her back and whispered, "We'll talk soon about the party."

Over breakfast they chatted about family and the winery. As the meal ended Izzy said, "Ellie's a terrific person. She seems like a good match for you."

"She's a hard worker. Creative and enthusiastic."

She rolled her eyes. "I mean personally. She's single, attractive, and you seem to click."

He furrowed his brows. "I don't think she's looking for a guy right now. She's going through some tough times. She's been on her own for a long time."

Izzy sipped her coffee and arched her brows over the top of her mug. "All the more reason she could use a strong partner."

"Did she say something about me?"

"No, nothing in that vein. It's my own observation. I think you two make a lovely couple. You're not getting any younger, you know."

He grinned and took out his wallet. "Yeah, I know. Neither are you."

"Oh, I've been down that road. I'm happy on my own. Plus, I'm never alone between Mom and Dad and the winery. Not to mention my law office."

"I could say the same," he said.

"You need a woman in your life." He narrowed his eyes. "Let me rephrase. I think you'd be happier with one, that's all." She flicked her hair off her shoulders. "I guess we better scoot, huh?"

He helped her with her jacket and paid the tab. He rolled her suitcase to the pier and gave her one more hug goodbye. "Give Mom and Dad a hug from me and come back soon."

"I will," she said as she turned to walk on board.

***

The week was packed with preparations for both upcoming weddings. Ellie spent a significant portion of her days on the phone with the brides. The

May bride was easy-going and made decisions quickly. The June bride, not so much. She was a bit more demanding and had a hard time deciding, making things more complicated than necessary. She had changed her mind about the menu and colors overnight.

Jack phoned to let her know the manager of the bakery wanted to meet with her on Friday. The paperwork would be finalized Thursday and she would be delivering the check and wanted to go over the equipment.

Thursday night as she was eating yet another chicken breast and salad, it hit her. In a week she'd no longer have a daily connection to the bakery. The place she had gone to each day for the last twenty years would no longer be her sanctuary. She felt tears moisten her cheeks before she realized she was crying. With a mixture of sadness and nostalgia tugging at her heart, she went to bed.

Friday she skipped the winery and spent the entire morning at the bakery getting ready for the new manager. She boxed the majority of the pans and tools, along with all of her recipes and those of her aunt. The fixtures and equipment were included in the lease, but The Flaky Baker would be outfitting the kitchen with their own tools. She unpinned the memorabilia from the walls and collected all the aprons.

The bakery would close for a week during the transition, starting tomorrow. She had the cupboards emptied and a stack of boxes stationed at the back door by the time Sweet Treats opened for the last day. Ellie spent the morning waiting on what seemed like every citizen of Friday Harbor. She did her best to keep a smile on her face, but was on the verge of tears throughout the day.

She was visiting with Annie from Knitwits when Blake came through the door. He gave her a grin and held up a bag. She took a break and followed him into the back room. "I brought you some soup for lunch." He slid bowls out of the bag and set them on the counter. "You look like hell."

"It's a hard day. I'm sad on the inside, but trying to be happy."

He put his hand on top of hers. "You've spent twenty years here. I'm sure it's more like your home than anyplace else."

Her vision blurred. "Exactly," she whispered. She undid the lid on her soup and tasted a spoonful. "Thanks, this tastes great."

"Are you sure you want to work tonight?"

She nodded. "Oh, yeah. I need to take my mind off all this." She waved her hand above her head. After another spoonful she said, "I love my new job at the winery. So much of me and who I am is wrapped up in this place."

"It all happened so fast, you probably haven't had time to process all of it."

"It helps to have a new challenge. It didn't hit me until last night. I've been too busy to think about it. I'm trying to think of it as a new chapter in my life and not the loss of something I love."

"Not to mention you're doing what's best for your health."

"That too," she said, tossing their takeout containers. "My levels have been improving. I needed to wallow a bit, I guess. I've got a lot of memories wrapped up in this old place."

"If you change your mind and want to stay home tonight, call me."

She shook her head. "Nope, sitting home alone is not what I need. I'll be there."

He moved to leave and saw the stack of boxes. "I'll load these up and take them to your house, if you want."

"That would be great. Could you stash them in the shed? You'll find some other boxes there near the door."

He moved his truck around back and made quick work of the pile. She took a deep breath and went to face more customers.

She had boxed the few remaining pastries in the case when Jack arrived. He introduced her to Connie Bass, the new manager. Ellie shook her hand and was greeted with a curt nod. "Would you care for a pastry or something to drink?" she offered.

Jack started to nod yes, but Connie said, "No, let's get down to business, shall we?" There was nothing relaxed about the woman. Her head darted around the building and she walked with a clip. The dour look on Connie's face and her deep wrinkles reminded Ellie of the shriveled apple heads she had noticed at the craft fair last Halloween. Connie's frumpy gray hair, harsh eyes, and grim face invoked the image of Ellie's mother, causing her to shiver.

Jack handled the paperwork while the two of them walked around the entire building. Jack checked off the equipment on the list as they identified and inspected each piece. After two hours, they reached the end of the list. "Everything looks to be in order. I'll need to meet with your employee tomorrow and go over a few things," said Connie.

"Sure, here's her contact information. She's expecting your call," Ellie said, handing him a note. "Cooper Hardware will be by this afternoon to remove the sign on top of the building."

"They need to get it out of here. We'll be installing our logo early next week." She reached inside her jacket and extracted an envelope. Here's your check, Ms. Carlson. It covers first, last, security, plus the inventory."

"Wonderful. And please call me Ellie." She held the envelope and chose to focus on a chance for a better future instead of the detached woman in front of her who would soon be running, and she hoped not ruining, the bakery. "I left my contact information in the office should you need anything."

"I don't expect we'll be in touch unless there's a problem with the building. All the equipment is under maintenance, so we'll contact them with any repair issues."

"Okay then, I guess we're done here," she said. She collected her things from the office and presented Connie with a set of keys.

Jack shook her hand and hugged Ellie. "If you need any help finding a place to live, let me know."

"I'm heading over to look at a condo now," said Connie, with a touch of superiority.

"Good luck, Ms. Bass. I'll stop in and see you when you reopen," said Ellie. "I'll lock the back. I'm parked out there."

She nodded and gave Ellie her card. The new manager followed Jack out front and locked the door. She heard Jack trying to make small talk with Connie, but she was already opening the door of her BMW.

Ellie gazed across the empty display counter and the vacant walls one last time. She trudged through the kitchen and rested her hand on the floor mixer. "Goodbye Sweet Treats," she whispered.

* * *

Ellie dropped most of the leftovers from the bakery at the church on her way home. She retained a box for Blake and deposited it in the kitchen when she arrived for her evening shift. She popped her head in the office and found Blake. "I left you some treats in the kitchen."

"Oh, thanks. How'd the handoff go?"

She wrinkled her nose. "The new manager, Connie, is a complete ogre from what I saw. She's cranky and surly. I feel sorry for Nicole. I hope Connie stays in the back and lets someone who's friendly interact with my wonderful customers. They like to chat and I can't picture Connie giving them personal service."

"Time will tell. Maybe she'll stay in the back, like you said. I'll check it out when they open and give you a full report."

"I didn't even mention working with her on weddings and events for the winery. I didn't want to prolong my time with her today." She stepped through the door and put her jacket on her chair and saw a vase of flowers in the middle of her desk. "Wow, what's this?" She plucked the card and read it. *Enjoy the next chapter, Blake.*

"Ah, how sweet." She bent to smell the fragrant pink and white bouquet. "Thanks for thinking of me."

He rose and embraced her in a hug. "It's going to be okay." She nodded against his shoulder and detected a hint of sage. Lingering, she breathed in the scent.

The tasting room hummed with activity all night, but she found time to visit with Jack and Lulu, who motioned her to their table. He handed her a folder and told her he found a few houses she could take a look at in her spare time. She thanked him and stashed the folder on her desk.

She helped Blake clean the tables and take all the dirty dishes to the kitchen before she rang out the register. As she prepared the report at her desk, the fresh scent of freesia filled the air. She admired the flowers and the considerate man who brightened her day.

Nineteen

Instead of an alarm waking Ellie Saturday, she was roused from sleep by the loud tweets of birds and a snort from Oreo. She hadn't had a Saturday off in years and vowed to lounge and enjoy it. After coffee and a long shower she fixed herself breakfast and perused the folder from Jack.

She'd calculated what she could afford and was happy to find most of the homes listed were in her budget range. One in particular caught her eye. It was only a half-mile from Sam's house and had a huge deck, though it lacked the stunning water view.

She put in a call to Jack to schedule an appointment. He surprised her and told her he could meet her at the property in an hour. She hurried to get ready and found Jack waiting on the gorgeous deck surrounded by lush plants. They perused outside and walked the length of the wraparound wooden deck, inspecting the boards. The yard was immaculate with mature trees and plants and several water features tucked in the midst of the greenery.

He led her through the French doors off the back of the house into the dining room. The house appeared bigger than it was, thanks to the open floor plan and high vaulted ceilings. The house had been built in the 1990's but the kitchen and baths had been remodeled. The large kitchen housed granite counters, stainless appliances, and a small island. It was accessed through archways leading to the great room and dining room. The master bedroom was behind a set of double doors. It was inviting, with access to the deck. Two nominal bedrooms shared another bathroom.

"What do you think?" asked Jack.

"I like it. I know I'd miss the acreage, but the yard is fenced and Blake said Oreo is always welcome at the vineyard. I like the idea of a one level house and smaller makes sense. It's been so well kept, it's like new."

"I thought you'd like this one. I think it's a great price and a terrific house. I don't think it will stay on the market long."

"It's near Sam and Jeff, not to mention Linda and Max. I like the idea of being so close to them. I can walk to their homes for a visit or to the water."

"Most of the furnishings stay, along with all the deck planters."

"You're kidding? I didn't realize the furniture was part of the deal. That makes it a steal."

"Have you talked to a lender yet?"

She shook her head. "No, but I need to, and soon. I figured what I could afford based on my income and this is in the range. I'll get to work on a loan Monday."

"Do you want to look at any of the others?"

She gazed across the wood floors in the kitchen and what looked like new carpet throughout and said, "No, this is the one."

Jack promised to draw up the offer contingent upon her receiving financing. He anticipated an answer Monday. She drove down the street and took the turn that led to Sam's house. She hated stopping by unannounced, but was too excited to wait.

Jeff was outside with the dogs and hollered out a greeting when she got out of the car. "Hey, Ellie. What brings you by?"

She jogged over to him. "I met Jack and put an offer in on a house down the street. I can't believe it." She danced on her toes and clasped her hands together. Bailey and Zoe darted at her and wrapped themselves around her legs. She bent and put a hand on each of them.

"That's wonderful, Ellie. Let's go tell Sam. She's in the kitchen." He led her around the back of the house. "Sam, sweetie, Ellie's here."

Ellie shared her news and Sam insisted she stay for lunch. She described the rooms and became more animated when she told them the furnishings came with the house. She helped set the table and as she worked she let them know she still hadn't heard from Ceci. Over salmon salads she filled them in on Connie. "They may have to rename it The Crabby Baker," said Ellie, with a snicker.

"I'm a firm believer in the power of the free marketplace. If Connie's attitude impacts business, I bet there willl be a change in management. You've been more than successful, so the corporate bean counters will know if Connie isn't performing."

"How's the barn coming along?" asked Jeff.

"It's ahead of schedule. Speaking of the barn, when Izzy was here she said Blake's family wants to plan a birthday party for him the last Sunday in April. It's a surprise. I've been too busy to let anyone know."

"We'll be there. Let me know how I can help," said Sam.

"We'll need to distract Blake all day. How about a fishing excursion?" she asked.

Jeff's eyes brightened. "That could be arranged. I'll get with Nate and figure something out."

"I better get going. I want to video chat with Aunt Ginny and Uncle Bob and tell them about the house." She lingered on the deck and wrestled with both dogs before leaving.

She snagged the mail from the box on her way to the house. An envelope with Dani's return address caught her eye. She ripped it open and scanned the card. Dani thanked her for the flowers and told her she was home now and doing better. She still didn't have her strength back, but was happy to be out of the hospital. Ellie smiled and held the card against her chest. She dashed into the house, her steps lighter as she called to Oreo.

She went from room to room in the old house, scanning the furnishings, realizing she wouldn't have much to move. With the exception of her televisions, a bed, and some cookware, the furnishings belonged to her aunt. She fired up her laptop and connected the video call.

Her aunt and uncle were happy she was considering a home of her own. "If you end up getting the house, we'll arrange for a moving company to pack up the stuff we want. We'll ask the kids to make the trip and go through things," said Ginny.

"Maybe we can talk you into having a yard sale for us," said Uncle Bob, with a wink.

"I'd be happy to do it. Let me know what you want to do."

"If we waited until summer, we could come to the island and do it ourselves," said Aunt Ginny, turning to gauge her husband's reaction.

"I don't think we need to mess with it, honey. Let's have the kids do the work."

They wanted to know about the winery and if Ellie liked her new job. Her excitement didn't escape them as she detailed the property and how busy her days had been organizing the upcoming weddings. "You look so happy, dear. I'm glad you found a new passion," said Aunt Ginny.

She shared Dani's card with them and let them know she was home from the hospital. "That's great news, dear. She's in our prayers."

"I love you guys. I'll talk to you next week," said Ellie, as she disconnected the call.

After dinner she curled up in the recliner with Oreo. "Do you think you could adjust to a smaller yard?" The dog thumped her tail several times and winked. "That's a girl."

* * *

Blake suggested they drive by so he could inspect the house on their way to town. Sundays the winery didn't open until noon and they were in the habit of doing breakfast after a couple of hours of work. Since the house was unoccupied, he stopped the truck to get a better look.

"What a great yard." He followed the deck around to the back of the house. "Wow, it's even better back here."

"I'm so excited. I hope it works out. I fell for the place. The only thing that would make it better is a view of the water, but I can't afford it."

"I think it's perfect for you. I'd live on the deck. It's situated to give you privacy and they've done a terrific job on the plants."

She babbled about the house throughout the meal. Blake listened and smiled, his eyes creasing as he laughed. "What's so funny?" she asked.

"You. You're so happy. The enthusiasm looks great on you."

She blushed. "Sorry, I'm excited."

"Don't be sorry. I'm thrilled for you. You deserve a home and all the good things that go with it." He checked the clock. "We better get moving."

He drove them to the winery where they spent the afternoon entertaining wine enthusiasts. Blake was able to handle the counter by himself most of the day and Ellie spent her time on the weddings. The June bride had stuck with her decisions for a whole week, so Ellie proceeded to rework the arrangements.

She also corresponded with Izzy about Blake's upcoming surprise party. Sam and Linda offered to invite the locals and keep track of their responses. Izzy was talking to the family about menu choices and cake flavors.

Ellie spent the evening planning how to organize her new house, hoping the offer was accepted and the financing was approved. As she went to bed she remembered to check for word from Ceci. The happiness and joy she'd experienced since finding the house dissolved as she read an email from her sister.

She shook her head and let out a sigh. Ceci said she was sorry to have taken so long, but the decision had been weighing on her. They had spent the weekend in Sunnyside visiting her parents. Ceci said she wasn't going to donate to Dani. One section stood out to Ellie. *I can't live like you, Ellie— alienated from Mom and Dad. I'm so sorry for Dani, but Mom has made it clear—if I do this, I'm out. I can't do that to my kids. She's been good to us and I don't want to ruin our relationship.*

Ellie tossed her phone on the night table. *So, too bad for my daughter. She can get sicker, suffer more, or die, but Ceci doesn't want to jeopardize Mom's relationship with her and the kids. What relationship?*

* * *

The winery was closed for tastings until Thursday. She and Blake had worked out a schedule where she'd be off on Mondays and Tuesdays. She slept in after spending most of the night staring at the ceiling, composing a response to Ceci. None of them were right, so she chose to leave it and come back to it after some deliberation.

While she was sipping her third cup of coffee, Jack called. He brightened the morning with news the offer had been accepted. He also gave her the name of a mortgage lender he had worked with in the past who he knew was reputable and fast. She put in a call to the guy as soon as she disconnected.

Gathering all the documents for the loan took up most of her day, but she finished the online application before the close of business. He promised to call her back once she'd been approved and the appraisal was complete.

As soon as she had attached her last document, she hustled to get ready for dinner. She was expected at Kate's in less than half an hour. She joined Spence in the kitchen and they visited while Kate put the finishing touches on dinner.

She commiserated with them about Ceci's email and shared the excitement of the possibility of a new house. Kate wanted to see it, so Ellie pulled it up online and the three of them gathered around the computer to take a virtual tour. "It looks brand new," said Spence.

"I love the open space and the tall ceilings, not to mention the deck in the backyard. It's lovely," said Kate.

The conversation turned to the bakery and Ellie filled them in on Cranky Connie. "I hope it works out. I don't want the bakery to end up with a bad reputation, after all these years," said Ellie.

"You don't need to worry about it anymore. It's not your problem," said Kate. "You've got so much to look forward to with your new position at the winery and a new home."

Ellie's smile filled her face. "Yes, I've got so many exciting events going on in my life now. If only I could figure out how to convince Ceci to help Dani."

Kate put her hand atop Ellie's. "Sweetie, I don't think you can do much more. It's Ceci's choice and despite what we think of her reasoning, it's hers to make. It's hard to accept, but not everything is fixable."

Ellie stayed late, soaking in the comfort Spence and Kate offered. Kate had lost her own daughter to suicide years ago, so her advice was meaningful. She would know, more than anyone, about feeling powerless.

Tuesday Ellie had an appointment to get her hair done and spent most of the day in town. A day off that didn't revolve around catching up on sleep was rare. She took delight in frittering away an hour at Sam's coffee shop and window shopping. She visited with Kate and fell in love with an exquisite mirror. "If this house deal works out, I want to get this. It would be perfect in the entry." Kate went to her desk and retrieved a tag.

"There," she said, taping the sold tag on the glass. "Now, it'll be safe until you know." Ellie opened her mouth to protest, but Kate said, "No arguments. I have a good feeling about your house."

Ellie noticed the new sign was already installed at the bakery and the front door was open. She wandered in and found Connie in the kitchen supervising the delivery of kitchen equipment. "Hi, how's it going?" asked Ellie.

"Busy. What can I do for you?"

"I was hoping to talk about utilizing The Flaky Baker as a vendor for events at the winery. I've got a couple of weddings booked and wanted to discuss cakes and pricing you could offer."

"I don't have time right now. The owner needs to decide anyway. I'll give you his card." She bustled to the office and smacked a card in Ellie's hand. "He's planning a visit, but not sure when."

"Okay, thanks. I'll give him a call."

Connie nodded and went back to barking orders at the delivery men. Ellie set out for her last stop at the market before calling it a day. After she put her groceries away, she decided to email the owner, rather than risk a game of phone tag.

She saw an email from Izzy saying they had decided on the chocolate and peanut butter cake for Blake's birthday and Lou's for catering. She knew peanut butter cups were one of his favorite treats, so the choice didn't come as a surprise. She opened her spreadsheet and slotted in the cake and dinner selections. Jeff's favorite band had confirmed they would be there, so she checked it off her list.

As she sat by the fire after dinner, she composed a response to Ceci. She told her she was beyond disappointed because Ceci was Dani's last hope. Ellie wanted her to realize the impact of her decision, but also explained she understood it was her choice to make.

I wish I understood why you value a relationship with Mom that means she dictates what you can do when you're an adult. I've lived my whole life wondering why my mother hates me. I've tried to figure out the hold she has on Dad and you. Now I'm thankful she isn't in my life, because I couldn't bear the thought of my decisions being controlled by her twisted rationale. I don't think you'd do that to your children and I'm not sure why you put up with it from her. I will always love you, Ceci, but I'm devastated for my daughter. I'll do my best not to let this come between us and my offer still stands for you to visit Friday Harbor this summer. Love, Ellie.

She took Kate's advice and slept on it. She made a few changes in the morning and sent it before she left for the winery. The busy week passed without a reply from Ceci.

On Friday she learned her financing was approved, pending the appraisal, which was slated to be done next week. She called Jack and he said if all went as planned she could be in the house in mid-April. As soon as they closed the winery on Sunday, they drove over to Sam's for dinner. She enjoyed cooking and always included the group of friends.

The thrill of the news about the house and the comfort of amazing friends surrounding her kept Ellie's thoughts off Ceci. Worries about Dani were relegated to the back of her mind. They stayed concealed there until she faced two free days with nothing to do. Unstructured time led to panic and worry, so she vowed to find something to keep herself busy.

Twenty

After wrestling with ideas to keep busy, she was surprised and thankful for an invitation to go boating Monday morning. Blake texted soon after she woke and asked if she was up for an outing. She called him back, eager for a distraction.

She and Oreo drove to town and met Blake for breakfast on the deck overlooking the harbor. He had ordered lunch from Dottie's Deli and packed a cooler with drinks. They spent the day winding along the coast of the island, enjoying the sunshine.

"I haven't been out on a boat for years," said Ellie. "I forgot how relaxing it is to be on the water."

"The views here are spectacular. I needed a break from the winery and this sounded better than anything else."

The motion of the boat, together with the warm sunshine and the gentle lap of the water against the hull, soothed her spirit. She stretched out on a seat and struggled to keep her eyes open behind her sunglasses. A faint breeze carried the perfect blend of ocean scents that couldn't be duplicated. Wet rocks and sand, salt, trees, and water merged together in an intoxicating perfume.

Ellie sensed a shadow across her face and opened her eyes to find Blake standing near her looking at the shoreline. "What do you see?"

"Sorry I woke you. We're getting close to Sam's neck of the woods, so I was getting my bearings to see if I could spot her place."

Ellie sat up and concentrated on the landmarks along the coast.

"There," she pointed, "I recognize the umbrellas on her deck."

He followed her finger and smiled. "Yeah, I got it now." He slowed the motor and suggested lunch. After feasting on sandwiches and salads, he turned the boat and headed to the marina. He picked up the pace on the way back and the wind carried the spray. Ellie perched on the front of the boat, enjoying the spritzing and the rush of the air, like a dog with her head out the window.

They pulled into the marina in the late afternoon and Blake maneuvered the boat into his slip. He went about the business of tying the lines to the cleats on the dock. "What a wonderful day. Thanks for inviting me," said Ellie. "I'm sure the romance of living on a boat has worn off by now, but it was a lovely way to spend the afternoon."

He chuckled as he worked. "I'm not sure I ever considered it romantic, but I'm definitely ready for a house that doesn't move. I'd also enjoy a bathroom bigger than a postage stamp."

"Do you need any help with anything?"

"Nah, I'm a pro at this now." He pulled on the last line and wrapped it around the cleat with ease.

She let out a sigh. "I'm going to take off. I'll catch up with you at work. I may come in for a few hours tomorrow." He met her and hopped onto the dock, extending his hand. He steadied her as she stepped from the boat to the wooden walkway.

"You, my friend, need a hobby. It's your day off tomorrow, enjoy it."

She smiled. "It's a new phenomenon for me, but I'll work on finding a diversion." She waved and strolled along the pier to the parking lot. When she loaded Oreo in her car, he was still standing by the boat and sent her home with another wave.

***

In the middle of her busy week, the lender called to let Ellie know the appraisal was complete and things were on track. He was shooting for a closing date in less than two weeks.

She and Blake had taken to stocking the fridge and making lunch in the kitchen most days. They limited lunch outings to once a week, but Blake insisted they celebrate the exciting news at Lou's. They chose a table on the deck, intent on enjoying the sunshine and the view. They split an order of fish and chips and shared a plate of crab cakes.

Blake offered her the last golden patty, but she declined. "When you're ready to move, say the word and I'll help you load things with my truck."

"That would be great. I know Nate and Jeff will be there with their trucks. I don't have much, so it should be easy." She nibbled on a fry, savoring the battered deliciousness she had missed. "Would you mind stopping by the market on our way back and snagging a few boxes?"

"Sure, not a problem. If you need more, let me know and I can pick them up in the mornings and drop them by on my way to work."

"Good idea." She pushed her plate away. "That was sinful, but delicious."

"Well, we better get back and finish our day," he said, plucking the check before she could reach for it. "My treat."

They found a few boxes in back of the market and dropped them at Ellie's house on the way to the winery. Oreo was excited to see them and begged to go. Blake couldn't resist her sad dog face and Ellie relented and let her hop in the truck. Blake had work to do in the vineyard, so Oreo spent the afternoon following him and sniffing her way across the acreage.

After a busy weekend of tastings and working on an upcoming anniversary party and twenty-first birthday bash, Ellie carved out some time to work on moving preparations. She consolidated her bakery tools and memorabilia into boxes she could stack in her new garage.

She worked in the kitchen and boxed all of her cookware and small appliances, vowing to eat salads or takeout until she was situated in the new house. She spent her days off cleaning the carpets and making sure everything was spotless.

She had few personal belongings and only a handful of decorative objects to pack. In her Sunday call with Aunt Ginny she found out the cousins would be coming in April to go through the house and arrange for movers. Ellie would be tasked with having a yard sale for the rejected items.

Aunt Ginny told her to sell what she could and keep the money for her new house.

As she contemplated the amount of furnishings in the house and all the junk in the barn and shed, she hoped the cousins found a home for everything. She didn't have time for a yard sale, but appreciated the gesture and knew it was important to her aunt and uncle.

She scheduled a meeting with the owner of The Flaky Baker, Milt Bigelow, on Wednesday. Nicole was behind the counter and she squealed when she saw Ellie. The two embraced and Milt emerged from the kitchen. Unlike Connie, he was warm and welcoming. He complimented her on the success of Sweet Treats and told her he wanted to continue her long tradition. He invited her in the back to sample some cake flavors.

"Where's Connie this morning?" asked Ellie, secretly delighted to miss her and be in the company of the blond and blue-eyed man, who looked more like a California surfer than a baker.

"She'll be in later this afternoon. She's getting settled in her condo."

Ellie nodded and considered the kitchen that was no longer her shelter. All of her personal touches had been removed, but the layout remained the same. She saw an array of cupcakes on the table. He pulled out a stool and invited her to sit.

He pointed out each flavor and she took a small bite of each. Mindful of her blood sugar, she was careful to consume miniscule amounts. She found all them to be tasty. Some combinations were not quite as unique as hers, but most were delicious and all of them were acceptable.

They discussed the pricing he could offer for events and Ellie was pleased with the discounts he proposed. "I anticipate being the liaison with the client. It would save Connie the, uh, time of interacting with clients. I'd need some photos of examples from you and may have to have her provide samples like these, if the client wants to taste."

Milt nodded. "Not a problem. I'll give you a book with the different sizes and shapes of cakes and the menu of flavors and frostings. It's full of pictures of cakes we've done. If you need samples, call Connie a day or two in advance."

"I'd prefer to pick them up and have clients sample at the winery. Uh, Connie is, um, so busy."

Milt grimaced. "I take it she's been less than cordial?"

Ellie gritted her teeth and nodded. "Yeah, she's uh, well, business-like and a bit cold."

His lips tightened and he shook his head. "She excels at production and keeping our costs in line. She runs a tight ship. She's been asking for a promotion for months and when this came up, I gave it to her. I'll talk with her some more about interactions and customer relations."

"Those are going to be what makes or breaks it here for you. Nicole is a wonderful employee, so she won't have trouble with her. But, if she's treated poorly I know she'll leave. My customers love to chat and if Connie's not willing to welcome them, you'll have a hard time in Friday Harbor. The island is different than the city or even the suburbs."

He sighed. "I may have made the wrong choice. I appreciate you telling me. I think I'll extend my stay for a bit and observe. I may have to rethink my assignments."

She took the sample book and literature. He suggested clients from the mainland could always visit one of his locations in the Seattle area for samples, if they wanted to save a trip. He also showed her the website where she could find their cake menu.

"I've got two weddings, a birthday, and an anniversary booked. I can give you the orders for everything except the June wedding now. I'm going to send my June bride to one of your sites in the city for samples and her final selection. She changes her mind. A lot." Ellie smiled and raised her brows.

"I'm familiar with the species," he said, laughing. "No problem. I would suggest the location in Queen Anne and recommend she work with Sue." He gave her his card and scribbled his personal cell phone on the back. "If you ever have a problem, please call me. I want you, of all people, to be a happy customer."

She nodded and put the card in her wallet. He wrote up the orders for the events Ellie had booked and gave her copies. He walked her to the door and reiterated to call him with any concerns or feedback from customers. "My goal is to be as successful as you were with Sweet Treats."

* * *

After another busy week, Ellie got a surprise call informing her the house could close early. She rushed to town and signed the sheaf of papers required for a mortgage late Friday and took possession of the keys to her new home. With a busy weekend at the winery, she had no time to move until Monday. The stacks of boxes staged around the house made Oreo antsy and made Ellie glad she didn't have to pack the rest of the house.

Blake came over Sunday night after they closed the winery and consolidated her piles of boxes from the house into one large organized square outside the garage. Nate and Jeff were going to meet Blake Monday morning and transport everything to the new house.

Ellie's cell phone rang while she and Blake were having a cup of tea after she made a salmon salad for dinner. She frowned and answered it. Blake watched the color drain from her face as she said, "Okay, Dan. I understand. I'm so sorry and I'll be there as soon as I can."

She hit the button to disconnect and stared across the room. "Ellie, are you okay?"

She shook her head. "That was Dani's dad. She's back in the hospital in bad shape." She took a breath as her chin quivered. "He told me…he said I should come if I want to see her. Uh, they don't think she'll make it this time."

Blake stood and sat next to her on the couch. He wrapped his arm around her shoulder and pulled her close. He felt the sobs rack through her before he heard the sorrow in her moans. "I'm so sorry, Ellie." He rested his head atop hers and let her cry.

He reached for the tissue box and held it for her. After wiping her eyes and blowing her nose several times, she cleared her throat. "I need to go to her."

"How about we see if Linda or Jen will go with you?"

He watched her face dissolve into tears as she nodded her head. He pulled out his cell phone and called Max. He walked to the kitchen cradling his cell phone against his shoulder as he carried their cups. While he explained the situation to Max he boiled more water.

When he returned he found Ellie still on the couch and Oreo cuddled across her lap. "I talked to Max. Linda wants to go with you and they're going to talk to Steve to arrange transport for the two of you. It will save you time and hassle. Sam's already called Becky, who insists you stay as long as you need."

She gave him a weak smile. "Becky is Sam's assistant and she lives in Seattle. Steve helped Sam out when Jeff was in the hospital and transported the family several times. I'm lucky to have such wonderful friends." She ran her hands over Oreo's back. "I need to pack a bag. Moving will have to wait." She shuffled to her bedroom.

While she gathered clothes and toiletries, Blake put in a call to Nate and gave him the news. The two of them discussed the situation and made arrangements to move Ellie in her absence. Nate offered to call Jeff and coordinate with him.

Ellie's cell rang while she was rummaging through her things in the bathroom. He heard her say, "That's great. I'll meet you there. Thanks so much, Linda."

She emerged carrying a plastic bag of bottles. "Linda called and said Steve's willing to take us over tonight. Becky's going to meet us at the marina and then I can get to the hospital late tonight, if they'll let me, or first thing tomorrow."

"I'll drive you there now."

She nodded, still pale and shaken from Dan's phone call. She wandered from the kitchen to the bedroom and finally grabbed her dad's old duffle from the coat closet. "I've packed everything, so I'm discombobulated and can't find anything." She tore out of her bedroom a few minutes later. "Oreo. I've got to have somebody watch her."

"I can stay here and take care of her and she can come to the winery with me. Not a problem."

"Are you sure? Sam and Jeff would take her, if it's easier for you."

He shook his head. "No, it's fine. I don't mind."

She put on her jacket and reached for the duffle. She gave Oreo a soft nuzzle and threw her purse on her shoulder. "Okay, I think I'm ready." She handed him her house keys.

Blake got them to the marina in less than ten minutes. Steve was readying his boat and Blake handed him her luggage. Max and Linda arrived and Steve took Linda's bag. Max embraced Ellie in a hug and gave Linda a kiss before surrendering her to Steve.

Blake put his hand on Ellie's shoulder. "Call me and let me know how she's doing." He pulled her close in a one handed hug. "Don't worry about anything here. Oreo and I will be fine."

A silent tear leaked from her eye and she gave him a faint smile. "Thanks, Blake. I appreciate everything." Steve offered her a hand and within minutes the boat roared to life. Max and Blake watched them leave, making out only the wake of white water in the moonlight.

Twenty-one

Becky met Ellie and Linda at the marina. While they loaded the luggage in Becky's SUV, Ellie put in a call to Dan. She disconnected and said, "He thinks tomorrow morning would work better. She just got to sleep."

Always generous and hospitable, Becky got them settled in her guest rooms and promised breakfast in the morning. Drained and shattered, Ellie fell into the plush bed. Her mind whirled with visions of Dani and what she would say to the poor girl. She fidgeted with anxiety. As soon as she drifted to sleep, she woke, drenched in sweat and kicked the covers to the bottom of the bed.

Apprehension filled her as she pondered the coming day and the real possibility of losing Dani. She longed for the comfort of Aunt Ginny, but knew it was too late to call. The last time she saw displayed on the clock was 1:31 and then she surrendered to exhaustion.

* * *

Ellie forced herself to eat a few bites. Becky drove them to the hospital. She made sure they each had her cell number to arrange rides whenever they were needed.

Linda helped Ellie navigate the labyrinth of hallways and they found Dani's room in the critical care unit. She checked in with a nurse and soon a middle-aged man approached them. "Ellie?" he asked. "I'm Dan Lawson," he said, extending his hand. The bags under his eyes resembled small purses and were a smoky purple color.

"Nice to meet you, Dan. This is my good friend, Linda Sullivan. Her husband is my doctor."

Dan shook her hand. "April, my wife, is in with Dani now. You probably didn't know, but after we exhausted our last hope with your sister, the doctors tried another kidney transplant from the list."

Ellie shook her head. "No, I wasn't aware. How long ago?"

"It was last week. She's rejected it and now her system is shutting down."

Ellie's eyes filled with tears. She told herself she wasn't going to cry, but it wasn't working. "Oh, no. I'm so sorry. Do you think it will upset her to see me?"

"No, I told her I called and you were coming. She seemed to perk up a bit."

Ellie smiled. "Would you like me to wait until April comes out?"

"No, let's go on back. We're only supposed to have two in there at a time, but I'll show you to her room." Linda gave her friend's arm a squeeze of support.

Ellie left Linda reading a book and followed Dan through the maze of glass cubicles and flurry of scrub clad men and women. He stopped and gestured to his wife. She stepped into the hallway, her face blotchy and red, looking as if she hadn't slept in a week. "April, honey, this is Ellie."

Ellie took her hand and couldn't speak. Tears rolled down her face. April embraced her in a hug and both of them cried. "I'm so sorry," whispered Ellie.

April only nodded as she released Ellie. She turned to the glass door. "Dani's in and out, but go on in and have a seat next to her. I'm going to get some coffee." She slid her hand in her husband's and they leaned on each other as they made their way to the exit.

Ellie went through the door and stifled a gasp when she saw all the tubes and wires connected to the shrunken form in the bed. Dani's face was drawn and gray, her lips drained of color. Her eyes were closed. Ellie rested her hand atop Dani's fragile arm.

"Dani, it's Ellie," she whispered, not wanting to startle her. "I'm here."

The girl's eyelids fluttered and opened. Instead of the hazel eyes she remembered, Ellie saw dull eyes staring back at her. Dani swallowed hard. Ellie reached for the water glass and brought the straw to Dani's lips.

Ellie saw her struggle to lift her head. She tucked her arm under Dani's neck and helped her ease forward a bit. She took a swallow and fell back on the pillow. "Your dad called me. I'm sorry I didn't know you were back in the hospital." She willed herself not to cry.

"It's okay," said Dani, in a tiny voice. Gone was the bravado she displayed in the bakery.

"Is there anything I can do for you?"

Dani gave a slight shake of her head and a tear glided down her cheek. She moved her hand and curled it around Ellie's. Dani's eyes closed. Ellie held her hand and watched her. She couldn't tell if Dani was sleeping or resting. Her eyes landed on a stack of books. She opened the topmost with one hand and began reading it aloud. It was a children's book, *Anastasia, Absolutely*. Ellie laughed a bit as she read about a young girl, Anastasia Krupnik, who mistakenly mails a bag of dog poop instead of the important letter her mother gave her.

When Ellie looked over the top of the book, she saw a smile on Dani's lips. She continued to read, positioning the book so she could hold it and Dani's hand at the same time. She was near the end of the book by the time Dan and April returned. April came into the room and said, "Those were her favorite books when she was a little girl."

Ellie looked at Dani, who appeared to be sleeping. "They're funny," she whispered, extracting the book and her hand. "Thank you for letting me sit with her."

April nodded and sat in the other chair and stroked her daughter's hair. "She's been through so much." She moved Dani's hair off her shoulders. "There's nothing more to be done."

"I can only imagine your heartache." Ellie's hand shook as she put the book back in the stack and stood. "I'll let Dan come in and be back later." She slipped out and Dan took her place.

She found Linda in the waiting room. Linda encouraged her to take a walk. They went outside to a garden area and wandered along the path. Linda linked her arm in Ellie's. They didn't speak as they walked among the flowers.

It was nearing the lunch hour and Linda reminded Ellie she needed to eat. They wound their way back through the hospital to the cafeteria. Ellie ate her soup and picked at a salad. "She looks horrible. She has no color and is beyond frail."

"It's heartbreaking. She's too young for such a tragic illness," said Linda.

Ellie pulled her phone out of her purse. She saw a voicemail from Aunt Ginny. As she listened, she felt the sting of fresh tears. Her aunt told her Jen had called to give her the news. She expressed her concern for Ellie and Dani and asked Ellie to call her when she could. She offered to come to the hospital.

Linda cleared their trays and accompanied Ellie back to the critical care unit. Ellie checked in and made the trek to Dani's room. April saw her through the glass and she and Dan rose. "She's been resting."

"Linda and I had lunch. I'm happy to stay with her if you two want to grab a bite."

Dan nodded and put his arm around his wife. "We won't be long."

Ellie, preferring to do something rather than stare at Dani, took up where she left off with Anastasia. She finished the book and moved on to another before Dani's parents returned.

They traded places and Ellie went to find Linda. She opened the door to the waiting room and took a step back in surprise. Sitting next to Linda was Ceci, who jumped to her feet when she saw her sister. "Ellie, I'm so sorry." Ceci ran to Ellie and put her arms around her. Ellie stood with her arms at her side.

"What are you doing here?"

"Aunt Ginny called and told me about Dani." She released Ellie. "I talked to Tim and told him I needed to help her. I came now and he's coming as soon as he can get a substitute."

"What do you mean help her?"

"I mean do what I should have done before Mom got to me. I want to donate my kidney."

Ellie's mouth dropped open. "If you're sure, we need to hurry." She grabbed Ceci by the arm and went through the door with her. The pair hustled to the nurse's station and in a frantic voice Ellie asked them to page Dr. Jacobs."

Several minutes later, Ellie saw a tall man in a white coat approach. The nurse pointed in her direction and he introduced himself. "Pleased to meet you Ms. Carlson. What can I do for you?"

"It's Ellie. This is my sister, Ceci. She had her test with Dr. Sullivan to be a donor for Dani. She originally said she couldn't, but changed her mind and is ready to donate now."

"Let's step into a conference room." He led the way to a door and motioned for them to have a seat. He explained Dani's condition had deteriorated to a level that prohibited surgery. "I'm sorry, but it's not feasible. Dani wouldn't survive the procedure."

Ceci let out a sickening moan. "No, no, no."

Dr. Jacobs gripped her hands in his. "I know this isn't easy for you to hear, but it's too late."

Ellie said nothing. Her body went cold and she trembled, her hands tapping against the table. Dr. Jacobs sprinted out the door and returned with a warm blanket, which he wrapped around her. "Ellie, you're in shock. Stay with me." He rubbed his hands over the blanket and encouraged her to take deep breaths.

Ceci continued to wail. Linda opened the door and rushed to Ellie's side. She breathed with her and wrapped an arm around her shoulder, speaking to her in a soft calm voice.

Dr. Jacobs turned his attention to her sister. "Ceci, try to calm down. Let's get a drink of water." He put his arm around her waist and lifted her from the chair and took her out the door.

Ellie was breathing normally and nodded at Linda. "Are you okay? What happened?"

Ellie relayed the bad news. "Oh, sweetie, I know you must be devastated."

Dr. Jacobs returned with drinks for both Linda and Ellie. "How are you doing?"

"Better, I think. Sorry, it's unbelievable."

"I know. It's a terrible situation and such a tragedy. Dani is a strong girl and has endured beyond all of my expectations. I feel horrible that I can't do more. We're out of time and options."

"Dan called me last night and said she wasn't going to make it. When Ceci said she was willing, I hoped it would save her."

He shook his head, sadness filling his eyes. "If there was a chance, I would do it. I don't expect her to last more than another day or so." He looked to Linda. "I'm truly sorry, Ellie."

Ellie nodded her head. "Me too," she whispered. Linda gave the doctor a knowing nod and he left the room.

Ellie crumpled against her friend and wept.

* * *

When Ellie had regained her composure she returned to Dani's room and Linda went back to the waiting room to find Ceci. Wanting to spare Dani's parents any additional suffering, Ellie didn't mention the ordeal with her sister. She was happy to find Dani awake and more alert.

Dan and April opted to get dinner while Ellie was with Dani. Dani asked Ellie questions about her life and in turn Ellie discovered more about Dani's childhood. April had stayed home with Dani and doted on her from the moment she had arrived. Dani relayed happy memories of growing up playing games and surrounded by love. April had read to her each night at bedtime and they spent many days at the library. Dani had spent time in and out of the hospital as a child and April always stayed with her. Dani told Ellie her favorite color—green and that she wanted to be an architect.

Soon Ellie noticed Dani grow weary. She grabbed a book and settled in to read. Dani said, "I know I wasn't nice to you when I came to visit. I was scared and angry. I'm sorry."

"I didn't notice," said Ellie with a grin. "It's forgotten." She bent and kissed the girl on the forehead. "I'm sorry too, Dani. For everything." She opened the book.

Dani's dry, chapped lips formed a small smile and she said, "It's forgotten."

***

When Ellie returned to the waiting room she recognized Tim from the pictures Ceci had shared. He and Ceci both sprang from their chairs. Ceci rushed to her. "I'm sorry, Ellie. I am so sorry." She turned to Tim. "This is my husband."

Ellie shook his hand. "Hello, Tim." She turned to Linda. "I'm tired and need to get something to eat. Are you ready to go?"

Linda nodded. "I'll call Becky right now."

"It's probably best if you guys go home. There's nothing to do here, but wait," said Ellie.

"We're happy to stay here with you," offered Ceci.

Ellie shook her head. "No, I think it's best you go."

Ceci hung her head. Tim said, "We'll be at your aunt's house in Mt. Vernon if you need anything."

"Okay, thanks. Tell them both hi for me. I'll call when I can." She took a few steps and Linda joined her.

The foursome rode the elevator together in silence and Ceci and Tim left them in the lobby to wait for Becky. "I can't talk to her right now. I'm furious and numb, not to mention exhausted."

"Becky said she saved us some dinner. We can eat when we get there." Linda guided them to a bench. Ellie leaned her head on her friend's shoulder and shut her eyes.

***

After dinner, Ellie fell asleep on the couch. Becky covered her with a blanket and turned out the light. She and Linda migrated to the kitchen and chatted in hushed tones while they cleared the dinner dishes. Rather than disturb Ellie and risk her not being able to sleep, they elected to leave her on the couch and tiptoed to bed.

In the early morning hours, Ellie's phone rang. Disoriented, she fumbled for it and saw Dan's number. "Hello," she said in a croaky voice.

"Dani's gone, Ellie. It happened a few minutes ago." He choked on a sob. "We'll let you know about a service."

She thanked him and disconnected. Pulling her legs up, she rested her head on her knees. Plagued with guilt and regret, her body shook with sobs as she cried for the daughter she never had the chance to know.

Linda found her in the same positon hours later. "Are you okay?"

Ellie shook her head as she rocked back and forth. "She's gone," she said, her voice thick with emotion.

Linda sat next to her and held her close. "Oh, Ellie. I know there's nothing I can say to make it better."

Becky came through the living room and gave Linda a questioning look. Linda shook her head. They convinced Ellie to eat a bit of breakfast after Brad left for work. "Do you want to stay here, sweetie, or go back home?" asked Linda.

Ellie shrugged. "I don't know." She used her fork to push the eggs around on her plate. "I need to call Aunt Ginny." After she ate a couple more bites, she shuffled upstairs to her bedroom to make the call.

While Ellie was busy, Linda called Max and shared the sad news. She had already been in contact with him about Ceci's visit and her change of heart. "I'll let everyone know. I need to give Steve a heads up so he'll be prepared if Ellie decides to come home," said Max. "Tell her we're all thinking of her."

Linda retrieved another cup of coffee and sat on Becky's deck. Becky took the opportunity to get some work done in her home office. Soon Ellie joined Linda, looking less disheveled after a shower. "Did you talk with your aunt?"

"Yeah, she said Ceci and Tim were leaving today to go back home." Ellie took a sip from her cup. "Aunt Ginny wants me to stay at her house when I go to Dani's service. They want to come with me."

"I know they would be a great comfort to you."

"I think we should probably head back to the island. I can get my move done and then make a trip back for Dani's service."

"I can give Steve a call and have him head over."

"I hate to impose on him. It's not an emergency at this point. Do you think Becky would be willing to drive us to the ferry in Anacortes? There's a 2:40 sailing."

"I'm sure she would. I'll ask her." She checked her watch. "We have plenty of time."

Linda returned with Becky, who was happy to make the drive. She insisted on treating them to lunch before they boarded. She stopped at a bistro in an old brick building in Anacortes. Linda guided the conversation to Ellie's new house. The shift worked wonders and over salmon salads and crab ravioli Ellie began to smile. Her energy heightened when she showed Becky pictures on her phone.

"I can't believe ya'll will be so close to Sam. That's wonderful." Becky oohed and aahed as Ellie flicked through the photos. "Brad and I will be coming for a visit this summer. I can't wait to see it in person."

Linda brought up the winery and Ellie bubbled with enthusiasm when she told Becky about her new job and working with Blake. "His family has me planning a surprise birthday party for him in a few weeks. I've been busy with it along with the events planned in May and June."

As they were climbing into Becky's SUV, Ellie's phone pinged. She looked at the text and said, "That was Dan. They're planning a memorial service for Dani in their hometown of Chelan on Saturday."

"Good thing you're heading home then. You can come back Friday and spend the weekend with your aunt and uncle," said Linda.

"Yeah, that should work." She put in a call to her aunt while Becky drove them to the ferry landing. Becky visited with Ellie and Linda, hoping to distract Ellie until it was time to board. She left them with hugs and wishes for safe travels.

The two women sat outside for the hour crossing. With the warmth of the sun, the view through the green islands was a healing balm for Ellie's broken heart. She let out a sigh. "I can't thank you enough for coming with me, Linda. It made a difficult trip much easier."

"No need to thank me, it's what friends do." She smiled and linked her hand in Ellie's.

"I'm going to take the ferry back on Friday and then come home Monday. I'll have to miss work, but I'm sure Blake will understand. Chelan is at least three hours from Mt. Vernon, so we'll have to take off early Saturday morning."

"You'll probably have some company. I know Max and I will be coming and I'm sure others will want to attend her service."

Fat tears spilled onto Ellie's cheeks. "Thank you, it means a lot." She squeezed Linda's hand. They were content to spend the rest of the journey in silence, letting the slow rhythm of the ferry and the breeze off the water carry away some of the stress of the past few days.

Twenty-two

Max was waiting to pick them up at the landing and after giving his wife a kiss, swallowed Ellie in a tight hug. "I'm so sorry about Dani." He released her and loaded their bags after helping them into the car.

He passed the turn for her house and Ellie said, "Did you forget me?"

"No," he said with a grin. "The guys went ahead and moved you while you were gone. Blake didn't want you to have to deal with it when you got home." He eyed her in the rearview mirror, but saw no signs of irritation.

"You mean I'm going to my new house?" Despite the fatigue of the past few days, her eyes danced with happiness.

"That's right." He put his hand on Linda's knee and squeezed. "We can stay and help you unpack. Sam and Jeff are going to meet us there."

"What about Oreo?"

"Blake's coming over with her as soon as he's done at the winery today." He made the turn for her new home. "Spence and Kate are bringing dinner."

Ellie slumped against the back of her seat. "Just when I imagined it couldn't get any better. You guys are the best."

He grinned into the mirror and pulled up in front of her house. Sam and Jeff were waiting on the deck. Max pulled a keyring from his pocket and presented it to Ellie. "Your key, madam."

A smile filled her face and she ran to the front door. The first thing she noticed was the gorgeous mirror she had found at Kate's shop. It was hanging on the wall in the entry with a giant green ribbon draped around it. She saw the card tucked in the corner and opened the envelope. *Welcome Home, Ellie. With love from Kate, Spence, and Blake.*

The boxes were stacked in neat piles in their designated rooms. A massive bouquet of gorgeous white blooms stood on the granite counter. She eased into the midst of the flowers and filled her nose with hints of jasmine and lily of the valley. She closed her eyes and let the fresh aroma of spring wash over her.

After breathing in the comforting scents, she tugged the card from the spike in the arrangement. She smiled when she saw it was from Jack and Lulu, congratulating her on her new home and wishing her many years of happiness. She slipped the card back into the holder and gazed around the kitchen.

Sam interrupted her reverie. "How about we help you unpack all of this and get rid of the boxes?"

Weary from the last few days, Ellie lacked the energy to tackle unpacking and took Sam up on her offer. She looked over the cupboards and gave Sam her preferences for locating dishes and pots and pans. Max and Jeff sliced through the tape and extracted the contents.

Linda followed Ellie to her new bedroom. Ellie saw her bed was not only set up, but made. She gave Linda an inquiring look. "Sam and Regi supervised the boys and did a few things." Linda decreed Ellie was to stretch out on the bed and shout out directions on where to store things. She took hold of a stack of clothes and hung them in the walk-in closet.

Blake arrived with Oreo in the midst of the unpacking and the dog made a beeline for her mistress. She jumped onto the bed and assaulted Ellie with licks, sprawling across her. Ellie laughed and wrapped her arms around the frenzied bundle of fur. She glanced up and saw Blake in the doorway. "Thanks for watching my girl."

"She was no trouble." He stepped to the edge of the bed and sat. He reached out and touched her leg. "I'm so sorry about Dani."

She tightened her lips and nodded, tears filling her eyes. He looked away and considered the room and said, "Hope you like where we put the bed. Sam and Regi chose this wall."

"It's perfect. Thanks for moving all my stuff and for the beautiful mirror." Tears streamed down her face. He inched forward and wrapped her in a hug. She rested her head against his chest.

He held her close while Linda organized the master bathroom. "You're going to get through this, Ellie. It won't be easy, but we're all with you. You aren't alone." He kissed the top of her head and squeezed her tight.

She wiped her eyes and said, "I've got to leave Friday, but I'll be back on Tuesday. Dani's service is in Chelan on Saturday."

"Take whatever time you need." They were interrupted by the doorbell announcing the arrival of Kate and Spence. Jeff was opening the door as Ellie came around the corner. The couple was laden down with boxes of pizza and bags from Big Tony's. As soon as they stepped into the entry, Nate honked his horn as he parked out front. He and Regi unloaded several bags and joined the party.

The kitchen was organized and the moving debris had been removed. Nate and Regi apologized for being late as they stuffed groceries into the fridge and cupboards. "We wanted to have this done before you arrived today, but got sidetracked," said Nate.

"How thoughtful of you," Ellie said, giving each of them a hug. "I can't get over everything you guys have done for me."

They spread the food across the island counter and stacked paper plates and plastic cutlery, along with containers of iced tea and lemonade. "Dinner is served," said Kate.

Spence added, "We decided to make it easy and made sure there's plenty of veggie thin crust in there for you, Ellie."

"Pizza sounds great. Thanks too for the mirror. I love it," she said, wrapping her arms around both of them. The rest of the crew filled their plates with salad and pizza.

"Jen and Sean will be by later. He's stuck at work and she's waiting for him. They're in charge of dessert, so it won't matter if they're running late," said Jeff. He walked across the dining room and opened the doors leading to the deck. "I think it's warm enough to eat out here."

"We'll have to take some chairs out there. I have to get some outdoor furniture," said Ellie, grabbing the back of chair.

"I think we can make do with what's out here," said Jeff, giving her a sly smile.

She marched to the doors and shrieked when she saw a glass table with wrought iron chairs and fluffy cushions the color of grasshoppers. She looked to the right at the area off the master bathroom. A set of three curved outdoor couches, with the same cheerful green cushions, encircled a pedestal fire pit. "Who did this?" She ran from the table to the fire pit.

"Guilty," said Sam and Jeff along with Linda and Max. "Jen and Sean were in on it too." Happiness and excitement radiated through their smiles as they watched Ellie's delight.

"Oh, my gosh. This is gorgeous and so perfect. It's too much, though."

"We got a great deal. We know this guy who owns a hardware store," said Sam, with a laugh. "We're so pleased you like it."

"I love it," said Ellie, as she plopped onto one of the couches. She eyed the fabric. "Dani told me her favorite color was green too." Her lips tensed as she ran her hand across the cushion. She glanced across the space and saw Oreo had claimed a cozy corner for herself.

After collecting platefuls in the kitchen, the group gathered around the patio table. Linda and Ellie carried ice and the drinks outside and set them up on the table. When Ellie turned around she noticed the grill. "Oh, wow, a new barbeque too. You guys are spoiling me."

The guys chimed in with lots of advice related to outdoor cooking and how it would be sacrilegious to have a deck without a grill. Jen and Sean arrived bearing boxes from Ellie's old bakery. She welcomed them with hugs and thanks. They munched on pizza while the others visited.

As dusk set in, lights sprang to life in the yard and all along the deck. Whimsical lights that changed color were tucked in planters and near the water features. The trees were lit from below and a few of the trunks were wrapped in mini lights. The backyard was gorgeous in daylight, but at night the effect was surreal. "I know you wished you had a water view, but you've got quite the private oasis here, Ellie," said Blake.

She smiled and the lights reflected in her eyes. "I was thinking the same thing."

Jen plated slices of chocolate cake and cheesecake. Jeff showed Ellie how to work the fire pit and the group gathered around to enjoy dessert. Blake shared a bite of the chocolate cake with Ellie, who had opted for a paper thin sliver of cheesecake. "They don't hold a candle to yours, but not bad," he said.

The twelve friends bantered back and forth, discussing the upcoming busy season, golf, fishing, and the latest books they were reading. Ellie watched the flicker of the flames, listening, but hypnotized by the dance of the yellow curls. As the adrenaline from the excitement of her house wore off, her eyes grew heavy. Sitting across from her, Sam noticed and yawned. "I think we better head for home. I've got an early morning tomorrow."

The others followed her lead and after discarding the takeout boxes and tidying the kitchen, each couple took their leave. Blake was the last one remaining and made sure the gas to the fire pit was off and the doors locked. "Come in tomorrow when you're ready. Sleep in, if you want."

"I may take you up on that," she said with a yawn. "I'm beat." She handed him a box of leftover pizza.

He moved to the door. "Oh, I almost forgot. We didn't have the keys to your car, so it's still at the other house."

She grinned. "I won't be getting far tomorrow. I can call Jeff or Linda to give me a ride." She held the door. "Thanks again, Blake. I don't think I'd have the energy for a move on top of the last few days. I'm happy to be here tonight. It's the perfect place for a fresh start."

He bent and petted Oreo. "See you girls tomorrow."

* * *

Ellie and Oreo showed up at the winery mid-morning. She had to use her key, which meant Blake was in the barn. Oreo darted down the path in that direction, while Ellie got to work. She found two more requests for weddings and a few responses to the ad they had posted for seasonal employees.

Blake appeared in time for lunch and confessed he'd been eating out while she'd been in the city. The kitchen was bare, so they made a trip to town for lunch. He nixed the idea of stopping at the market for groceries since Ellie was leaving again on Friday. "We'll eat out for a couple more days and get back on track when you come home."

As they were finishing lunch at Soup D'Jour, Linda popped in for a takeout order. She visited with them while she waited and they discussed the trip to Chelan. "So, Max and I are going to take the SUV and Sam said they could take theirs too. That way between the two of us, we could take you and your aunt and uncle. I'd rather you didn't have to hassle with driving."

Relief flooded Ellie's face. "That would be wonderful. I know it's going to be a hard day without the stress of traffic."

"We were going to ask Blake to stay at our house with all the dogs. I think Regi and Nate are going to take Jen. That means it'll be you against five dogs. Kate has to stay and work, so she and Spence can back you up, if you need it." She smiled and raised her brows at Blake. "We leave Friday and we'll be back late Sunday night.

He puffed up his chest. "Do you think five dogs scare me?" He chuckled. "I'd watch twenty dogs if it meant I could stay at your house, Linda."

They settled the logistics and Linda waved goodbye as she left with her bag of lunch for the staff at Buds and Blooms.

Ellie worked late that night and the next day, trying to get things caught up before she left again on Friday. Both new weddings were for July and her June bride had made her cake tasting appointment in the city. Everything was set for Blake's surprise party and for the May wedding. When she left Thursday night, her desk was clear and all her emails had been answered.

Friday morning the two vehicles boarded the ferry and made the trek across the blue water to Anacortes. Aunt Ginny had lunch ready when they arrived. They spent several hours catching up on island news and getting to know Sam and Max. Nate and Regi were taking the late ferry, so they planned for an evening arrival in Chelan.

Sam researched lodging and the group agreed to rent a large house together on Lake Chelan, rather than a mass of motel rooms. It was lovely and more economical than five motel rooms. Uncle Bob and Aunt Ginny insisted on treating the group to dinner after they checked in at the house.

There were five bedrooms and Ellie claimed the one decorated with cartoon characters. She and Jen would be sharing the twin beds. Had the reason for the visit not been such a somber one, she would have enjoyed the lake view from the wall of windows in the living area. She was happy to see her uncle so animated as he sat on the deck visiting with Jeff and Max.

She wandered into the bedroom her aunt and uncle were using and found Aunt Ginny reading. She motioned to Ellie to join her on the bed. "How are you doing, sweetheart?"

Ellie snuggled beside her and rested her head on her aunt's shoulder. "I'm dreading tomorrow. Dan and April have been quite cordial to me, considering the circumstances. I feel awkward. Everyone will wonder who I am and why I'm there."

"You're there for Dani. I doubt anyone will be paying much attention to you."

"Ceci's not going to show up, is she?"

"No, dear. She did consider it, but I suggested it would be better if she stayed home. She feels horrible, I know, but tomorrow is not about Ceci."

"She has a streak of my mother in her, doesn't she? Always has to be about her."

Aunt Ginny nodded. "It's something Ceci's going to have to live with the rest of her life. Knowing she could have helped Dani if she would have acted sooner won't be easy for her."

"Maybe it will make her realize how rotten our mother is. I can't figure out how she wields such power over Ceci and Dad. It makes no sense." She fell silent and her aunt stroked her hair.

"I've always felt pieces of me were missing. Dani was one of those pieces and now she's gone forever. My mom took delight in persecuting me and each time she spewed her hateful words, tiny bits of me were chiseled off. I'll never understand her."

"I think you've spent enough of your life worrying about why your mother behaves the way she does. My heart breaks for you, for Dani, for her parents. I can't imagine their sorrow."

"I know. I feel selfish when I realize the depth of their loss compared to mine. Dani was lucky. She told me how much she was loved, especially by April. They were terrific parents. Better than I could have been at that point in my life."

Aunt Ginny smiled. "Well, then you know you made the right decision, don't you?"

Ellie nodded and patted at the wetness on her cheeks. "I'm glad you guys are here." She drifted to sleep, watching the flames in the fireplace and listening to the soft flick of the pages as her aunt continued to read.

Twenty-three

It took Ellie a few minutes to adjust to her surroundings when she woke the next morning. She saw a mound under the quilt and recognized Jen's hair on the pillow of the other bed. She had a hazy memory of being guided to her room by Jeff and Max last night.

She tiptoed out of the bedroom and into the kitchen. She found Sam and Jeff having coffee and watching the lake activities. "Good morning," said Sam. She moved to the counter. "How about a cup of coffee?"

"Thanks, sounds wonderful." She watched Sam doctor it with fat-free half and half and the natural sugar substitute Ellie favored. "You're amazing. Don't tell me you went to the store already."

Sam grinned. "Actually, Jeff went early this morning and got a few necessities."

Ellie took her cup and set it down next to Jeff. She looped both arms around him from behind his chair. "Thank you for taking such good care of me."

He smiled and patted her hand. "Are you ready for today?"

She slid into the chair next to him and Sam sat on the other side. "As ready as I can be. I feel a bit uncomfortable, not knowing Dani."

"You played an essential role in her life and you have nothing to be embarrassed about. You did the best you could and gave her the gift of wonderful parents," said Sam.

"That's why we all came with you today. You're not alone and don't need to feel awkward. We'll be with you," said Jeff.

Ellie finished her coffee and excused herself to get ready. When she emerged from the bathroom, the house had awakened and was bustling with activity. Jeff and Max were in the kitchen cooking breakfast for everyone. Uncle Bob was regaling them with stories while they worked.

Nate and Regi were enjoying their coffee on the deck. Ellie slipped outside and greeted them with hugs. "Sorry I missed you last night. I fell asleep early."

They were soon joined by Jen, fresh from her shower. Jeff hollered, "Breakfast is ready. Come and get it." They gathered around the huge dining room table and feasted on pancakes, eggs, and bacon.

One by one the group left the table to shower and dress. The service was at eleven o'clock and they arrived more than an hour early. The chapel was a quaint white Victorian home surrounded by lush grounds. A huge rose garden dominated the landscaping. One of the staff members greeted them on the porch and Jeff explained Ellie's relationship to Dani.

The quiet man directed Ellie to a pew reserved for family. She motioned her aunt and uncle to join her. The others slid into the pews behind the family section. A slide show filled a huge screen on the front wall. They were treated to photos of Dani as a baby and watched her grow throughout the years. She had excelled in art and was featured holding many of her drawings with ribbons and awards.

Ellie watched the pictures of Dani with her parents and others, whom she guessed were her grandparents, as a couple of dogs and school friends glided across the wall. Dani radiated happiness, despite her obvious illness in some of the photos.

The chapel was soon overflowing with friends and extended family members. People stood along the sides and in the back. An oversized picture of Dani, along with a number of her paintings and drawings were displayed on a table below the screen. Ellie fixated on an exquisite jade green urn and a glass sphere with a stunning swirl the color of emerald within it.

The slide show ended and the pastor stepped to the podium. He said a prayer and spoke about Dani's life, cut too short by an unrelenting disease.

After he spoke, Dani's uncle gave the eulogy. He shared cheerful anecdotes from her childhood and her love of books and art. He talked about Dani's strength throughout all the procedures she endured in the hope of curing her illness. He opened the floor to others and several teachers and classmates spoke of their love for Dani. Ellie noticed Dr. Jacobs standing along the side.

Ellie kept her hand tucked in Aunt Ginny's throughout the memorial. She dabbed at her eyes throughout the speeches and found those of Dani's friends most touching. As the remarks ended, the pastor urged the crowd to file by the first pew and pay their respects to the family. He invited the guests to attend a light luncheon reception in the adjacent room.

Ellie was thankful she was in the second pew. Throughout the service she tried to focus on the speakers and keep her eyes off the back of Dani's parents in front of her. April wept softly with Dan's arm around her. He wiped his eyes often, but April's body trembled the entire time.

Dani's parents stood as mourners filed by, offering hugs and condolences. Ellie waited in the pew and watched as her friends from Friday Harbor spoke to Dan and April. She was surprised when she sensed a hand on her shoulder and saw Izzy. "What are you doing here?"

Izzy whispered Blake had called and told her the news. She was only a couple of hours away and wanted to pay her respects. She hugged Ellie and said, "I'm going to get back home, but know I'm thinking of you. I'll catch up with you in a few weeks."

Over an hour later, family occupied the only pews in the sanctuary. Most of them filtered into the reception room, leaving Ellie the opportunity to speak with April and Dan.

First, she introduced Aunt Ginny and Uncle Bob, explaining she had come to live with them when she was pregnant. They both expressed their sympathy and made their way to the reception. Ellie took a seat next to April and the threesome stared at the photo of Dani.

"Thank you for letting me be here today," said Ellie. Her throat constricted and she swallowed trying to moisten it. "Thank you even more for giving Dani such a loving home. I wanted her to have a better life and seeing all this I know she did." They both gave her a weak smile. "I'm devastated I wasn't able to help her myself or find anyone to help. I'm so sorry." She swiped at the tears and choked on a sob.

"Dani told us how much she admired you. She was impressed you owned a bakery. She knew she was rough on you when she came to the island, but she was scared. She was happy you came to see her," said Dan.

April wiped her face with another tissue. "Thank you, Ellie. For giving us Dani. We loved her more than anything and will always be grateful to be her parents."

Dan moved to the display. "Dani wanted you to have this to remember her. It's a keepsake made from Dani's cremains."

The smooth cool glass filled Ellie's hand. "She told me green was her favorite color. It's mine too." She ran her fingers over the polished surface. "I'll treasure it always. Thank you."

Ellie hugged them both, unable to speak. She followed them into the reception and forced herself to fix a small plate of food. She glanced around the room and spotted her friends. She squeezed into the space they had saved her and picked at her lunch. She placed the green sphere on the table and told them about Dani's wishes.

The group found Dan and April and said their goodbyes before they left for the house. Ellie claimed a chair on the deck and spent the afternoon lazing in the sun and watching the early season boaters glide across the water. Occasional visits interrupted her solitude, but for the most part, her friends gave her privacy.

The guys manned the grill for dinner and served up chicken and steaks. They enjoyed a casual meal together before gathering around the fireplace. Ellie put in a call to Blake and thanked him for telling Izzy. He reported the dogs were having a grand time romping through Linda's yard and chasing each other. "I'm going to spend tomorrow night with my aunt and uncle and catch the ferry Monday. I'll be back at work Tuesday."

The grief and strain of the day left Ellie weary. She wished everyone goodnight and turned in early. Not wanting to chance forgetting Dani's glass sphere, she wrapped it in layers of clothes and tucked it in her suitcase.

She crawled into bed and wondered if she should have called Lance. She had no desire to speak to him, but reasoned a note would be appropriate to let him know about Dani's passing. With one problem solved, she shut her eyes and fell into a deep sleep.

* * *

They opted for an early start the next morning and stopped to eat on the road. They made it to Mt. Vernon close to the lunch hour. After a short respite at Bob and Ginny's, the group headed for the ferry. Aunt Ginny sent them with a care package of muffins and cookies she had in the freezer, along with hugs for all of them.

Ellie spent the rest of the afternoon and evening discussing the logistics surrounding vacating the old house and a subsequent yard sale. Prior to Dani's death, the cousins had arranged to be on the island this weekend, but had postponed it. They would be arriving at the end of the week. Bob and Ginny planned a trip in early summer to visit the property one last time.

Ellie offered to get in touch with Jack about listing the property and asking his advice on a price. Uncle Bob went to bed early and the ladies stayed up to watch a movie and continue their visit.

"We can't wait to get a look at your new house. I love the photos you sent, but want to see it for myself," said Ginny.

Ellie dashed from the kitchen where she was fixing a pot of tea. "I forgot to tell you what was waiting for me when I got back last week." Ellie went on to tell her about the guys moving her, the new patio furniture and grill, and her gorgeous mirror.

"I'm so glad you're surrounded by kind people. It makes us happy to know you're thriving. You deserve joy, Ellie."

Ellie smiled through her tears. "I never believed I was worth anything until I came to live with you and Uncle Bob. Watching the slideshow of Dani yesterday I saw how it should be. Her parents loved her and protected her. You and Uncle Bob did that for me."

"You, my dear, were definitely worth it. We couldn't love you more if you were our natural child. Ted and Caroline are the ones who lost out." She took a sip of tea. "You're building your life now— with your new home and new job. Grab all the adventures that come your way. You're no longer a sad teenager, lost and confused. You don't need the approval of your parents. What you've been through has only served to strengthen you." Ginny squeezed Ellie's hand in hers. "You're a smart and resilient young woman—one who will succeed in whatever she chooses."

* * *

The next morning Aunt Ginny drove to the ferry landing. Ellie dispensed fierce hugs before she followed the passenger walkway. Concern swept over her when she held Uncle Bob's frail body. "You need to rest up. I think we've worn you out traipsing all over Washington."

"I will, sweetheart. I plan to go home and take a nap. We'll be on the island for a visit before you know it." He embraced her one more time and planted a kiss on her cheek. "Love you, Ellie."

She looked for them when she went upstairs on the deck. They waved one more time and then walked arm and arm to the parking lot. While on the ferry, she sent Spence a text and asked for Lance's address. She planned to get a card in the mail as soon as possible.

She scrolled through her emails to check on things at the winery. Before she was done reading, the ferry pulled into Friday Harbor. She toted her suitcase downstairs and waited on deck for the docking process. Linda met her with Oreo in tow, and drove the pair home.

She unpacked, threw in a load of laundry, and pondered a spot for Dani's glass sphere. She placed it on her nightstand, liking the idea of remembering Dani each night before she went to bed. She took a few minutes to sit on the couch she now owned and soak in the atmosphere. Oreo was happy to join her and nestled close to Ellie. She'd spent so little time at home, she hadn't absorbed the accomplishment. When things quieted down, she swore she'd have a proper party to thank all her friends for the work they had done to help her get through these past few weeks.

She took a quick inventory of her fridge and cupboards and scrawled out a list. After tossing the clean clothes in the dryer, she took off for the winery. She planned to spend an hour getting organized for the coming days. Blake was gone by the time she arrived, so she had the place to herself. She looked through the stack of papers on her desk, replied to several emails, and read over the applications Blake had left for her review.

His handwriting was miserable, but she took the multiple stars on the sticky notes on two of the applications as his stamp of approval. She read through them and agreed they sounded like strong candidates. She put in a call to each of them to schedule an interview. They needed to have them on board and ready to roll by the first of May.

She ran through the event checklist for Blake's party one more time, noting the cake was her responsibility. She'd need to carve out some time to bake early the morning of the party. It was only two weeks away and the days between now and then were going to be demanding. She had made arrangements with Ethan to work Sunday, since Blake didn't know it yet, but he'd be tied up fishing.

The rooms were reserved at the Bed and Breakfast and Sherrie knew to keep it a secret. Blake's family was scheduled to arrive on Saturday night, while Blake would be busy at the winery. They vowed to stay out of sight until Blake was in the water. She grinned as she looked over the plan, knowing how shocked Blake would be to see his whole family.

She penned a concise message to Lance, letting him know about Dani's death and stuck it in the outgoing mail. She made sure the interviews were scheduled in Blake's calendar and led Oreo to the car. She dashed into town and filled her grocery list. By the time she returned home, she had to cycle the clothes through the dryer again to get rid of the wrinkles. She made a quick omelet for dinner and ate it on the deck. As she enjoyed the simple meal, she delighted in the backyard. The gentle tinkling sound of water calmed her while she took pleasure in the visual display of plants and flowers. It was peaceful and beautiful—and all hers.

The sky gathered darkness and she ignited the fire pit, enchanted by the graceful flames. She made a pot of tea and chose one of the quilts her aunt had made. Nestled in the corner of the couch, she sipped tea and gazed in admiration at the subtle illumination of her private sanctuary. The twinkle of white in the trees, the soft pools of light along the deck and pathways, and the gentle flicker of the fire bolstered her sprits.

Calmness and tranquility replaced the tension and fear that had plagued her mind and body over the last several weeks. Despite semi-healthy eating, her blood sugar numbers had been erratic. She vowed to add more exercise to her daily routine and take advantage of her new backyard to relieve stress. There was nothing more she could do for Dani. She had to move forward and concentrate on her own health. She gave herself permission to abandon the past. The anxiety of her parents always lurked in the back of her mind and she needed to put an end to it. Family, as in Aunt Ginny and Uncle Bob, friends, her new house, her new career, and her health were where she would focus her energy.

Twenty-four

The days at the winery rushed by in a blur. On the days she worked, she arrived early and took to walking the acreage for exercise. Some mornings, Blake joined her. Blake spent his working hours on the list of to-do items for the barn, while she handled the office. Fueled by warm weather, the weekend tastings were well attended. Tourists desiring to beat the crowds ventured to the island in April and early May. The tiny bridal boutique was set up and ready for business. All the linens, tables, chairs, and serving necessities had been delivered and inventoried.

Ellie, with Linda's guidance, recruited a crew of experienced servers to assist with events. They all had jobs in local restaurants, but had agreed to do events on their off hours. She slotted in those she would need for the weddings and events scheduled, including Blake's birthday.

Her cousins completed their work at the house and the movers packed and transported the furnishings. Ellie was left with odds and ends to sell at a yard sale. Regi helped her amass a few high school students to help and together they arranged everything in the large shop. She scheduled a cleaning service to get the house in shape to list with Jack's realty firm. Ellie knew her weekends would be busy starting in May, but couldn't squeeze the yard sale in any earlier. Regi and Nate came to her rescue and offered to handle the sale while she was at work.

Before she knew it, the weekend of Blake's party arrived and with it, his huge family. Amid a flurry of protests, Nate and Jeff convinced Blake to take Sunday off for a fishing expedition. Over dinner at Sam's one night

Nate said, "Come on, Blake, you're not going to get a weekend off all summer. You deserve one day of fishing with the guys before next weekend."

Blake hemmed and hawed, but finally caved to the pressure and agreed to the trip. The guys were tasked with keeping him at sea for the duration of the day and would bring him back in time to clean up for dinner at Linda and Max's house. In order to lure him to the winery for the surprise, Ellie would call him with a feigned emergency once he had a chance to dress for dinner.

Ellie was up at the crack of dawn to bake nine layers of rich chocolate cake batter. She needed three cakes to provide enough for the guests. She was in the midst of mixing the decadent frosting when Nate texted to let her know the boat had cleared the harbor. She finished assembling the cakes and put them in the fridge to chill. After a shower and a light breakfast she texted Izzy with the all clear signal.

She had been at the winery for less than ten minutes when the Griffin family arrived, in full force. Izzy made the introductions of her three sisters plus Henry, husband to Esther. She looked at the group and added, "Lauren's husband, Ken, is working and couldn't be here today." Ellie welcomed all of them.

Another car pulled in and parked and Izzy said, "It's Mom and Dad." She motioned them over and said, "Ellie, please meet Helen and Gene Griffin." By way of a greeting, Helen wrapped her in a hug and Gene smiled and sandwiched her hand between his. "Wonderful to meet you. Izzy's told us so much about you. Thank you for doing all this," said Helen.

Ellie considered the whole family as they formed a circle around her. Shannon, the youngest of the four sisters, stood out from the others. Her hair was a mass of frizzy braids. She paired a long loose floral skirt with a t-shirt emblazoned with a recycling logo and covered it all with a long net-like sweater. She topped off her ensemble with black combat boots. All the others wore jeans and shirts or blouses, looking ready for a day of work. Izzy appeared to be ready for a board meeting, albeit in jeans, but sported a gorgeous button down blouse and matching jewelry.

The four sisters, along with Henry and Gene, set up tables and chairs in the main section of the barn. Helen took charge of the table linens. Linda came through the barn doors with flowers and soon Regi, Kate, Sam, and Jen arrived to lend a hand.

Izzy took the liberty of introducing the group of friends to her family, proving to have an excellent memory. The group made quick work of the setup tasks. Ellie stood back to admire the festive space, smiling with satisfaction. "It looks terrific." The white tablecloths were decorated with simple fresh flowers, using blue accents. Ellie added a few candles to each table to enhance the ambience. She turned on the twinkly lights wrapped around the beams, followed by the chandeliers, and the strings of clear globe lights strung overhead. The glow added to the atmosphere and cheerful feeling of the space.

It was nearing two o'clock and Gene suggested he treat everyone to lunch in town. Ellie opted to stay and wait for the band to arrive for their sound check and rehearsal. She also needed to finish the ganache on the cakes and let them chill again. Izzy promised to return with a takeout lunch for her and led the spirited group to the harbor.

Ellie dashed home, finished the cakes, and checked on Oreo. Since all the dirty work was done, she changed into her party outfit. She'd done a bit of shopping after she sold the bakery van to a local plumber and found several new pieces for her work wardrobe. She had lost a few more pounds, which had done wonders for her waistline. She put on a pair of black jacquard pants and paired it with a raspberry silk shell. A cropped black jacket, a bit of silver jewelry and a pair of strappy black sandals finished off the ensemble. Using Jen's techniques, she put her hair up, added a bit of make-up, and some dangly silver earrings before heading back to the winery with the cakes in tow.

She stashed the chocolate masterpieces covered in mini peanut butter cups in the fridge and double checked the tables. Lou arrived to ready his buffet area, followed by the band. While they were in the midst of stringing cables across the stage area, the Griffins arrived. Izzy produced a salad and pint of soup for Ellie and made her sit to eat it.

The group sat and listened to the band run through a few numbers, clapping at the end of each song. During a brief silence Helen said, "Gene, dear, let's head back and everyone can get freshened up and changed." She turned to Ellie. "We'll be back before five and ready for the surprise."

Ellie gathered the remnants of her lunch and said, "Sounds perfect. All the guests will be here before five. I think we're on schedule and ready."

Izzy was visiting with Lou while helping him set up the buffet. Izzy's car was needed to transport the family, so Shannon offered to leave her Prius in the lot for Izzy to drive and caught a ride with her parents. Ellie retrieved some extra napkins from the closet upstairs and joined Izzy at the buffet tables. Izzy turned and said, "I'm staying a few extra days and would love to see your new house. Blake told me it's fantastic."

Ellie's radiant smile revealed her delight. "I love it. I'd be glad to have you visit. You could even stay with me, if you'd like."

"Oh, I wasn't trying to wangle an invitation." She paused and tilted her head. "It would be fun. Are you sure?"

"Yes, I'd love to have you. I'm technically off tomorrow, so plan to get settled in whenever you check out."

Lou's staff arrived with the servers Ellie scheduled for the event. She turned her attention to them and Izzy took her leave. "I'll hurry and change clothes. I'll be back in a jiffy."

Guests began to arrive and parked behind a storage building, so as not to pique Blake's attention when he was called to the winery. Ellie welcomed each of them to the barn and ushered them to the bar. Everyone was assembled, save for Blake's fishing buddies. The fictitious dinner was slated for six-thirty and the plan was to lure Blake to the party around five-thirty.

Izzy returned, decked out in a becoming off the shoulder top and black ankle pants. The cobalt blue of her shirt set off her eyes and her shoes were to die for—strappy heeled sandals embellished with tiny rhinestones. She looked much younger than Esther, wearing a plain dress, in a soft pink color. Helen chose a burgundy flowing pants outfit and Lauren wore a stunning lace covered dress in silver. When they all stood next to Shannon, the contrast was striking. Shannon's hair remained the same mess of braids and she'd kept her black combat boots. Over a different flowing skirt, she wore a long sweater with fuzzy threads of yarn sprouting all over it. Although the look was unflattering, Ellie admired her moxie—Shannon wasn't afraid to march to her own drummer.

Ellie's phone pinged with a text from Nate. *Just docked at the marina. Blake will be busy with the boat and we're all heading home to clean up.* She grinned and tapped in a quick reply. Izzy caught her eye and Ellie gave her a wink to let her know the plan was in action.

Ellie kept her eye on the clock and after twenty minutes, she stepped outside, away from the noise to make the call to Blake. She rehearsed it one more time before she poked the button. The phone rang and went to voicemail. She left a message to have him call and hung up. *Crap, he must be in the shower.* She took a slow stroll from the barn to the pavilion, waiting for her phone to ring. She could hear the hum of activity from the barn and knew she'd have to quiet them down.

Max and Spence drove by and hid their vehicles with the others. The fishing group, dressed in their party clothes, hurried to the barn. She gave them a wave and pointed to her cell phone. After a few minutes of gazing at the lush grounds and the restored barn, she heard the ringtone. Taking a breath she answered, "Hi, Blake. Sorry to bother you."

"No problem. I was in the shower when you called. What's up?"

"I stopped by work on my way to dinner to check on the inventory in the barn and noticed water on the floor. I think you better come and take a look. I'm not sure where it's coming from."

"Oh, shit. I've got to get dressed. Turn the valve off it you can. I'll be right there." His voice frantic, he added, "Give the plumber a call and find out if he's available. We may need him."

"Okay, will do. See you in a few." She hung up, satisfied he didn't suspect her subterfuge. She hurried back down the path to the barn and went to the stage.

She took the microphone from the stand and said, "Hey guys, could I have your attention." The chattering came to a stop and the group focused on Ellie. "Blake is on his way and thinks we have a water leak." The group chuckled. "So, let's all move along the walls over to this side." She pointed to the area. "I'm going to turn off the party lights, so he won't suspect anything. We'll need to be quiet until he gets inside." She glanced at the buffet table. "I can't do much to disguise the delicious aroma of Lou's food, but maybe Blake won't notice."

The group shuffled around the perimeter and Ellie took her place next to the door and the light switches. Once the guests were in position, she doused the party lights and turned on the usual overheads.

They didn't have to wait long before they heard the rumble of Blake's truck. The door slammed and he rushed to the barn. "Did you get in touch with Pete?" he asked, as he strode through the door.

Ellie said, "Yes, he said he'd be happy to come out." Little did Blake know, Pete was already in the barn.

As soon as Blake made the turn for the restroom area, Ellie flipped the switches and amid the twinkling lights, the crowd erupted with "Surprise."

The shouts stopped him midstride and he turned to look at them. His face broke into a wide smile when he realized his family was there. He rushed to his mom and lifted her off the ground in a hug. After embracing his dad, he did the same with all the sisters and Henry. Ellie watched the sheer amazement on Blake's face as he took in the group of friends. In a sea of laughter and hugs, he greeted each guest.

Izzy took to the stage and said, "Thank you all for coming. For those of you I haven't met, I'm Izzy, Blake's oldest sister. We wanted to wish him a Happy Birthday and also congratulate him on the opening of his beautiful winery and event space. Someone get him a glass of wine," she waited while he was handed a glass. "Please raise your glasses and join me in wishing my baby brother the happiest of birthdays." After sips were taken and wishes bestowed, she added, "I'd like to ask Ellie to join us." She motioned her to the stage.

Ellie's face reddened and her heart pounded. All eyes were on her as she made her way through the crowd. Blake took her hand as she stepped up the two small risers. "Our family is so proud of what Blake and Ellie have done here. They've worked tirelessly to develop this wonderful new venue.

Isn't it gorgeous?" Hoots and shouts of praise came from the guests.

"Join me in congratulating Ellie and Blake on a wonderful job. We wish you only happiness and success." Glasses clinked again, followed by a rumble of applause. "Lou is set up and ready to serve at the buffet table. We need someone to start the line. Please help yourself and fill your plates." The sounds of laughter and the movement of chairs mingled with the light notes of music from the band.

The mass of well-wishers meandered toward the food. Ellie played hostess, visiting with the guests and slipping behind the bar to help fill glasses. In deference to Jeff and many of the guys, she made sure they were stocked with a selection of beers, in addition to the Griffin wines and Island Winery vintages. She refilled the lemonade and iced tea decanters and visited tables to make sure guests were comfortable.

She leaned against one of the wooden supports and took in the activity. The candles flickered on the tables and with the canopy of lights overhead, it made for a magical setting. With a happy glow on his face, Blake was surrounded by his family in the buffet line. She sipped her tea, thankful for the cool breeze filtering in through the open doors.

She didn't hear Izzy approach and flinched when she touched her arm. "Sorry, Ellie. I want to make sure you sit next to Blake at the family table." She linked her arm in Ellie's. "Come get a plate and relax for a bit."

She let Izzy lead her through the maze of tables and slip her into the line in front of Blake. He turned and saw them. "There are two of my favorite girls now." He bent and gave each of them a quick brush on the cheek. "My sources tell me you two are the main culprits in charge of this shindig."

Izzy held up her hand. "I engaged Ellie's services, but all this is on her." She waved her hands across the expanse of the barn.

"It's a great way to test our party planning skills, don't you think?" asked Ellie.

He grinned and his eyes twinkled in delight. "You did a fabulous job, as always."

He gazed around the room as they inched forward. "I'll even forgive you for giving me a heart attack about the water leak. I fell for it, hook, line, and sinker. What a terrific surprise."

"Speaking of hooks, how was fishing today?" she asked.

"It was great. We had a fun time on the boat and perfect weather. This has been one of the best days I can remember." He put his arm around her. "Thanks for doing all this. I know it can't have been easy, with everything else you've been going through."

"You are most welcome. It was a pleasant distraction and working with Izzy was terrific. I'm glad you're having fun."

They reached the plates and Lou loaded them up with all of his tasty selections. Ellie convinced him to cut back on the portions for her plate, but he insisted she sample his creations.

They wound their way through the tables and slid into the chairs at the large family table. Ellie was overdue to eat and was beginning to feel a bit shaky. She dug into a crab cake and enjoyed a mound of fresh spinach salad. She took a bite of the crab macaroni and cheese and shoveled the rest onto Blake's plate. "I don't want to push my luck," she said. "My numbers have been better and I want to keep it that way."

He took a sip of wine and said, "I meant to tell you earlier, you look terrific tonight. Your hard work shows."

She blushed as she forked a bite of crab ravioli. "Thank you. I treated myself to a few new things to wear to work." She swallowed and added, "Izzy's going to stay at my house for a few days."

He rolled his eyes. "Are you sure? You don't need to do that."

"Yes, I'm sure. She's a cool big sister." She watched Shannon eat salad and roasted potatoes. "I didn't realize Shannon was a vegan. With all Lou's crab concoctions, I'm afraid there isn't much for her to eat."

He smirked. "She's a vegan at the moment. Shannon goes through…phases, let's say. She's living in Eugene now and working at a vegan café and volunteers at a food co-op, so she's immersed in the life." He laughed and added, "Good thing Mom and Dad support her with their greedy capitalistic money, or she'd be living in a cardboard box."

"You have to admit she's brave to risk being so different from all of you."

"Brave, but unrealistic. She's a hypocrite. She lectures us on the evils of money and business, but has no problem taking rent money my parents give her, not to mention her new car. A Prius, of course, but still." He shook his head.

"It was sweet of her to make the trip and come for your party."

"I guess. She grates on me. I work hard and she judges me, yet would be perfectly happy to sit in the park all day and listen to her granola friends play music. As long as Mom and Dad pay for everything."

She looked across the table at the dark haired beauty talking to Izzy. "Is Lauren married?" she asked, in an attempt to shift topics.

He smiled. "Yeah, she's married to a great guy, Ken. He's in insurance and had to go to a conference, so he couldn't come. They've been married about two years, I guess." He gazed at his two sisters. "I miss seeing her. Before she got married she hung out at the winery a lot."

She saw Esther and Henry in conversation with Blake's parents. "Esther is sweet, but a tad shy."

"Yeah, she's always been quiet. She's never worked and is a wonderful cook and homemaker. Henry's in banking and they're both on the reserved side, but steady and reliable."

Soon the servers cleared the dishes from the tables. Ellie excused herself to ready the cake. Blake gripped her arm as she stood. "Did you make my birthday cake?" He raised his brows.

"I sure did." She smiled and patted his hand. "I'll bring you the first piece."

She supervised the placement of the cakes amid the mobile table Linda had decorated with fresh flowers. She inserted a few cake sparklers in the top of one and added a knife and server to the table. After she lit the cheerful candles, one of the wait staff wheeled the table to the front, near Blake.

As soon as the guests saw the glow of the sparks, they quieted and watched. The band played the well-known tune and the entire room joined in and sang birthday wishes to Blake. The special sparklers extinguished on their own and Ellie cut the first few slices of her work of art. She made sure

Blake's slice was generous, but asked the servers to cut thin pieces to make sure they had enough cake to serve everyone.

He dug into the mountain of chocolate cake, separated by dense ribbons of whipped peanut butter frosting sprinkled with candy pieces. The whole thing was covered in a lavish coating of chocolate ganache. "Best. Cake. Ever. It's incredible."

She declined a piece of her own, but accepted the bite he offered. She let the decadent concoction linger in her mouth, enjoying the sweetness. She closed her eyes and swallowed. "It's quite yummy."

Praises were murmured as the guests devoured the entire cake. Blake made his way from table to table, visiting with friends and thanking them for their part in the surprise. The band began to play and several couples took to the dance floor. While Ellie supervised the wait staff in clearing tables and offering coffee and tea, she watched Kate and Spence glide across the dance floor, as if floating together.

She slipped into a chair to visit with Sam and Jeff and let out a sigh. "Tired?" asked Sam.

"Yeah, my feet are killing me. I'm not used to traveling in shoes like this," she held up a foot with the heeled sandal. "It's been a long day." She slipped out of her shoes and stretched her toes. She saw Blake and Lauren dancing and laughing. "But totally worth it."

"We had a great day fishing and from the look on his face, he had no idea what was waiting for him here," said Jeff. "You did a great job."

The band transitioned to a slower melody and Ellie felt a tap on her shoulder. Blake stood with his hand out. "Dance for the birthday boy?"

She made sure her feet were in her sandals and took his hand. "Only because it's your birthday." He led her to the dance floor as the first notes of Blake Shelton's "Home" filled the air.

As he slid his arm around her, he looked down and smiled. "Thanks for such a great party. I can't believe you did all this right under my nose."

"I'm glad we pulled it off. Your family wanted to do something special for you." She inhaled his clean scent as she rested her head against his collar. She relaxed as she let him lead her to the gentle words of song.

She gazed overhead and said, "You've done a great job with the barn. It's the perfect setting for a wedding. So romantic and dreamlike with all these lights. I can picture a bride and groom dancing here."

"You're the one with the lights." He tipped his head back and took in the clear glass bulbs strung in a zigzag pattern, along with the elegant chandeliers Ellie had chosen. "You're right though. It's totally romantic."

"Our first wedding's only a couple weeks away."

"She's the good bride, right? Not bridezilla."

Ellie laughed. "Yeah, but bridezilla has calmed down. I hope she stays that way." The song ended and she pulled away.

He drew her closer with a firm hand on her back. "One more. I'm having fun."

Despite her sore feet, she smiled and wrapped a hand around his neck, wishing he didn't smell so enticing.

Twenty-five

Ellie didn't get home until after midnight and took pleasure in sleeping in on Monday. Blake's family invited her to meet them for brunch before they left on the ferry. She eyed the clock and saw she had plenty of time to get ready for the blood draw appointment she had at the hospital. She longed for a cup of coffee, but settled for a cup of hot water and took it outside. While she sipped, Oreo bounced through the yard on her morning exploration ritual. The dog was acclimating to the smaller yard and finding her favorite spots.

Birds chirped as Ellie savored the view. She ran through a list in her head of the things she needed to complete for the upcoming yard sale. After brunch she planned to label and price items and stop by the bank to get some change. She needed to pick up a gift certificate from the Cliff House for Nate and Regi. She wanted to treat them to a special evening for their willingness to run the sale in her absence. A bird indulged her with a show as he bathed in a puddle while she finished drinking her water.

After getting ready, she checked the guest room and found it immaculate and ready for Izzy. She jotted down her list from memory and added a few groceries before heading to the harbor. She was in and out of the lab within minutes. With time to spare, she made a beeline for Sam's coffee shop. She made a point of walking by the bakery and ran into one of her old customers coming out the door. He toted a pastry box and told her she looked fantastic and he missed her. She thanked him and waved to a couple of other regulars before strolling to Harbor Coffee.

It was a pristine morning filled with sunshine and a light breeze. She visited with Hayley for a few minutes and then took her coffee to the deck. The warm brew revived her as she surveyed the harbor. She savored the taste and reflected on last night's party with a smile. It had been a wonderful evening full of fun and celebration.

She blushed as she recalled Blake's kiss at the end of the evening. He'd been drinking wine all night. She and Izzy were the last ones in the barn. She gave him a hug goodbye and in turn, he kissed her right on the mouth. A long and hungry kiss. In his tipsy state, he didn't possess the necessary sense to apologize or even appear ashamed at his boldness. She was embarrassed, but didn't say anything. She was anxious to see if he remembered it in the morning.

She finished her coffee and wandered to the Front Street Café. The Griffin crew occupied a huge table on the patio. She took the chair to which Blake gestured, next to him. He greeted her with, "Morning, Ellie." No mention was made of the smooch he had bestowed.

Over the clatter of dishes and silverware, the siblings joked and teased each other. They raved about the party and the new venue. "Now with the winery in shape, you need to do something about the house. I hate to think of you living on that boat," said Helen.

"I will, Mom. I'm fine, don't worry." He reached for her hand and gave it a gentle squeeze.

She focused her attention on Ellie. "Blake tells me you have your first wedding in a few weeks."

"Yes, I'm excited. It was perfect to have the party last night. It gave us the opportunity to rehearse for our first real event. It's a small wedding, so I'm not too concerned. We have a large one in June, which may prove more challenging."

"I'm sure you two will handle it well. All your friends told me the tourist season picks up around Memorial Day. I imagine you'll have a fruitful summer."

Gene plucked the ticket from the waiter's hand. "It's on me." He dug into his wallet for his credit card and added, "Helen and I told Blake he needs to bring you to visit our winery. Maybe after harvest when things die down a bit?"

"That would be lovely. I'm sure I'd enjoy it."

Lauren, who was seated next to her father, whispered in his ear. "Hey, everybody, quiet down, Lauren has something to say."

Lauren looked around the table and took a deep breath. "Ken wanted to be here when I told you, but I'm not sure we'll all be together soon." She smiled and blurted, "We're going to have a baby."

Helen brought her hand to her chest and Gene kissed Lauren on the forehead. The excitement raised the chatter to a new level. Blake strode to Lauren's chair and lifted her out of it, spinning them both in a slow circle. "I can't wait to be a new uncle."

She was due in December and Lauren promised to let them know the sex of the baby when they had the tests in the coming months. Tears sprang from Helen's eyes as she hugged Lauren. Blake whispered to Ellie, "They've been trying to get pregnant for a year. They weren't sure it would happen, so it's exciting."

The group dispersed when Blake reminded them they had to get in line for the ferry. After hugs and kisses from the family, Izzy stood with Blake and Ellie as they waved goodbye from the dock.

Izzy was going to spend a few hours with Blake at the winery and made plans to meet at Ellie's house in the late afternoon. Ellie made quick work of her errands. After dropping groceries at home, she and Oreo drove to the old house.

While she trudged through pricing objects, Oreo rocketed for the pond and spent her time leaping through the meadow. Hours later, covered in dust, Ellie finished the task. She hollered for Oreo, who came running and they took off for home.

She took another shower to wash the grime away and made a fresh pitcher of iced tea. She heard the bell ring from her perch on the deck and found Izzy and Blake at the door. Izzy tilted her head and said, "He insisted on coming."

He toted her suitcase and garment bag to the guest room. Ellie gave Izzy the grand tour. "What a terrific place." She followed Ellie outside. "Oh, this is even lovelier than Blake described."

Blake tossed a ball for Oreo while Ellie fixed iced teas. After a never ending game of fetch, Blake plopped into a chair. "I forgot to mention, we went for coffee at Sam's this afternoon. She invited all of us to come tomorrow night for dinner. Jeff's going to grill the fish we caught."

"Speaking of dinner, I picked up some chicken to grill. Would you care to join us, Blake?"

"I never refuse a home cooked meal." He laughed as Oreo nudged him with the ball. "I'm worn-out, girl." He petted her head.

Ellie gestured for Oreo to leave him alone. "I think I'll put you to work on the grill, if you don't mind." She stood and said, "I'll get started on a salad, if you'll light the flame."

They enjoyed a simple meal on the deck and turned on the fire as the sun dipped into the water, taking with it the streaks of gold and orange light. Izzy took great delight in the garden lights and Ellie made a pot of tea to share. "I understand why Blake raved about this. What a serene place to spend your evenings," said Izzy.

"I thought I'd miss the old place, but it didn't take me long to adapt. I'm glad it came with so much furniture. It made it easy to move in and feel right at home."

"I've got meetings in Seattle starting on Wednesday, so if it's okay I'll stay through tomorrow night. I'm taking the early ferry Wednesday," said Izzy.

"That works for me. I've got a doctor's appointment tomorrow. It won't take long and I'm sure you'll figure out how to entertain yourself."

"We could put her to work," said Blake, with a laugh. They heard the sound of a cell phone over his laughter.

Izzy pulled hers from her pocket and excused herself to take the call inside.

Through the glimmer of the flames, Blake caught Ellie's eye. "So," he said, looking to the side and lowering his voice. "I, um, sort of remember maybe, uh, kissing you last night."

She said nothing, taking a bit of pleasure in his discomfort. She hid the smirk on her face by taking a sip from her mug.

"So, anyway, I'm sorry. I think I drank too much wine last night." He paused and waited for her to respond, but all he heard was the sound of water trickling over rocks in the garden. "I apologize, if you were offended."

Izzy came around the corner and joined them. Ellie gave Blake a knowing smile and said, "I wasn't offended."

His eyes widened and he suppressed a laugh. Izzy looked at one and then the other. "What did I miss?"

"Nothing," they both said in unison.

A chill saturated the air and rather than retrieve a quilt, Ellie chose to turn in for the night. "You're welcome to stay and enjoy the evening. I'm pooped from my day of yard sale prep. I'll see you in the morning."

Ellie fell asleep as soon as her head rested against the pillow. She woke early and elected to take Oreo for a walk through the neighborhood. They walked all the way to Max and Linda's driveway. They detoured at the Harbor Resort to let Oreo leap through the water. Ellie sat on a bench and listened to the soft lap of the water as she watched the dog delight in the game. On the way back, her cell rang.

"Hi, Aunt Ginny." As she listened her hand began to shake and her legs trembled. The color drained from her face and she looked for a place to sit. She leaned against a tree for support as she listened to her cousin calling from her aunt's phone.

"I'm so sorry, Stan." Her voice faltered as she continued the conversation. "Tell Aunt Ginny I'll work on things here on the island. I'm happy to come to Mt. Vernon if she needs anything." She listened for a few more moments and then added, "Please tell her I'll call her later tonight."

She disconnected and clutched her stomach, while she slid down the trunk of the tree, coming to rest on the dew soaked ground. Oreo sensed her distress and leaned against Ellie, whining. The sobs came from deep within her chest and tears streamed down her face with abandon. At that moment she sensed the hole in her heart would never heal.

* * *

She didn't remember the walk home. She stumbled through the door and found Izzy in the kitchen reading the paper. Izzy looked up from the article she was reading, saw the ashen color of her face, her vacant look, and her dirty clothes. She rushed to Ellie. "What's wrong? What happened?"

Ellie's throat was tight and dry, her face leached of color. She croaked out, "Uncle Bob." Izzy filled a glass with water and made Ellie take a drink. She led her to the table and put gentle hands on her shoulders to lower her into the chair. "He's gone."

Izzy furrowed her brow. "What happened?" She pulled her chair close and kept her hand on Ellie's.

Ellie took another sip from the glass. Despite the waterworks from her eyes, there was no moisture in her mouth and her throat tightened. "Aunt Ginny found him on the steps this morning. He was already gone by the time the ambulance arrived. Heart attack they think."

Izzy hugged Ellie to her and felt her body heave and shake as she wept. "I'm so sorry, sweetie," she whispered. She continued to hold her until the sobs quieted. "How about you take a shower?"

Ellie let Izzy guide her to the master bath. Izzy hung her robe on a hook and turned on the shower. "I'm going to call Linda and Max. If you need something, yell for me."

Ellie cried while she let the hot water cascade over her. The drumming of the water masked her sobs. She planted her palms on the smooth tile and let her aching head rest against the wall. She had to pull herself together. Aunt Ginny wanted his memorial on the island he adored, where she would scatter his ashes. She turned and tilted her head so the spray would hit her face, hoping the warmth would relieve her stuffy nose.

Ideas tumbled through her mind as she considered venues for the memorial. As she dried her hair with a towel, she decided it would be best to call Blake and ask if he'd let her do it at the winery. They didn't have any events booked until the middle of May, so she could make it work.

She wrapped herself in her fluffy robe and found Izzy in the kitchen making eggs. She took the plate Izzy offered and poured herself a cup of coffee. She sat and after her first bite, slammed her hand on the counter.

"Damn, I forgot I have a doctor's appointment."

"Oh, don't worry. I called Linda and Max said he'd stop by the house. He said he had your test results and everything was fine. They're both coming over this morning."

Ellie let out a sigh and ate a few more bites. Izzy joined her and said, "I called Blake to let him know and he said not to worry about work."

Ellie nodded. "Stan, my cousin, said Aunt Ginny wants me to work on a memorial here for Uncle Bob. She wants to scatter his ashes here." Tears moistened her eyes as she took a sip from her mug. "I'm going to ask if Blake will let me have it in the barn."

"Oh, I'm sure he would."

"With the season opening, we're going to be busy. I need to find out how soon Aunt Ginny wants to do something."

"It would be a wonderful tribute to your uncle to have it in the new barn you've spent so much time creating. I'm sure we could work it all out. I'm happy to stay on and help at the winery, if need be."

Ellie smiled and said, "That's kind of you, Izzy. I appreciate it." She excused herself to get dressed.

As soon as Izzy tidied the kitchen the doorbell rang. Max and Linda greeted her with a hug. "How is she?" asked Linda.

"Shocked. Her aunt wants a memorial on the island, so she's preoccupied with all of those tasks right now." She offered them coffee. "She's in her room."

Max took his bag and knocked on her bedroom door. "Ellie, it's Max. May I come in?" He heard a mumbled response and opened the door. She was dressed and sitting in a chair, petting Oreo.

After expressing his condolences, he went about taking her vitals and blood pressure. He smiled when he told her what a terrific job she'd been doing with her diet. "I've been logging all my numbers." She connected to the app on her phone and showed him the statistics. "I'm sure today my blood pressure is up, but it's been better. I wanted to incorporate more exercise. I was walking this morning." Tears welled in her eyes. "That's when I got the call about Uncle Bob."

Max sat on the bed facing her. "I know how hard it is to lose someone you love. I don't think the void left is ever filled. It sounds cliché, but in time the pain subsides. You'll think of Uncle Bob each day for months or years and then somewhere down the road you'll go a whole day without thinking of him. That's when the healing begins."

"I thought of him as my dad. He saved me. I owe him and Aunt Ginny everything." Silent tears streaked her cheeks.

"Children deserve to be loved and protected. He did that for you. He loved you. I'm sure they didn't look at it as if you owe them anything."

Ellie wiped her eyes and nodded. "Thanks, Max."

He turned his attention back to her chart. "It's important, especially in times of stress, to stick to your good habits. Eat healthy meals and exercise. Don't skip any meals. You're doing great." He eyed the lab report. "If you increase your exercise a bit, I think you'll get these numbers in the lower range, which would be ideal."

"It's been getting easier…until today. For years, I've dealt with stress by baking. Right now I feel an incredible urge to get in the kitchen and whip up some treats."

Max smiled. "As long as you give them away, it won't be a problem." He closed the cover on her file and grinned. "I know several guys who'd be happy to take them off your hands." He put a hand on her shoulder. "You're going to get through this. If you need anything you call one of us, day or night. We'll be here."

He left her to finish getting ready and joined Linda and Izzy on the deck. They gave him a questioning look and he nodded in return. In a low voice he said, "She's okay. I think we need to keep an eye on her. We may have to remind her to eat and not let her spend too much time alone."

They heard the gate open followed by Blake rounding the corner. "How's Ellie doing?"

Max filled him in and Izzy brought him a mug of coffee. Izzy revealed Ellie's idea about having the memorial at the winery. "I'm staying tonight, but have to leave on the early ferry tomorrow. I could come back if you need help at the winery," she said.

"It depends on how Ellie feels about working." They continued talking in hushed tones, so as not to disturb Ellie. "It might be better for her to be at work and have a distraction than to sit here alone all day," said Blake.

They heard footfalls and saw Ellie come through the door. Blake rose and enveloped her in a hug. "Is there anything I can do?" he asked. "Izzy told me about the memorial and it's fine to have it at the winery. Whatever you need."

She felt safe in his firm hold and whispered her thanks. "I'll call my aunt later and find out what time frame she's thinking of for the service. If it's not right away, I'll probably make the trip over to visit her for a few days."

He released her and led her to join the others gathered around the patio table. Max gave Ellie a hug before leaving for his office, while Linda remained and brought a tray of tea to the table. The foursome discussed the best dates for a memorial and Ellie scribbled notes. After finishing a cup of tea, she went in her bedroom to call her aunt.

Linda and Izzy went to the kitchen in search of the makings for lunch. As they were eyeing the contents of the fridge, Jeff and Sam came through the door toting bags from Soup D'Jour. While the group sorted through containers of soups, salads, and sandwiches, Ellie emerged from her bedroom.

After hugs from Sam and Jeff she settled into a chair with lunch. "Aunt Ginny likes the idea of doing the service next week on Tuesday. It gives me a week to get it planned." She raised her brows at Blake.

"Totally doable," he said. All her friends nodded in agreement.

"Linda can do the flowers. They love Lou, so I'd like him to do the food." She took a spoonful of the soup, letting the warmth ease her throat. "Jeff, could you talk to Pastor Mark for me? They always attended your church and I know Uncle Bob would like him to officiate."

Jeff assured her he would call and let her know. Ellie planned to have The Flaky Baker do some cupcakes and cookies. After airing her concerns about dealing with Connie's crankiness, Blake offered to call the owner directly.

"I hate to put it on you, but I'm not sure I could take her attitude right now."

"Make a list of what you want and I'll handle it."

She jotted a note and handed it to him. "Here you go. Thanks for doing this and for letting me use the barn."

Sam made a list while they talked so all the items for the service would be covered. Before Blake left to go back to work, Sam invited everyone to dinner at her house. "Spence and Kate will come and so will Regi and Nate. Jeff's going to swing by and talk to Jen, but I'm sure she'll be there." Ellie felt the sting of new tears, but this time they were of happiness.

Twenty-six

After a lovely dinner and the comfort of friends, Izzy drove Ellie home. They sat by the fire pit and visited, until the fatigue of the day caught up with Ellie. She slept, comforted by Izzy's presence.

Sad to see her pseudo-big sister leave in the morning, Ellie elected to go to work. She kept busy catching up on mail and focusing on the details of the upcoming wedding. She fielded a call from Lou confirming the food for the memorial service. The funeral home in Mt. Vernon had been in contact with Blake to follow up on the logistics and Pastor Mark had confirmed.

She looked over her list, amazed things had come together overnight. She and Blake made a lunch from the groceries in the kitchen. While they ate, he told her Milt at The Flaky Baker was happy to handle the order for her uncle's funeral. He assured Blake they would have the order delivered to the winery early Tuesday morning.

After lunch she received three more bookings for summer events and got to work on her checklist for each of them. The phone rang as Ellie was ready to close the office. It was Nicole from the bakery calling to express her sympathy and let her know Milt put her in charge of Ellie's order.

They chatted for a few minutes and Ellie promised to call her and catch up over coffee soon. "Thanks so much for calling, Nicole. I'll see you next week."

She sighed and turned around to find Blake waiting behind her. "How about dinner tonight? I'll cook at your place."

"I was about to say, I'm too beat to go out. A meal I don't have to cook or go to sounds perfect. I'm not sure what I have, but I know I have the makings of a salad in the fridge."

"Don't worry. I'll bring everything I need. I'll see you in about an hour." He locked the door after her.

She and Oreo made it home and she put in a call to Aunt Ginny. Oreo cruised the perimeter of the yard while Ellie lounged on the deck, talking. Aunt Ginny was a bit weepy, but happy to hear about the plans for the service. All of her children were staying at the house, so she had a lot of company.

"I love you, Aunt Ginny. I'll meet you at the ferry on Monday and book the rooms you need. Talk to you soon." She hung up as Oreo bolted for the door.

Blake stood laden with bags from the market. She helped him unload things into the fridge. "I think you went a little overboard for one meal, don't you?"

"I didn't want you to have to worry about shopping for a few days."

"That's thoughtful of you." She plucked out two containers of no sugar added ice cream. "Oh, this looks yummy."

"I hope you can have it."

She checked the label. "Yeah, I can. Not every night, but for a treat." She finished putting the groceries away. He fixed them both iced teas and insisted she sit on the deck and relax while he put the meal together.

She took advantage of the quiet and called Sherrie to book rooms at the Bed and Breakfast. She found four rooms there and The Lighthouse near the harbor had the other four she needed. Blake came through the door to light the grill as she hung up the phone.

While they waited for the grill to warm up, they talked about the upcoming weekend. "I meant to tell you, Jeff's friend with the band wants to book a concert in the pavilion in June or July. I told him we'll waive the rental fee and tag along on his promotion. I think it'll be a popular event. They're going to try to get a prominent musician to come. We'll see how much luck they have, but I think it will get some people out to the winery." He retrieved the salmon from the kitchen and put it on the grill.

She helped him set the table and said, "I didn't tell you, I booked three more events, so every weekend in June is full. We'll have to target July for the concert."

He smiled and wiggled his brows. "Great news. When things settle down we need to finalize the Harvest Festival for September."

"I know. I've got the mockups done, but we need to nail down the details. Then there's the holiday season."

He went back to his kitchen duties and returned with a salad and brown rice risotto. He opened a bottle of wine and checked the salmon. A few minutes later he ushered Ellie to the table. She clinked her iced tea with his wine glass and thanked him for dinner. She took a bite of the risotto and said, "This is scrumptious."

"Thank my mom. I called her and asked for a healthy side dish to go with the salmon."

"You outdid yourself. It's all tasty."

After dinner he lit the fire pit for her so she could relax while he cleaned up the dishes. While he toiled in the kitchen she fielded calls from Linda, followed by Sam and Regi, all checking in on her. She collected her mail, which she had forgotten for the last few days.

She sifted through the junk mailers and saw an envelope from Ceci. It was postmarked at the end of last week. She ran her finger under the flap and opened it to find an attractive floral card. Dusk was chasing the sun into the ocean, so she squinted to read the handwritten note on all sides of the card. By the time Blake returned with ice cream, tears were streaming down her cheeks.

The cheerfulness on his face dissolved into worry as he set the ice cream down and hurried to her side. "What's wrong?"

She pointed to the card and let him read it. He scanned it, moving to the doorway to enhance the readability. He closed the card and sat beside her. "Her timing sucks all the way around."

Ellie nodded, lips tight. He picked up the bowls of ice cream. "Eat this, it'll help." She took the spoon and slid a bite of it into her mouth. He did the same. "Not bad for no sugar."

They sat, spooning in the frozen dessert and letting the twinkle of lights and the flicker of flames do their magic. Darkness enveloped the space and without a moon, the garden lights were more brilliant. She finished and wiped her eyes with her napkin.

Blake gripped her hand in his. "She's trying to say she's sorry for what happened to Dani. I know it isn't enough. It'll never be enough, but it's all she can do at this point."

Ellie squeezed his hand. "I wish she would have stood up to Mom sooner. If Ceci had a backbone, Dani would still be alive."

He continued to hold her hand. He felt the vibrations hum through her body. "My mother is hideous and cruel. How many lives does she get to ruin? If someone had to die, why the hell couldn't it be her? Who would miss her? Oh, I forgot, Teddy, of course. She's created another waste of a human being in him. My dad's a complete moron to stay with her all these years." She used the tattered napkin to wipe her eyes again. "Maybe he hates me too, like she does." She stood and paced around the seating area. "It's not enough she destroyed my childhood, but she's still screwing things up for me."

She plopped back down on the cushion. "Poor Aunt Ginny, the only real mother I've known, has to go through this. I love her so much, but I don't want to intrude. Her real kids are with her and I feel like an outsider with them. They look at me like the pitiful stray their parents took in. All of this is so unfair and it all leads back to my despicable mother and my pathetic excuse for a father. I used to fantasize she'd die from some horrid disease and my dad could find someone who was kind to him. How come people like her never suffer a consequence and people like Dani and Uncle Bob are dead?"

After her tirade, she let her head slump onto Blake's shoulder. The grief that weighed on her over Dani's death coupled with the anguish of losing Uncle Bob drained every ounce of energy from her. She'd been teetering on the edge of a cliff and Ceci's card had sent her spiraling into the abyss. Tasks had served to distract her, but here in the quiet shadows, the dark waters of despair and anger threatened to submerge her.

He slipped his arm around her and she tucked her legs into the curve of the couch. "Your aunt might like to come and stay with you after this is over. I think it's always harder for people who've suffered a loss after family leaves. She'll need the support in the coming weeks and months."

She sighed and said, "She'd like that, I think. I'll mention it when she's here." Her eyes were puffy from crying and she shut them, embracing the stillness. Within minutes the gentle sounds of the garden lulled her to sleep.

He knew she needed her rest and hated to wake her. As it got later, the air chilled. He tugged the quilt she'd relegated to the back of the cushions and covered them both. She stirred, but only nestled closer. He watched the flames until his eyes grew heavy and closed.

* * *

Hours later he flinched in his sleep and woke. He couldn't make out the time on his watch, but knew it was late from the crisp, still air. He scooched out from under Ellie and with gentle hands lifted her. Her eyes fluttered open and then shut.

He took slow steps through the house to the master bedroom and set her atop the bed. He covered her with the quilt and tucked it around her shoulders. She grabbed his arm and whispered, "Don't go."

Oreo had followed them indoors and was in her dog bed next to Ellie. He looked at the dog, hoping for guidance. He tiptoed through the house, locked the doors, and doused the lights. After taking off his shoes, he padded back to the bedroom. He spied the recliner in her room and dragged another quilt off the back of it. He sat with care and worked the mechanism, gritting his teeth as he waited for it to squeak. The noise didn't disturb Ellie, so he pushed the back to fully recline.

His back was sore from sleeping outside and the recliner was more comfortable than he expected. It was four in the morning, leaving him only a few hours to suffer.

* * *

Ellie sensed the soft slivers of dawn through her eyelids. She opened her eyes and saw Oreo nestled in her bed. She pulled the quilt up and noticed she was dressed and on top of her bed. Confused, she frowned and propped herself up against a mound of pillows. She saw Blake sprawled in her chair.

She stifled a gasp and crept out of bed. Oreo sprang from her own bed and followed Ellie to the kitchen. She put a pot of coffee on to brew and recalled last night. The outburst about her parents and utter fatigue that followed came back to her. She had a vague recollection of Blake carrying her and surmised he must have been concerned about leaving her alone.

She settled in with her coffee and let Oreo roam outside. She decided to fix omelets and let Blake sleep until they were ready. As soon as she had them plated, he rounded the corner. "Morning, Ellie."

She looked up and said, "I've got breakfast ready."

"Smells great," he said, helping himself to coffee. He took a chair next to her at the island countertop. "I wasn't sure what to do last night. I hope you're not creeped out I slept in the recliner."

She laughed. "Sorry I was such a spaz last night."

"When I carried you to your room, you said not to go, so I thought I'd better stay close. How are you feeling this morning?"

She blushed as she shoveled a bite into her mouth. "I feel better. Sorry, I think I was half asleep and probably wasn't making much sense. Thanks for watching over me."

"Anytime." He stuffed a wedge of toast in his mouth. He finished his plate and said, "If you need to take today off, I can handle things." He collected his dishes and put them in the sink.

She shook her head. "No, I'm fine. I need something to do." She took a gulp of coffee. "I'll meet you at work."

"Okay, I'm gonna get cleaned up. See you there." He gave her a wave and headed out the door.

* * *

After Blake grabbed a shower and changed he stopped by the hardware store. He found what he needed and saw Jeff at the back counter. "Hey, how's it going?"

Jeff looked up from his paperwork. "Oh, hey, Blake. Ready for Friday?"

Blake nodded. "I think so."

"How about a coffee? I was about to head across the street."

Blake checked his watch. "Um, okay. I can spare a few minutes." He signed the charge slip for his purchase and followed Jeff to Sam's coffee shop.

They ordered and took a seat at a table. Sam was busy baking in the back and shouted out a greeting to them. Jeff took a sip from his cup and said, "So, did your truck break down at Ellie's last night?"

Blake choked on his drink and sputtered coffee on the table. He coughed and said, "Uh, no. I made her dinner and then she got worked up over her uncle and Dani again. She had a meltdown and then collapsed. She asked me not to go, so I slept in the recliner."

Jeff's eyes narrowed and he nodded. "Ellie's like my own sister. I don't want her hurt by anyone. She's had enough pain in her life for twenty people. What are your intentions with her?"

Blake's eyes widened. "Wow, you get right to the point. Number one, I would never hurt Ellie. I know she's been through a lot and right now she's fragile."

"And vulnerable."

He nodded. "I have feelings for Ellie, but I'm not sure she's even looking for any kind of a relationship. We're friends and work together. We spend a lot of time with each other. Izzy likes her and thinks she's great. I think she's great. She's strong and smart. I'd like to think we could move beyond friends someday, but I'm not going to rush it. I was hoping it would come about naturally."

Jeff's serious lips turned up with a hint of a smile. "Smart plan. Remember she's special." He stood and smacked Blake on the back. "Good talk."

Blake looked up and said, "How'd you know I was there?"

"Small town. Newspaper delivery comes by early in the morning."

Blake laughed and nodded. "Got it." He grabbed a coffee to go for Ellie and followed Jeff to the sidewalk. The two men waved as Blake climbed inside his truck.

Ellie was on the phone when he arrived. He set her coffee in front of her and she mouthed her thanks. He jumped into the golf cart, followed by Oreo, and headed to the vineyard.

Nate arrived with a delivery as Blake was returning from checking the old home, which was the next project. He met the brown box truck at the storage building. As Nate hefted the boxes from the truck onto his dolly, he quizzed Blake about being at Ellie's this morning.

Blake grinned and said, "Jeff grilled me about the same thing already this morning."

"I think of Ellie as my little sister and look out for her when I can. It's important to me that she be treated well."

"Like I told Jeff, I cooked her dinner last night and she got upset when she opened a card from her sister. I stayed outside with her until she fell asleep. Well, uh, we both fell asleep. I carried her inside and she asked me to stay, so I slept in the recliner."

Nate put his foot on the dolly and steered it inside. "No funny stuff, then?"

Blake shook his head. As with Jeff, he explained he had feelings for Ellie beyond friendship, but hadn't acted on them. "I'm taking it slow, waiting for things to develop. I'd never harm her." He acknowledged she was in a fragile state and vowed to do nothing to upset her.

"Sorry, man. She's been dealt a shitty hand and we want to protect her from any more distress. She's a great person and deserves to be happy." He handed Blake the signature board. "We think you're a great guy. Just don't hurt her."

The two shook hands and Nate drove away to his next stop. Blake shook his head and looked at Oreo, resting on a pallet. "What? Are you going to lecture me about your mom next?" Oreo cocked her head and gave a low growl in reply.

Twenty-seven

A steady stream of visitors at the winery kept Ellie busy through the weekend. Along with Ethan, they had hired two other staff members for the busy season. Nate and Regi reported success with the yard sale and dropped off a cash box to Ellie Sunday afternoon.

"There are only a few odds and ends left. I could load them up and take them to the donation center," offered Nate.

"That would be terrific, if you find the time. There's no rush at this point. The house is cleaned and ready to show. Jack's got the listing paperwork and I'm going to have Aunt Ginny sign it when she's here." She hurried to the office to lock up the cash box and retrieve the gift for them.

Along with a lavish dinner at the Cliff House, she presented them with a case of wine, tied with a huge ribbon. "I can't begin to thank you," Ellie said, as tears threatened. "I'll be forever grateful."

Regi gave her a hug, followed by Nate. "It's what friends are for," he said, wrapping his arm around her. He hefted the box of wine and they snaked through the busy tasting room, leaving Ellie to finish her day.

Ellie rang out the register while Blake ran through the cleaning procedures with one of the new staff members. While she was making out the deposit, he stood in the doorway. "I think we deserve pizza tonight. How about I pick some up and bring it by your place?"

"Sounds better than foraging for something in the fridge. I better get a veggie on thin crust."

He phoned in the order and took the deposit to make on his way to Big

Tony's. When she got home she changed clothes and gathered table settings for outdoor dining. She counted out the yard sale cash and put the money in an envelope, surprised at the handsome total.

Oreo announced Blake's arrival. She put the salad in a bowl and he toted the pizzas outside. Ellie rested her feet on one of the chairs while she ate. "Feels great to sit and relax for a bit."

"I'm exhausted, but it was a lucrative weekend." They continued discussing work and the new staff. "Tomorrow Ethan and I will get the barn set up for the service. I want you to stay home and focus on your family. We'll have everything ready for Tuesday."

"I was planning to set up in the morning. They won't be here until the afternoon."

He shook his head. "No, you stay home and relax or do something you enjoy." He reached for her hand. "Please let me help you."

She let out a deep breath. "It's hard to accept help. I'm used to doing things for myself."

He stroked her arm with his fingers and tightened his grip on her hand. "Maybe you need to reconsider your stance." He pulled her to her feet and put his arm around her. "Let's sit by the fire."

They sat side by side on one couch and Oreo hopped onto another. Ellie sighed and tightened her lips. "I'm afraid to rely on anyone. It took me a long time to trust Aunt Ginny and Uncle Bob. They made it easy, but I was fearful if I got attached, I'd have to leave or they'd leave me. I never considered myself part of my family when I was growing up. I was an outsider. I was rejected to the point I was abandoned. So, I guess, I don't know, it's hard to explain."

"It's your form of self-protection. Don't get attached and then you can't get hurt again. I get it."

The light of day had slipped away and with it came the comfort of darkness. With only the flicker of the flames and the garden lights, it was easier for her to reveal her feelings. "Yeah, I think you're right. If I don't care about someone, they can't hurt me."

"Don't you get lonely?"

"Sometimes." She stared across the yard. "But it's better than the pain of rejection. I worry if I make a mistake or do something wrong, I'll be dumped. The stress of being perfect is too much."

He hooked his arm around her shoulders and she leaned her head against him. "You don't have to be perfect. You have a close-knit group of friends. Jen, Jeff, Linda, Nate. They've all known you for years and you've remained attached to them."

She nodded her head against his chest. "Yeah, but there's a part of me I never shared. None of them knew the reason I came to the island or that I had a baby. I was terrified I'd be cast aside, so I hid anything that might be objectionable."

"We all know now and nobody ran away, did they?"

She felt a tear slide off her cheek onto his shirt. "I guess."

He chuckled and said, "Nate and Jeff think of you as a sister. I can vouch for that."

"What do you mean?"

He explained about the visit from both of them and the questions about staying the night at her house. "Apparently the island has its own information superhighway."

She felt her face flush, thankful for the dimness of the night. "Oh, boy. Sorry you were subjected to the interrogations." She laughed and added, "It's comforting to know they're looking out for me."

"They wanted to know my intentions."

"Hmm. What did you say?"

He twisted a strand of her hair around his finger. "I told them I had feelings for you that went beyond friendship, but I'd been a gentleman."

"After everything you know about me, you're still attracted to me?"

He sighed with exasperation. "None of those things matter, Ellie. You're an incredible person. Honest, smart, hardworking, kind. Not to mention beautiful. All the things you've been through make you who you are. I love spending time with you."

"I enjoy your company too. I find you downright charming. Do you think it's a wise idea to, uh, escalate our friendship with you being my boss?"

"I've given it a lot of thought. I even consulted an attorney."

She laughed and tilted her head. "So you talked to Izzy?"

"She's an attorney. A damn fine attorney." He smiled. "You could report to my parents, since they're my partners. We could also sign an agreement that would protect the business if things didn't work out between us. They call them love contracts."

She snickered. "Seriously? I've never heard of such nonsense."

"Yeah, some of Izzy's corporate clients use them. Basically it says two people are in a consensual romantic relationship, to protect from sexual harassment claims."

"I've heard it all now."

"I'm willing to risk it, without the paperwork." He kissed the top of her head. "But I'm not in a hurry. You need to get through the next few days. I'm not going anywhere."

"Promise?" she asked.

"Promise."

* * *

Blake persevered and Ellie stayed home on Monday. She baked some muffins and cookies to have on hand for her family. While they were in the oven she put together a veggie tray along with a platter of cheese and fruit for snacks.

Kate invited her to an early lunch, which they enjoyed from the patio at the Front Street Café. Regi had told Ellie how she wished Kate had been her own mother and listening to her, she understood why. Kate had been through every mother's worst nightmare when her daughter committed suicide close to twenty years ago. "It took me a long time to move forward, Ellie. Don't be too hard on yourself. You've been dealt two horrific blows within weeks of each other."

Kate didn't say anything new or profound, but it was the way she said it that comforted Ellie. Like a mom. She didn't tell her everything would be okay. Instead she reassured Ellie she was strong enough to endure it.

The mixture of emotions swirling within made Ellie's stomach churn.

She did her best to eat the chicken salad, but only managed half of her plate. Gripping her cold glass of tea, she said, "What do you think about me dating Blake?"

Kate's whiskey colored eyes danced with joy. "I think it sounds marvelous. He is a wonderful guy." She paused and said, "What do you think? That's what matters."

"I like him…a lot." She flipped the cloth napkin around her fingers, back and forth. "I'm scared though. I love my job and if something goes awry I wouldn't want to jeopardize it."

"What's the worst that could happen, in your mind?"

Ellie shrugged her shoulders and tugged at the napkin. "I guess he'd leave."

"Sweetie, that's a risk we all take, no matter what. You've survived being on your own before, you could do it again. I know it's scary, but you're jeopardizing the chance at maybe a lifetime of happiness and togetherness." She reached for Ellie's hand and separated her from the napkin. "Protecting yourself from a possibility of pain isn't living. It's just existing. If the worst happened, we'd all be here for you and you'd survive."

Tears burned Ellie's eyes as she listened and nodded. Kate looked into her eyes. "You are worthy of being loved, of having a wonderful partner in your life, of creating a home and family together with someone like Blake. Think of the magic and happiness that could be yours. Be brave, Ellie. It's easier than living with regrets."

The waitress brought their ticket and Kate released Ellie's hand. The ferry was due in less than twenty minutes. Ellie dabbed her eyes dry while Kate slipped her credit card in the folder. "When this stressful week is over, promise me you'll give the idea consideration and not let fear paralyze you."

"I will." She hugged Kate tight wishing, like Regi, that she was her mom too.

* * *

Kate left her at the ferry and promised to be at the service Tuesday. Soon cars Ellie recognized thumped across the metal apron. She waved and waited for the caravan to find parking spots.

Aunt Ginny opened the passenger door and wrapped Ellie in a long hug. Both of them cried and clung to each other. The rest of the family hung back, giving them a bit of privacy as Ellie put her arm around her aunt's slender shoulders and guided her to a bench.

They gazed at the harbor, taking in the boats gleaming in the sun and the captivating water view. "I've missed the island," said Ginny. "We loved it here." She plucked a tissue from her pocket and wiped her eyes. "We should have come and visited more after we left."

Ellie held her aunt's hand as they bathed in the tranquility under the shade of a tree, letting the gentle bob of the boats in the harbor hypnotize them. Crepe myrtle trees were bursting with colorful blooms and a few joggers sprinted past on the harbor path. A gentle breeze drifted by, bringing the salty smell of the water. The only thing missing was Uncle Bob.

Aunt Ginny stole a look back at the parking area and saw her brood of children and grandchildren, noting a few of the great-grandchildren were restless. "How about you show me your new house and I'll let the kids go about exploring on their own? They can get settled in their rooms and do whatever they want for a few hours."

Ellie's smiled widened. "I'd love it."

They walked back to the group and Ellie gave them directions to the two different properties she had booked. The group split up and went their separate ways with a plan to meet for dinner.

Ellie took the long way home and explained where Linda and Jeff now lived. She drove into her driveway and Ginny said, "I love the house being so close to your friends." She opened the front door and Oreo darted for her aunt, covering her with doggie kisses.

After a tour through the inside, Ellie led her aunt to the deck. "Oh, it's gorgeous. I'm thrilled for you, Ellie."

Ellie settled her into a chair and left her to admire the plants while she fixed them iced teas. She put a few cookies and muffins on a plate and carried it all outside. Aunt Ginny raved about the cookies and Ellie enjoyed one of her healthy muffins. "I'd love for you to come and stay with me in my new house for a few days. I know you'll have company for a bit, but when they leave."

Her aunt finished her cookie and said, "I'd like that. I'm tired of being hovered over right now and could use a break from all the company. Maybe next month?"

"Anytime. We've got lots of events booked for weekends all summer, but I could finagle some time off during the week." Ellie filled her in on the weddings and upcoming concert at the winery.

"I need to sign those papers for Jack while I'm here. The kids want to take me to visit the house one last time while they're here." Fresh tears stained her cheeks. "I suppose I should."

The conversation drifted to current events, the bakery, and Ellie's new job. "Have you met any nice eligible men?" asked her aunt.

Her face reddened. "Well, there's Blake. He and his family own the winery. He's made it clear he has feelings for me."

Ginny's eyes twinkled and she grinned. "What about you? Do you have feelings for him?"

Ellie nodded. "I think I do." She took another gulp from her glass. "I'm scared though."

"You've had a lot of disappointment in your life. I fault your mother…and your father for that. Don't let their shortcomings color your life. Not everyone will abandon you. Is your happiness more important than the fear you feel?"

Ellie pondered the question. "Yes."

"Then he's more important. Courage is not avoiding things that are hard or scary, it's moving forward in the face of fear. I know you're courageous. Look at what you've done."

Ellie smiled. "You think so?"

"I know so. I don't want you to look back and regret this chance. I'd love to meet him. Ask him to join us for dinner tonight."

"Really?"

"Yes, I need to check him out." Her aunt broke off another piece of cookie. "I could use the excitement."

Ellie sprang from her chair. "I'll call him and see if he's available." She hurried inside.

Oreo stayed at Ginny's feet. "What do you think, girl? Is he a keeper?" Oreo thumped her tail in quick succession.

* * *

Blake insisted on picking Ellie up for dinner. He had quizzed her about intruding on her family time, but she persuaded him and told him it was her aunt's idea. He arrived early and waited on the deck while she finished getting ready. Her cousin Stan was treating the whole family to dinner at the Cliff House and she had been trying on several outfits. She hadn't been out to a fancy dinner in years and had been fussing over her clothing choices for over an hour.

She found Blake in the backyard throwing the ball for Oreo. He wore a navy suit with a blue shirt the exact color of his eyes. She stood on the deck watching him play with the dog. Sensing something, he turned and saw her. He dropped the ball and Oreo swooped to retrieve it.

"Wow," he said. "You are gorgeous." He hurried to the deck. "I've never seen you in a dress."

She blushed and said, "I haven't worn a dress in years. Kate talked me into this one."

He took her hand in his and admired her. "She has impeccable taste."

"We better get going." She hollered for Oreo and locked the doors. After opening her door, Blake settled into the driver's seat.

They were the last to arrive and Ginny motioned them to the seats next to her. After introductions around the table, they took their chairs. Aunt Ginny whispered to Ellie, "I like him already. Plus he's a handsome devil."

Ellie stifled a laugh and listened to the chatter around the table. It ended up being a fun celebratory night, not one filled with sadness. Uncle Bob would have loved the gathering. They told funny stories and relived memories from their childhood, made all the better by the man they treasured and missed.

Blake and Ellie were the last to leave the parking lot. Ellie was quiet, immersed in reflection. He drove and didn't try to make conversation. He pulled in the driveway and walked her to the door. "Come in for a bit? I still have ice cream."

"How can I resist?" He turned the key in the lock and shoved the door open for her.

Oreo greeted them and then settled back into her bed. Ellie leaned her arm on the wall and flicked off her shoes. "I'm going to change."

"I'm happy to help," he said, wiggling his eyebrows at her.

She laughed and said, "You know where the ice cream is."

He took off his jacket and tie and busied himself dishing the ice cream into bowls. He took them outside and turned on the fire. She joined him on the couch and tucked her feet into the cushion. "Thanks for going to dinner." She took a bite, letting the creamy dessert linger in her mouth. "Aunt Ginny likes you."

"She's sweet." He spooned another mouthful. "And obviously an excellent judge of character."

She giggled as she swallowed. He finished his bowl, deposited it on the table, and slipped his arm around Ellie. "I could stay here like this forever." He turned and looked into the flames reflected in her eyes.

"Me too," she said, nesting her empty bowl in his.

He leaned closer. She inched forward. The fragrance from the peonies along the deck mingled with Blake's fresh citrus scent to form an intoxicating combination. Her pulse quickened as the space between them decreased. The air hummed with energy as his hand caressed the back of her neck. He wove his fingers through her hair and she felt a strand fall as it came undone from the pin. Goosebumps covered her arms as the rough stubble of his cheek brushed against her neck. He skimmed her jaw with his lips and she took a quick breath when his soft lips met hers. His mouth was cool, from the ice cream, and she tasted a hint of chocolate.

A sizzle of electricity jolted through her body as his kiss deepened. Her heart raced and his strong fingers dug into her scalp. He shifted his hands to the side of her face and released her lips, resting his forehead against hers.

"I take it this means we're dating?"

She broke out in a loud laugh. "Yeah, I'm in." She locked her hands behind his neck and pulled him close for one more kiss.

Twenty-eight

Tuesday morning Ellie hated to take a shower. She could still smell Blake on her pajama shirt. She smiled, remembering snuggling with him last night on the deck. Guilt washed over her and wiped the smile from her face. It was Uncle Bob's memorial service today—she shouldn't be happy.

She contemplated her feelings as she let the warm water cascade over her shoulders. By the time she was done, she realized Uncle Bob would want her to be happy. He would be overjoyed with the idea of her having a man like Blake in her life. She didn't need to wallow in sadness to prove how much she loved Uncle Bob—he knew he was loved.

On the deck, she sipped coffee and picked at one of her muffins, while she scrolled through her phone. She saw a text from Blake. She smiled as she read, *Morning, Ellie. I know today will be hard and I wanted you to know I'm thinking of you. I'm at the barn now and everything is ready to go. I'll see you soon, Blake.*

She took her dishes inside and changed into a new black dress. She tied a sheer black and green scarf like Kate had taught her and slipped on a silver bracelet. She arrived at the winery before anyone else. The tasting room doors were locked, so she followed the path to the barn. She heard her name and saw Blake under the cover on the pavilion.

"Hey," she said, making her way toward him. She noticed he was wearing another suit.

He wiped his hands on a towel and greeted her with a chaste kiss. "You look pretty." He rubbed her shoulders. "You doing okay?"

"I think so," she said with a smile. "Did you set the lunch up out here?" She surveyed the tables, covered with green table cloths and adorned with simple flowers.

He nodded. "With the amazing weather, Lou and I made an executive decision. I was making sure things were ready."

"I'm early, do you need any help?"

"No, we're all set. Pastor Mark should be arriving soon. The funeral home brought your uncle out early this morning. He's in the barn." He linked his arm in hers and they traversed the length of the path.

The soft light from the chandeliers lit the space and a green draped table stood in front of a grouping of chairs, along with a podium for Pastor Mark. A wooden urn sat atop the table next to a wonderful picture of her uncle smiling and dressed up for an occasion several years ago. The fresh smell of flowers wafted through the air and Linda's expert hand was evident in the arrangements scattered throughout the barn. Easels with photos of Uncle Bob throughout the years were positioned near the entrance. Ellie signed the guest book and perused the family pictures. She smiled at his baby pictures and those of his young family. Tears stung her eyes when she saw the photos of herself. Her finger grazed the edge of one depicting her working alongside her aunt and uncle in the bakery, covered with flour.

Blake put his hand on the small of her back. "Are you okay?"

She nodded. "Yeah, it all looks terrific. Thank you." He slipped his arm around her and she rested her head on his shoulder. "Will you sit with me today?"

"I'd be happy to." He tilted her chin with his finger and kissed her. The sound of footfalls prompted them to turn.

Izzy stood before them, smiling. "I take it this means you finally came to your senses and asked this gorgeous woman out?"

Blake grinned and Ellie blushed. Izzy rushed to them and flung her arms around both of them. "I'm thrilled. You two make a perfect couple."

Ellie returned her hug and said, "Thank you so much for coming back for the service. It means a lot to me."

"Of course. I'm glad to be here and plan to torment Blake for a few days."

"Yeah, she's going to help out, so you take as much time as you need with your family."

They were interrupted by the arrival of Pastor Mark. He hugged Ellie and drew her aside where they talked in hushed voices. He led her to one of the private rooms Blake had set up for the family.

Soft instrumental music filled the barn and calmed Ellie's nerves. Soon others arrived and Blake and Izzy helped to usher them to their seats. Surrounded by children and grandchildren, Aunt Ginny appeared at the door and Blake led the group to Ellie. They took advantage of the refreshments Blake had arranged on the table and the children watched a television show. Blake put his arm around Ellie. "We've got about five minutes before it starts. I'll come back and get you when it's time."

Aunt Ginny's eyes widened as she watched Blake leave. She whispered to Ellie, "I'm so happy for you, sweetie. He's a fine man, I can tell."

Ellie smiled, despite the somber day. "I think so too. His sister is here today. I'll introduce you after the service."

"Your uncle would be so proud of you and what you've done here. This barn is incredible." She paused and gripped Ellie's hand. "He'd also be thrilled you found someone special like Blake, who makes you happy."

Blake came through the door and told them it was time to be seated. Aunt Ginny walked between her two sons, trailed by her daughter and the extended family. Blake linked his arm in Ellie's and they followed the procession to the family section. Pastor Mark opened the service with a prayer and spoke about Bob's life. He highlighted the major events of his lifetime including his marriage, the birth of his children, Sweet Treats, and the blessing of his niece coming to be part of his family.

Ellie dabbed at her eyes and Blake's arm tightened around her. Several islanders took advantage of the invitation to use a microphone and tell stories about her uncle. The crowd chuckled at some of the funny stories and nodded when others spoke about his generosity and kindness. When the reminiscing was done, Pastor Mark invited the guests to attend the luncheon in the pavilion. Some of Uncle Bob's favorite music from the 1950's and 1960's played in the background and guests made their way to address the family.

Blake remained by Ellie's side as what seemed like the entire population of the island shook hands or hugged her. Lou was one of the first in line and had tears in his eyes when he told her how much he admired Uncle Bob. "He was a great man, Ellie. He thought the world of you." He visited with the others and then hurried to check on lunch preparations.

Ellie held it together until her closest friends stood before her. Jeff, Linda, Nate, and Jen had known her uncle longer than she had. They held her and hugged her, wrapping her in love, recalling youthful memories. They were the last group and together with Kate and Spence the dozen friends strolled together to the pavilion while Frank Sinatra singing "My Way" drifted across the grounds.

Long after all the other guests left, the group of friends remained and spent the afternoon with Aunt Ginny, visiting and basking in the perfect weather and scenery. After Izzy was done taking care of the barn and helping Lou clean up the buffet area, she joined the table. Blake made sure wine glasses were filled and kept the pitchers full of lemonade and iced tea. The group nibbled on Lou's leftovers and Nicole's wonderful dessert trays while they chatted.

Nate offered to take Aunt Ginny into town. She wanted to stop by Jack's and sign the papers for the house. Ellie linked arms with her aunt and walked her to the parking lot. "Your friends are delightful. You have been blessed, my dear. Those pieces you talked about that left you feeling wounded and incomplete…I think you found new ones. They might be different pieces than what you started with, but they're better. You've made a wonderful life here, Ellie. You're not missing many pieces now."

Ellie tilted her head toward her aunt. "Only because of you and Uncle Bob. I never would have survived without both of you."

Tears welled in Aunt Ginny's eyes. "I'm going to go back to my room and rest tonight. We've got a long day ahead of us. You take care of your uncle tonight and we'll spread him in the waters he cherished tomorrow."

Ellie opened the door and helped her aunt settle in the seat. "I'll meet you at the marina in the morning." She waved as she watched Nate and Regi drive away.

By the time she walked back, the group had broken up and was getting ready to leave. Ellie made them all take leftovers home. Izzy rode with Sam and Jeff, who had offered to let her stay at their place while she was visiting. She and Blake took a walk and ended at the barn, where she took the urn from the table. She held it with both hands, nestled in the crook of her arm.

Blake walked her to her car. "I've got a few things to do and then I'll be by to check on you." He bent and brushed his lips over hers. "Do you need me to bring some dinner?"

"There's plenty left from Lou's. Will that work?"

He nodded and helped her place the urn in the passenger seat. He encircled his arms around her and held her in a long hug. "Today was a wonderful tribute to your uncle. I wish I could have met him. I can tell he was admired."

Her cheeks glistened with tears. "It was a beautiful service. I'll be forever grateful for your kindness in letting me have it here and doing such a terrific job."

He kissed her forehead. "It's the least I can do." He released her and after she got behind the wheel, he bent down. "I'll be at your house within in an hour. Get some rest and call me if you need anything."

She drove away, watching him in her rearview mirror. Her eyes drifted to the urn. "I wish you could have met Blake. I think he could be the one."

* * *

After shucking her funeral clothes, Ellie took her iced tea to the deck and played ball with Oreo. The flawless weather that had made a perfect day continued into the evening, providing a gentle breeze and what was shaping up to be a gorgeous sunset. The doorbell sounded and she found Blake, carrying bags from the winery. He hoisted them onto the granite island. "This was all I had to carry all the leftovers."

They worked together reorganizing her fridge to pack in the containers of Lou's food. She left the pink bakery boxes on the counter. He opened one of the bottles of wine he included and poured himself a glass. "You should have enough to feed your family while they're here."

"More than enough. They're leaving on Thursday. I'll be late, but I'll be at work as soon as they catch the ferry." She retrieved plates from the cupboard and dished up leftovers to reheat for their dinner. He carried them outside and sighed as he dropped into the chair with a groan.

She toted their glasses and joined him. "You sound exhausted. I'm sorry you had to work so hard today." She ruffled his hair as she sat his wine in front of him.

"I'm fine, but ready to call it a night and relax." He took a bite of Lou's crab ravioli and moaned. "That hits the spot."

The garden lights flicked on while streaks of pink and violet lingered in the twilight. She looked through the trees to the perfect slice of the horizon. "Beautiful."

He glanced at the vista and then focused on her. "I agree." He reached for her hand and held it in his.

After they finished, she cleared the dishes while he readied the fire pit. She refilled his wine glass and freshened her tea, before settling into the couch. She burrowed closer to him and rested her head on his shoulder. Blake ran his hand up and down her bare arm and she heard the steady thud of his heart. The indigo blanket above twinkled with a scattering of stars. Her eyelids struggled to stay open. The hush of night lulled her as she resisted sleep.

The chime of the doorbell startled her. "I'll get it," he said. He moved from under her and Oreo followed. He found an older man at the door he couldn't place, but assumed he must be one of the family members accompanying Aunt Ginny.

"I'm looking for Ellie," said the man. He paused and added, "I'm her dad, Ted Carlson."

Stunned, but now wide awake, Blake said, "Uh, did she know you were coming?"

Ted shook his head. "No, I learned about Bob's passing and came for the service." He hung his head. "I saw you there with her. I sat in the back and left as soon as it was over. I've been driving around trying to muster the courage to come here."

Blake extended his hand. 'I'm Blake Griffin."

Ted shook his hand and smiled. "Sorry to barge in so late. I've been sitting in my car across the street. I'm not sure what to say to her."

Ellie rounded the corner and came up behind Blake. "Who is it?"

Blake shifted to give her a full view of the man at the door. She squinted and lines formed in the middle of her forehead. She recognized the eyes, but her brain was slow in making the connection. She considered the short gray hair and the lined face, but kept focusing on his eyes. "Dad?"

"Yeah, Ellie. It's me. I know I don't deserve it, but I was hoping you'd talk to me."

Ellie's legs trembled and her pulse quickened. She stood staring at him and then rushed to close the space between them and wrapped her arms around him. She felt his strong grip on her back and smelled the scent she'd missed for so long.

Tears streamed down Ted's face as he shook with sobs and held his daughter. She pulled away and took his hand. "Come in."

He walked through the entry and into the kitchen. "You've got a lovely home, Ellie." He saw the urn atop the counter and reached out his hand to touch the smooth wood. "Bob," he whispered. Sorrow filled his eyes as he ran his hand over the surface.

Through blurry tears, Ellie watched her father. She knew she'd found the most important piece she'd been missing. She led him outside, "Let's sit out here. It's a perfect night."

ACKNOWLEDGEMENTS

I love returning to Friday Harbor and enjoyed writing Ellie's story. She endured a horrible childhood and had much to overcome. Her story makes me realize how fortunate I am to have a wonderful mother. As with the other books in the series, Ellie's journey involves personal growth and the strength to conquer her past, with the underlying themes of forgiveness and hope.

Each time I write a book in the Hometown Harbor Series, it makes me want to move there! When I hear from readers the setting is always mentioned-they love the island and the community of friends. I've tried to bring the locale to life for you and although it's only for a few hours, I hope you enjoy your time in Friday Harbor.

I'm indebted, as always, to my early readers. They are always so excited to read my first draft. I'm usually tired of it and ready for someone else to wade through the pages. Theresa, Dana, Jana, and Ruth worked to find errors and provide valuable feedback. My editor, Mary, has taught me so much since my first book.

I'm fortunate to know a wonderful photographer, Skip Reeves, at Silver State Photography who did a great job on my new author photos. Kari at Cover to Cover Designs is unbelievably talented and came through with another beautiful cover. Jason and Marina at Polgarus format all of my books and do outstanding work.

I'm grateful for the support and encouragement of my friends and family as I continue to pursue my dream of writing. Reviews, especially from readers who appreciate my books, are important in promoting future books. If you enjoy my novels, please consider leaving a positive review. It's easy to do on Goodreads and I'm thankful for all my readers who have taken the time to do so. Here is the link to my author page on Goodreads, where you will find my books. https://www.goodreads.com/TammyLGrace

Remember to visit my website at www.tammylgrace.com where I've posted book club questions for all the books in the Hometown Harbor Series. I post frequently on Facebook and would love to connect with you there! https://www.facebook.com/tammylgrace.books

The best way to thank an author
is to write a review

Thank you for reading the fourth book in the Hometown Harbor Series. If you enjoyed it and want to continue the series, follow the links below to my other books. I'd love to send you my exclusive interview with the canine companions in the Hometown Harbor Series as a thank-you for joining my mailing list. Instructions for signing up for my mailing list are included below. Be sure and download the free novella, HOMETOWN HARBOR: THE BEGINNING. It's a prequel to FINDING HOME that I know you'll enjoy.

All of Tammy's books below are available at Amazon

Cooper Harrington Detective Novels

Killer Music

Hometown Harbor Series

Hometown Harbor: The Beginning (FREE Prequel Novella)

Finding Home

Home Blooms

A Promise of Home

Pieces of Home

I would love to connect with readers on social media. Remember to subscribe to my mailing list for another freebie, only available to readers on my mailing list. Visit my webpage at http://www.tammylgrace.com/contact-tammy.html and provide your email address and I'll send you the exclusive interview I did with all the canine characters in my books. I encourage you to follow me on Facebook at https://www.facebook.com/tammylgrace.books/, by liking my page. You may also follow me on Amazon, by using the follow button under my photo. Thanks again for reading my work and if you enjoy my novels, *I would be grateful if you would leave a positive review on Amazon.* Authors need reviews to help showcase their work and market it across other platforms.

**If you enjoyed my books,
please consider leaving a review on Amazon**

Hometown Harbor: The Beginning (FREE Prequel Novella)

Finding Home (Book 1)

Home Blooms (Book 2)

A Promise of Home (Book 3)

Pieces of Home (Book 4)

Killer Music: A Cooper Harrington Detective Novel (Book 1)

Praise for Tammy L. Grace, author of The Hometown Harbor Series and the Cooper Harrington Detective Novels

"This book was just as enchanting as the others. Hardships with the love of a special group of friends. I recommend the 4 part series as a must read. I loved every exciting moment. A new author for me. She's Fabulous."

— *MAGGIE!, review of Pieces of Home: A Hometown Harbor Novel (Book 4)*

"Killer Music is a clever and well-crafted whodunit. The vivid and colorful characters shine as the author gradually reveals their hidden secrets—an absorbing page-turning read."

— *Jason Deas, bestselling author of Pushed and Birdsongs*

"I could not put this book down! It was so well written & a suspenseful read! This is definitely a 5 star story! I'm hoping there will be a sequel!"

—*Colleen, review of Killer Music*

"Tammy is an amazing author, she reminds me of Debbie Macomber… Delightful, heartwarming…just down to earth."

— *Plee, review of A Promise of Home: A Hometown Harbor Novel (Book 3)*

"This was an entertaining and relaxing novel. Tammy Grace has a simple yet compelling way of drawing the reader into the lives of her characters. It was a pleasure to read a story that didn't rely on theatrical tricks, unrealistic events or steamy sex scenes to fill up the pages. Her characters and plot were strong enough to hold the reader's interest."

—*MrsQ125, review of Finding Home: A Hometown Harbor Novel (Book 1)*

"I thoroughly enjoyed this book. I would love for this story to continue. Highly recommended to anyone that likes to lose themselves in a heartwarming good story."

—*Linda, review of Pieces of Home: A Hometown Harbor Novel (Book 4)*

Made in the USA
Middletown, DE
25 November 2019